BAD
KIDS

ZIJIN CHEN is a bestselling author of crime fiction. *Bad Kids* has been adapted into one of China's highest-rated online TV shows of all time, with over five billion topic posts on Weibo. He lives in Ningbo, China.

MICHELLE DEETER is a translator based in Manchester, UK. She holds a bachelor's degree in international relations from Carleton College and a master's degree in translation and interpreting from Newcastle University. She translates and interprets both technical texts and works of fiction.

ZIJIN CHEN

BAD KIDS

**TRANSLATED FROM THE
CHINESE BY MICHELLE DEETER**

x

PUSHKIN VERTIGO

Pushkin Vertigo
An imprint of Pushkin Press
Somerset House, Strand
London WC2R 1LA

Huai Xiao Hai by Zijin Chen
© Zijin Chen 2014
All rights reserved
English translation © Michelle Deeter 2022

Ordinary Chinese edition published by Shanghai Insight Media Co., Ltd
English language translation rights arranged with Shanghai
Insight Media through New River Literary Ltd

First published by Pushkin Press in 2022

3 5 7 9 8 6 4 2

ISBN 13: 978-1-78227-762-0

Designed and typeset by Tetragon, London
Printed and bound by Clays Ltd, Elcograf S.p.A.

www.pushkinpress.com

BAD
KIDS

1

The stone staircase led straight up the peak. A city wall, supposedly built during the southern Ming dynasty, traced the side of the wide path. In its heyday, the wall had been tall and imposing, but it had become less impressive after hundreds of years of weathering and decay. A company had reconstructed it recently, making it wider and sturdier. Visitors liked to hold onto it while climbing.

Sanmingshan was the most famous mountain in Ningbo. It had been a military stronghold in ancient times, but had been made into a nature park.

It was the first Wednesday in July, and the park was practically empty. Zhang Dongsheng knew this would be the best day to take his parents-in-law for a nice outing.

"Mum, Dad, let's get to that observation point, then we can take a break," he said. Carrying a hiking backpack and a fancy camera, he looked every bit the filial son-in-law.

They soon reached a platform the size of several basketball courts, about midway up the mountain. There they stood under a shady tree and took in the view.

Zhang's mother-in-law inhaled the fresh air. She smiled with satisfaction. "I have always wanted to come here, but it's too crowded on holidays like May Day and National Day. We are lucky that Zhang Dongsheng can take us here in summer, when nobody else is around!"

She was right; there were hardly any people. They were alone on the large platform. Well behind them were a few souvenir

7

shops where some tourists were eating snacks or seeking shade, and about thirty yards away, three kids in their early teens were clowning around near a pavilion. Zhang dismissed them all as unimportant.

"Here, have some water," he said, pulling out bottles from his backpack and handing one to each of them. "Dad, the view is really nice, I should take a photo of you and Mum here."

Zhang's father-in-law gruffly agreed, and the couple stood together and smiled. Zhang took one shot, then considered the scene.

"The wall is blocking the view a bit. Why don't you sit on it instead? Then I'll take another photo from that angle; it will look better," he cooed.

"Just take one more and then let's keep going. I don't like having my picture taken," the old man replied, irritation creeping into his voice. Still, he moved to the wall as his son-in-law had asked, not wanting to dampen his enthusiasm.

The wall was low and wide; people rested on it all the time. The old man settled and put his hands in his lap. His wife sat next to him and placed her hands on his arm. Zhang smiled eagerly, directing them with one hand while holding the camera in the other. He put it down and walked towards them. "You're too stiff. Try to look like you are happily married!"

"Just take the picture," Zhang's father-in-law said, embarrassed. His wife smiled and did her best to look more loving.

Zhang's eyes swept the area carefully one last time. Nobody else was there. The tourists at the shops were not looking in their direction. This was his moment!

Still smiling, he shifted their position by placing his hands on their shoulders. Then without warning, he grabbed their legs and lifted, sending them hurtling down the mountain. They screamed loudly as he stepped beyond their reach.

Zhang was overcome with shock for a few seconds. He went back to the edge and looked down. "Mum! Dad!"

There was no response. There was no chance of surviving the fall.

He turned and ran towards the shops. People had heard the screams and hurried to see what was going on.

Zhang's voice became panicked. "Help! Help! There's been an accident!"

But he allowed himself an inward smile. He had waited almost a year for this moment. He had committed the perfect crime—nothing could compare to the "accident" he had choreographed.

2

Summer had started and Zhejiang University campus was practically empty.

Professor Yan Liang, a PhD supervisor in the Mathematics Department, had just finished a meeting. It had dragged on so long that it was time for lunch. He invited two of his students, a man and a woman, to join him.

The three left the campus. As they walked, Yan turned on his phone, which had been off during the meeting. He saw that he had three missed calls, all from Xu Jing, his niece, and a text message: *Uncle Yan, when you see this message, please call me back as soon as possible.*

He frowned. He did not know what it was about, but it was clearly urgent. Xu Jing's father, Yan's cousin, was a retired director of China Tobacco. Yan had not been that close to his niece during her childhood, but that changed when she was accepted at his university. They were on the same campus so he made sure to look after her. It was on one of her visits to his office that Xu Jing had met Zhang Dongsheng, a mathematics student. He was Yan's favourite student and so Yan was delighted when Zhang and Xu got married. He felt like he was not just Xu Jing's uncle, but her matchmaker. But every time he thought of how Zhang had wasted his talent by becoming a schoolteacher, Yan sighed inwardly. Zhang was a star student—he had a gift for mathematical reasoning and Yan had expected him to do great things.

Zhang had been given the opportunity to go straight into a PhD and Yan had hoped to be his supervisor. But instead Zhang had taken a job. When Yan had tried to persuade him to consider further study, Zhang explained that his family could not afford any more debt. He needed to earn money as soon as possible to pay off his student loans, and to be able to marry Xu Jing. Not long after that, Xu had used family connections to get a job at China Tobacco and Zhang had found a job teaching maths at a middle school in Ningbo.

Just as Yan was about to text Xu back, the male student said, "That old person looks as if she is injured!"

Yan stopped what he was doing and they rushed to help. An old woman was lying on the pavement at the corner. There was blood on her hands and her knee. She clutched her leg and wailed. Yan was about to help her, but the student stopped him, "Wait a minute, Professor Yan!"

"Why?"

He whispered in Yan's ear. "Haven't you read the news? A lot of people are pretending to hurt themselves and then they accuse the person who helps them of injuring them in the first place. Then you have to pay them compensation."

"Yeah, you shouldn't get involved," the female student agreed.

The old woman heard what they were saying and extended her hand to Yan. "Please help me. Please, I fell down on my own."

The students were still trying to keep Yan out of it. He was indecisive, as he remembered reports of those scams and he thought his students had a point. At that moment, a burly man jumped off his electric bike and went to the aid of the old woman. "What are you doing, standing there? If you hit her you should be taking her to the hospital!"

The students instinctively distanced themselves from the woman, claiming they had not touched her.

The burly man frowned, "Even if wasn't your fault, you should still help her, shouldn't you?"

"Why aren't you helping her then?" the male student shot back.

"Me?" It took a moment for him to resume his self-righteous attitude. "I have to get to work, otherwise I would be helping her already!" He spotted the university badge around Yan's neck and clucked his tongue. "You call yourself a teacher?"

"Yes, I'm a teacher and these are my students," Yan answered.

"What is the world coming to? Not even the students and staff at Zhejiang University are willing to help someone in need!" The burly man sighed dramatically.

Yan wanted to argue with him, but stopped: he felt guilty about not helping the old woman.

Seeing Yan's expression change, the man continued, "I'll be your witness if anybody asks you for money. I can take a video with your phone." He took it without waiting for a reply and tapped the screen a few times. "OK, it's ready, Professor. Now nobody can say you pushed her."

Yan took a few seconds to think before deciding it was all right: with multiple witnesses and a video, it would be fine. Yan and his students helped the woman stand up.

"Thank you, thank you! You are such good people!" The woman gripped Yan's hands and took a few faltering steps.

"I think you'll be OK," Yan said warmly. "Do you want us to help you get to the hospital?"

"No, thank you, I can walk. I don't want to burden anyone. Thank you!" She let go of his hands and started to walk faster and faster until she was practically running.

The male student stared at her receding figure, as his initial shock gave way to anger. "Look at her sprint! You're lucky nothing happened this time. I think you would have lost a few hundred back there, if we had not been around. But once we said the word 'hospital', she vanished. What a con artist!"

The other student agreed.

Yan stood still, scratching his head as he tried to figure out what was wrong. "But something did happen just now." The ex-cop raced through the details in his mind and then it clicked. "Wait! My phone! They took my phone!"

The three of them looked around for the burly man, but he

was long gone. Meanwhile, the grinning granny had hopped onto her own electric bike that was parked further down the road and was speeding away.

And that was why Professor Yan was unable to reply to Xu Jing when she needed him most.

3

A message had been carved into one of the front row desks in Classroom 4. It read:

If you wish to be the best, you must suffer the bitterest of the bitter.

The first part of the evening independent study period was over but Zhu Chaoyang was still leaning over his desk, focused on his practice questions for tomorrow's final exam in mathematics. There was no need to cram since he almost always got a perfect score. Still, he had a passion for numbers that compelled him to solve problems, whether or not they would help him on the test. He would probably sail through Physics, Chemistry and Biology without studying tonight. His scores in Chinese Literature, English and Government would not be too shabby either.

Two hands slammed on his desk with a loud slap. Zhu Chaoyang nearly jumped out of his skin. He looked up to see a girl with short hair giving him a withering stare.

He returned the disparaging look. "Ye Chimin! What's your problem?"

"Mrs Lu is looking for you," she spat. Chaoyang stood up angrily, but knew better than to pick a fight with her. He was known to be a wimp and he had to tilt his chin up to match her gaze. It was bad enough to be the shortest, scrawniest, wimpiest boy in his class. Getting his butt kicked by a girl who was taller than him was too much for his ego.

Chaoyang let out a loud cough, using the sound to fart

14

surreptitiously in her direction. A few seconds later, he made a show of covering his nose at the smell. "Ugh, Ye Chimin, can't you warn us before you let one rip?"

She looked horrified. "You idiot!"

Chaoyang laughed and stuck out his tongue at her. He swaggered to the teacher's office, but by the time he entered, his confidence had evaporated. He was probably going to be in trouble, even though he did not know why.

Mrs Lu, the form teacher, was in her forties and was tall and thin. She rarely smiled. All of the students were afraid of her, even Chaoyang. (She taught English, his worst subject.)

He could tell that she was in a bad mood and he shrank instinctively, like a turtle retreating into its shell. "You wanted to speak to me, Mrs Lu?"

Mrs Lu continued to read the homework assignments on her desk, not giving him a shred of her attention. Chaoyang scrunched the trouser legs of his school uniform with his hands, growing more nervous by the second. Was she too irate to acknowledge his presence? Was something else bothering her: hearing problems, indigestion, divorce? Mrs Lu ignored him for five whole minutes. Chaoyang couldn't stand it.

When she was finished with her marking, she looked up. "Why did you break Ye Chimin's camera?"

Chimin was a journalist for the school newspaper, so she frequently brought a camera to school.

Chaoyang looked utterly confused. "What camera?"

"Did you break the camera lens on Ye Chimin's camera?"

"I've never touched it!" Chaoyang said, bewildered.

"Still denying your crimes, I see?"

"I… I didn't do it," he stammered, not knowing how to convince her of his innocence.

Mrs Lu was enraged. "I know you're lying! Ye Chimin saw you take her camera from her desk and knock it against the classroom wall. When she got it back, the lens was broken."

"That's impossible! I never touched her camera! Ever!" Chaoyang protested. The conversation was utterly absurd.

"Enough. She already said that you don't need to pay her for a new lens, so you don't need to lie any more."

"I…" He was so distressed he had to fight back tears. The accusation was completely unfounded—he had been solving problems at his desk during the entire evening study period. He was used to being bullied for his height, for his shabby clothes and for being the child of divorced parents. But he could not fathom why he was being accused of breaking a camera.

Mrs Lu watched him carefully. Her gaze gradually softened. "Go back to your studies, you have exams tomorrow. I'm dropping the matter. But consider this a warning, Zhu Chaoyang."

Chaoyang wanted to protest again but gave up. The accusation was bizarre, but it wouldn't help to argue with Mrs Lu. The best thing was to ask that snake Chimin about it later.

4

The bell rang as Zhu Chaoyang returned to the classroom. He looked hatefully at Ye Chimin. She took a moment to smile triumphantly at him before bending over her textbook.

Chaoyang returned to his desk, dejected. Fang Lina, who shared a desk with him, poked him lightly in the elbow. She was one of the few people he got along with in his class. Now she spoke in a hushed tone. "Don't draw their attention. I want to tell you something."

Chaoyang fixed his gaze on his workbook as he whispered, "What is it?"

Fang Lina kept her head perfectly still. "Did Mrs Lu just ask you about Ye Chimin's camera?"

"Yeah."

"Looks like she blamed you for it."

"Huh?"

"When I finished eating and came back into the classroom, I saw Chimin and the class monitor looking at the camera. Chimin said that she dropped it and the lens broke. Then she said she was going to tell Mrs Lu that you did it."

"You've got to be kidding me," Chaoyang said, his anger rising. "She lied to a teacher! I never touched her stupid camera. I'm going to tell Mrs Lu."

"Please, don't tell anyone. I don't want to be their next target," Lina begged.

Chaoyang frowned. After thinking about it, he agreed, "OK."

"At least you know what happened. Don't tell anyone!"

"I won't."

"She's gone way too far this time," Lina said.

"But why did they want to blame me?"

17

"I think when she broke the camera, she was afraid that her dad would be furious. He's a captain in the police and he used to be in the military. It doesn't matter what she does: if she makes a mistake, he hits her. But her dad won't punish her if she says a classmate did it," she explained.

"She got me in trouble just so she could stay out of trouble!" Chaoyang grumbled. Then his expression changed. "But she's too old to be spanked, isn't she?"

"I dunno. Her dad basically treats her like a boy. One time she came to class with a bruise on the side of her face. She said her dad had slapped her."

Chaoyang snickered at the thought of Chimin being punished. "That explains her butch haircut. Maybe she has that dazed look in her eyes because of all of the slapping!"

At that moment, the two realized that they had forgotten to whisper. Mrs Lu was standing right in front of them.

"You seem to be having a lot of fun for a study session!" Mrs Lu said.

Lina hung her head, not daring to breathe.

Zhu Chaoyang took the fall. "It's my fault, I distracted Lina."

"You have exams tomorrow! You need to focus!" Mrs Lu commanded. Chaoyang could swear he felt cold air coming from his teacher—she must have freezer chests for lungs.

He was despondent about being told off again by his form teacher, as he was still seething about being blamed for something he hadn't done. He had survived the torture of the second independent study session when he headed towards the toilet and saw Chimin washing her thermos. He couldn't resist smacking the sink in the same way that she had slapped his desk earlier. "Why did you accuse me of something I didn't do?"

Chimin sized him up briefly and went back to her rinsing out her flask.

"Bitch," he said, and started to walk away.

All of a sudden, Chimin started crying loudly. He looked back, surprised. Talk about melodramatic! He was even more confused when she filled her thermos with cold water and poured it over her own head before running away. He went to the toilet as quickly as possible and returned to the classroom to get his things. He saw Ye Chimin in the teacher's office, wailing at Mrs Lu. Two other teachers were trying to console her.

Mrs Lu spotted him and used her most threatening voice. "Zhu Chaoyang, get in here!"

He quivered at the sight of her, but he had no choice.

"What's gotten into you? Pouring water on Ye Chimin's head?"

"What?!" Zhu Chaoyang stared at Chimin, then looked back at his teacher. "I didn't do anything, she did that to herself!"

Suddenly, he realized what was going on. There was no point in fighting because it was her word against his. Ye Chimin's hair was soaked and she was crying bitterly. Mrs Lu had believed her the first time around, so it wasn't surprising that she would now.

"I'm going to speak to your mother about this," the form teacher warned.

Chaoyang looked stricken. "But... I really didn't do it, she did it to herself."

"You'd better change your tone, or you can forget about your final exams," Mrs Lu said severely.

"I didn't pour water on her. She did it herself, honestly," he said, his lip quivering.

"Again you won't admit what you've done! I've never seen a student like this before! Just because you ace your exams doesn't mean we'll let you off for bad behaviour. I want to speak with your mother tomorrow—otherwise you don't need to bother to come for the exams."

Chaoyang dug his fingernails into his palms. This was the worst day of his life.

He watched as Mrs Lu guided Ye Chimin back into the classroom, telling her in soft tones not to be intimidated by the bully.

When Chimin disappeared through the doorway, Mrs Lu came back and spoke to Zhu Chaoyang: "Your mother explained your situation to me at the beginning of the year. Your parents are divorced, your father does not discipline you and your mother works away from home a lot, so you spend a lot of time alone. Last time she spoke with me, your mother asked me to be firm, but I never expected you to do something like this."

"I didn't do it," Chaoyang said, his voice cracking.

Mrs Lu took a deep breath. She knew that he was a good student but once she made up her mind, she never backed down. "You can't keep denying what you've done. Tell your mother to come to school in the morning, I *must* speak to her."

"But… she has to work."

"Then she will have to take a day off. Go home and call your mother. Explain that she has to come to school tomorrow, otherwise you will not be allowed to take your exams."

He stood still.

"Go home! Now!" Mrs Lu shouted, pulling him along by his arm.

When he had reached the door of the office, he couldn't stand it any more. "I'm sorry, I was wrong. I won't do it again. Please, Mrs Lu, let me take my exams tomorrow. I'm sorry, I will never bully Ye Chimin again. Please."

The other two teachers liked Chaoyang very much and helped him make his case. "Don't be so hard on him, he's admitted it. Let him write an apology letter and be done with it. He needs to take his exams, after all," one said.

Mrs Lu sighed, but was finally persuaded by them and Chaoyang's tears. She made him write an apology letter promising not to do it again before letting him go.

He slung his backpack on his back and headed home, exhausted. On the way he ran into Ye Chimin who gave a cruel smile. "Who gave you permission to be top of the class? My dad shouts at me for not being number one and it's all your fault. We'll see who's really the best tomorrow then, huh?"

He finally understood why this had happened. She was jealous of his exam scores! She did this just to cut him down!

He glared at her briefly, and kept walking.

He desperately wanted the term to be over.

5

After Chaoyang had finished his last exams, school ended and everyone went home. It was finally summer. He felt he could say goodbye to a thoroughly rotten year.

He was home alone that afternoon in their shabby apartment, which measured barely 650 square feet. The floors were covered in a plastic material that was popular in the '90s and the walls were unpainted. The place smelled a little musty. A steel fan creaked, providing a feeble breeze against the heat. Chaoyang had taken his shirt off to cool down. He was sitting on his bedroom floor, reading *Home Remedies to Increase Height*. He would give anything to be a little bit taller.

He had seen an ad for the book and bought a mail-order copy for 20 yuan. There were all kinds of tips. Chaoyang had gone through the list and underlined the key points. The first thing he would do was stop drinking carbonated drinks, because the book said they leached calcium from the bones. He drew a star next to the tip and vowed never to drink soda again.

He was fully absorbed in the book when he heard an urgent knock on the door. He stuffed the book on the shelf and went to the door. He opened the door but left the steel security grille locked. He could see a boy and a girl who were roughly his age. The boy was a head taller than him, at about 5 feet 5 inches; the girl was shorter. They both seemed frightened.

"Are you looking for someone?" Chaoyang asked hesitantly.

"Zhu Chaoyang, I can't believe you still live here!" The boy beamed. "Remember me?"

Chaoyang took a closer look. "Ding Hao! What are you doing here?"

"We need your help. Quick, open the door!"

He opened the grille, and Ding Hao quickly guided the girl in and closed both doors. "Can I have some water? I'm super thirsty."

Chaoyang got them glasses of water and Ding Hao downed his. The girl took small sips, her face expressionless. She resembled an ice sculpture.

"Who is your friend?" Chaoyang asked Ding Hao.

"You can call her Pupu. She's my sister. Not my actual sister, but we're family now." He looked at her. "Pupu, this is Zhu Chaoyang, the guy I've been telling you about. We were best friends at school. But we haven't seen each other in… five years now."

"Hi," she said.

Zhu Chaoyang felt awkward sitting in front of a girl half naked. He got his shirt and returned to the kitchen. "Ding Hao, how did you get so tall?"

"I dunno," he said, chuckling and scratching his head.

"You guys looked really frightened when I answered the door. What's happened?"

"Long story," Ding Hao said, swinging his arms in a familiar carefree way. "Someone wanted to nab us and we jumped out of a van to get away."

Chaoyang looked alarmed. "Were they traffickers? Should we call the police?"

"Nah. They were…" Ding Hao stopped. He laughed to ease the tension. "It's a long story."

"Seriously, what happened? Where did you go to school for the past five years? The teachers all said you moved to another city and I thought I'd never see you again. You left without even saying goodbye."

Ding Hao grew serious and looked at Pupu, who did not give any indication that she cared what he said.

"What?" Chaoyang was starting to get creeped out.

Ding Hao lowered his voice. "You really don't know why I moved?"

"How would I know when you never told me?"

"It's because... my parents were arrested."

"What are you talking about?"

Ding Hao made a face. "My parents killed someone, they were caught, and they were executed."

"What!" Chaoyang's eyes widened and he studied them both more carefully. "Why didn't I hear about this?"

"The teachers probably didn't want you to know that a former classmate was the son of murderers," Ding Hao said in an attempt at a joke.

"Don't talk like that. Your parents might have killed someone, but that has nothing to do with you. Umm... why did they do it?" Chaoyang asked, although he wasn't really sure he wanted to know the details. He was trying hard to think of a way to get rid of them. He didn't want any trouble. It had been years since he had seen Ding Hao and he didn't really know anything about him now. Chaoyang was home alone, anything could happen.

Ding Hao blushed. "I still don't know. Someone told me that it happened like this, but I don't know if it's true: my mum cheated on my dad, and he wanted her to find a girlfriend for him or something. So my mum tricked a college student into helping her. The kind student helped my mum home after she fainted on the street; then my dad raped the girl. Apparently they both killed her to cover it up, but they were caught. So they were executed by a firing squad."

"Oh..." Chaoyang was shocked at Ding Hao's far-fetched story. He felt nervous and certainly wanted them to leave, but he couldn't think of a good way to do it. He kept on talking. "So where have you been all this time?"

"At an orphanage in Beijing. People don't want anything to do with children of murderers, none of my aunts or uncles would take me. I had no choice. Pupu's just like me, she didn't have parents or a guardian, so she had to go to the orphanage, too."

Pupu looked up at Chaoyang, then turned her head away. They sat in an uncomfortable silence. They both had murderers for parents! Again Chaoyang regretted opening the door. He should have hidden in his room and pretended not to be home.

"So, how did you get here? Beijing is really far away," he finally said.

"We ran away," Ding Hao said. "We didn't want to stay at the orphanage, so we escaped and made our way here. Pupu is from Jiangsu and she didn't want to go back. I couldn't think of anywhere else to go, so we came here. I was too chicken to contact my relatives. I knew they would just call the police. We planned to spend a few days here and then move on, but then a bunch of stuff happened. This morning—" He suddenly clammed up.

"What happened this morning?" Chaoyang pressed.

"We kinda ran out of money, so we begged on the side of the road," Ding Hao said after a pause.

"You did *what*?" Chaoyang could hardly believe that this was his best friend from primary school. He had seemed like a perfectly normal kid years ago, but now his story suggested that he was with the wrong crowd.

"I knew that you would think less of me if I told you. But we didn't have a choice."

"No, no, I don't think less of you," Chaoyang fibbed.

"Really?" Ding Hao brightened. "Then a van came along, it said... what did it say on the van again, Pupu?"

"City Enforcement," she said coldly.

"Yeah, that's it. They said we couldn't beg and we had to move along. So we started walking, but we were hungry, so we bought something from a bakery. And then another van came, and those guys were from the Civil Affairs Bureau. They told us they wanted to contact our parents. No matter where they took us, they would find out that we ran away, and they would just put us back in the orphanage. So Pupu said she had to pee, and they stopped the van for her, and we ran off. We happened to be close to your house, and I recognized where we were, so we took a chance and knocked on your door. I can't believe that you are still living here!" he finished.

After hearing all this, Chaoyang was even more anxious. Ding Hao and he were good friends before, but that was a long time ago. He tried to think of a plan of action. Kicking them out might be dangerous, but if they stayed too long, what would happen then?

"What… uh… are you planning to do?" Chaoyang stammered.

Ding Hao shrugged. "I might try and find some work, but Pupu is too little. She's only eleven; she should be at school."

"And you shouldn't? You're only thirteen!"

"Man, I hate school. I want to start working as soon as possible."

"But nobody would hire you. You're not old enough to work."

"If I don't tell 'em, they won't know, will they? I'm tall enough to pass for sixteen," Ding Hao smirked.

Chaoyang finally brought up the awkward question. "So what are you planning to do… in terms of sleeping? My place is small, I mean… you know…"

"I won't freeload off you really, I promise. But if it's OK, we would like to spend the night here," Ding Hao said.

"Oh…" Chaoyang looked away awkwardly.

Pupu spoke up. "Ding Hao, forget it. Let's go."

"We left our bag in the what-d'ye-call-it van, remember? I don't think we'll find a place to sleep tonight," Ding Hao stage-whispered to Pupu.

"There's always a way," she said.

Ding looked at her, back at Chaoyang, and then stood and laughed jovially. "OK, then, we'll leave. See you around, Chaoyang. I'll come back after I find a job."

Chaoyang led them to the door, his brows knitted in concentration.

"When I start making money, I'll take you to KFC," Ding Hao said with a grin. He waved goodbye and had started to walk away when he turned around again. "Oh, wait, I have some candied haw berries for you in my bag! It's a snack from Beijing, I bet you've never had it before. I thought if I had the chance to see you…"

Pupu rolled her eyes at Ding Hao. "You left the bag in the van, remember?"

Ding Hao smoothed his hair awkwardly. "Next time, I guess. Take care, mate! Bye!"

"Wait, guys," Chaoyang said. He felt a pang of guilt—after being best friends in primary school, how could he not help? When an older student had bullied him, Ding Hao had stepped up and taken a beating for him. Chaoyang ran away but Ding Hao never blamed him for it, saying it was better that only one person got hurt. Now his worries were rejected because of their past friendship. "You can stay over tonight. My mum works at a tourist attraction and only comes home once every few days. She won't be back for two days, so you can stay here."

"Really?" Ding Hao asked hopefully.

"Yeah. We can all squeeze into my room. Pupu can have the bed and you and me can sleep on the floor."

Ding Hao turned to Pupu. "What do you think, Pupu?"

"I don't want to bother anyone," she said, shaking her head.

"It's fine," Chaoyang hurriedly said.

Pupu was quiet for a moment. Then she nodded, her face still serious. "Well, OK. Thank you, Brother Chaoyang. If you want us to go, you can tell us at any time."

He blushed.

6

"Pupu, you're a pro at making noodles. This is delicious!" Chaoyang said between bites.

"Yeah, she helped out in the kitchen at the orphanage, she knows her stuff," Ding Hao said.

Pupu, expressionless as usual, sat at the table and took small nibbles of her noodles. She had only said a few sentences since she arrived. Chaoyang was not entirely sure why, but he wanted to make a good impression on her. "Pupu, you're not eating very much. Do you want something else?"

"No thanks," she said.

"She doesn't eat much," Ding Hao explained. "Plus it's so hot outside, I don't think either of us is really hungry."

Chaoyang saw that Ding Hao was polishing off his third bowl of noodles, but didn't comment.

"So... Pupu, you went to the orphanage for the same reason as Ding Hao?" he asked cautiously.

"Duh," Ding Hao said. "It's the same for everyone at the orphanage. No parents, no guardian."

"Oh," Chaoyang studied his friend's happy expression. He didn't think he would be so upbeat if he were in their shoes. "So how did Pupu's parents die?"

She dropped her chopsticks on the table and stared at him.

"Sorry, I shouldn't have asked," Chaoyang said hastily.

She didn't answer, but picked up her chopsticks and slurped a mouthful of noodles.

Ding Hao laughed it off. "Never mind. You're one of us now, so it doesn't matter. Right, Pupu?"

When she did not say anything, Ding Hao took her silence as agreement and spilled the beans. "Her dad killed her mum and her little brother, and then he was caught. Got the death sentence."

"He didn't do it!" Pupu's response was loud. "I told you before, my dad never killed anyone."

"But the support workers all said he did."

"They don't know anything. Right before he died, my dad told me I had to believe him that he didn't kill my mother. He told me even if he fought with my mother sometimes, he loved me and he would never take my mother away from me," she said.

"But then why did the police arrest your dad? Police officers don't make an arrest until they are sure they have the right person," Chaoyang asked innocently.

"They get the wrong guy all the time! My dad told me they forced him to stay awake and interrogated him for days, until he had to admit to killing them just to make the torture end. But he didn't do it! I was only seven, but I remember my dad saying it was too late to change anything, and all he wanted was for me to know that he was innocent." Despite her impassioned speech, her face showed no emotion.

Chaoyang did not know what to say.

"Brother Chaoyang, do you have a camera?" Pupu suddenly asked.

"A camera? What for?"

"My dad told me I should take a photo of myself once a year and burn it so that he would receive it in the afterlife. Every year on the anniversary of his death, I take a photo of myself and write a letter to him. Then I burn them so he can receive them."

"Oh, so you need to take a picture so your dad can see how you're doing?" Chaoyang wanted to make sure he understood her correctly.

"Yeah. Burning stuff is the easiest way to communicate with dead family members, everybody knows that," she noted with exasperation.

Chaoyang bit his lip. "I don't have a camera. We might have to go to a photography studio."

"How much is that gonna cost?" Ding Hao asked anxiously.

"Maybe… fifteen yuan?"

"Fifteen yuan…" Ding Hao frowned as he thought about it. Then he became resolute. "We have to take a photo, I know it's important. Fifteen yuan is not that bad. Don't worry, Pupu, I have a little money."

She nodded.

Everyone finished their noodles. They stayed at the table and kept talking; it didn't take long before they were comfortable with each other. The visitors were envious when they heard about Chaoyang's top scores at school. Then they described the journey from Beijing to Ningbo, although they clearly did not enjoy sharing some parts. Zhu Chaoyang couldn't begin to imagine how difficult it was to get by as runaways. Sometimes they had had to charm people into giving them money; when that didn't work, they had shoplifted. When they told him about that, Chaoyang felt his stomach tie into knots again. He looked involuntarily towards his mother's room, where he knew a few thousand yuan were lying in an unlocked drawer. He resolved to move the money to a safer place when they weren't looking. The two didn't seem to be suspicious about him, which was reassuring.

The phone rang and Chaoyang went to his mother's room to answer it. After he hung up, he hesitated for a few seconds, hid the cash between the wall and the back of the bedside table, and placed a short piece of yarn between the door and frame before he closed it. If he discovered the yarn on the floor, he would know that the door had been opened. "My dad just called," he said. "He wants me to go see him at his office. Um… where will you guys hang out in the meantime?"

Ding Hao looked surprised but then smiled, "No worries. We can just walk around your neighbourhood until you come back."

Zhu Chaoyang felt relieved. They didn't seem to have bad intentions—perhaps he should trust them more.

7

YONGPING SEAFOOD OFFICE

About twenty miles east of the city centre was an industrial estate, where several seafood cold-storage facilities were located. A fair-sized building on the western side had a large sign: "Yongping Seafood". Its main office was hazy with smoke, as the owner Zhu Yongping played cards with five other wealthy men who owned businesses nearby. The table was a mess of snacks and cigarettes.

"That's a clean sweep!" Zhu shouted gleefully. He collected the 4,000 yuan and put it in a neat pile.

"It must be your lucky day, Yongping. How many times have you been dealer?" Yang Genchang asked.

"This makes up for last time when I kept losing," Zhu laughed. He shuffled the cards.

"You ought to give some of it to your son," Fang Jianping reprimanded him.

"I give him money, sometimes," Zhu Yongping said defensively, dealing the cards.

"Bullshit!" Fang said. "The other day I took Lina to the bookstore to buy some books and we ran into your son, reading on the floor. I asked him what he was doing there and do you know what he said? He said it was hot and the bookstore had air-conditioning. He has to go to the *bookstore* just to keep cool."

Zhu Yongping's face turned a delicate shade of pink. "I give him money, but he and his mother are frugal."

Fang arranged his cards as he spoke. "You're not giving him much. Lina sits next to him in class, and she says the boy wears the same three or four shirts all the time. You're here flashing your luxury brands and buying the prettiest clothes for your wife and your daughter. Meanwhile your son is dressed like a beggar. Just because you divorced your first wife, doesn't mean you should forget that he exists."

"I heard he's the best student in his school. He's the kind of kid any father would be proud of. He's actually doing really well at school unlike our kids," Yang Genchang added.

"Best in the whole school?" Zhu sounded genuinely surprised.

"Are you kidding me? You didn't even know that he had the best exam scores in the whole damn school?" Fang said contemptuously. "Your little princess Jingjing was held back a year, but you still kiss the ground she walks on. You don't even give your son the time of day. I would kill to have a kid half as smart as your son."

The others all took Fang's side.

"I'll call him in a few days and give him money," Zhu said in an attempt to save face.

"Why wait?" Fang replied. "Your wife is at the zoo with your daughter, right? Call him and tell him to come by, then I can ask him to tutor my daughter so she can get her grades up."

"We know your wife won't let you contact him, and they're always around so you can't see him much. Isn't this the perfect day?" Yang said. "Maybe during those tutoring sessions, they'll develop feelings for each other, and in a few years you and Fang will be in-laws. Your son will drive the family Bentley and you'll have a stake in Fang's factory. You'll be loaded."

Everyone laughed. Ashamed, Zhu called his son.

8

"Hello, Father. Uncle Fang, Uncle Yang, everyone," Zhu Chaoyang greeted the men when he entered his father's office.

"Look at how polite your son is! He's a little gentleman, unlike my good-for-nothing son," Yang Genchang joked.

"Pour them tea," Zhu Yongping said, ruffling his son's hair with pride.

Chaoyang did what he was told.

Fang Jianping rearranged his cards as he spoke. "Chaoyang, my daughter is ranked twentieth in the class. With her grades, I'm worried she won't be able to get into a good high school. You two sit next to each other, so can you help her out next time she needs it?"

"Sure, of course," he agreed.

"Thank you, Chaoyang."

"That's all right, Uncle Fang."

The others were deeply impressed by how polite he was. It was rare to find such a respectful teenager these days.

"Your dad doesn't give you money very often, does he?" Fang continued his attack.

"He does... sometimes."

"How much did he give you this time?"

"This time?" Chaoyang was confused. He looked at his father.

"The summer break just started, I didn't give him anything yet," Zhu Yongping explained hastily.

"When was the last time your dad gave you money?" Fang was not letting it go.

Chaoyang looked at his feet. "Lunar New Year."

"How much?"

"Two thousand."

It was a pitiful sum. Laughter rang out in the room.

Zhu studied his cards but failed to hide his embarrassment. "Money was tight then, I gave a little less than normal."

"Your dad won over ten thousand playing cards today you know. He's going to give it all to you. Remember, Yongping, your wife isn't here, and she doesn't even know this money exists. We promise we won't tell her," Fang announced.

The others murmured, liking Fang's plan.

"You're right. Son, sit over here. Let's see how much your dad wins today," Zhu said, caving in to the pressure.

Yang was the dealer for the next round. As he shuffled the deck, a well-dressed woman in her early thirties entered, followed by her grumpy nine-year-old daughter. A jade bracelet dangled on Wang Yao's wrist and a platinum necklace adorned her neck. She had the keys to a BMW in her hand.

"I'm exhausted," she exclaimed, throwing her keys on the table and making a show of massaging her arms.

"You're back!" Zhu Yongping exclaimed, standing up to hide Zhu Chaoyang behind him.

"This camera is old and the battery doesn't hold a charge. We took a few photos and then it stopped working. There wasn't any point in staying at the zoo. Buy me a new camera tomorrow, honey, this is a relic." Wang Yao dumped the camera on the table with a look of disdain.

"Sure, sure. How about you go home, then? We're going to play for a few more hours," Zhu said quickly.

She wasn't interested in card games, but noticed her husband was acting strangely and fixed her gaze on the boy sitting behind him. It only took her a second to recognize it was Zhu Chaoyang, the boy from his first marriage. She glowered at Zhu Yongping.

Chaoyang was just as quick to recognize her: the woman who stole his father away. He could easily guess who the girl was, but he pretended not to notice her.

The card game had stopped. Everyone was watching Wang Yao's face.

The little girl spotted Zhu Chaoyang and pointed at him. "Daddy, who's that back there?"

"It's…" Zhu Yongping looked more pained than ever, "… it's Uncle Fang's nephew."

The men laughed at his clumsy lie.

"Brilliant, just brilliant. From now on, you're Mr Brilliant," Yang said, his voice dripping with sarcasm.

"Don't laugh!" Fang said, with a deadpan expression. "It's true. Chaoyang calls me Uncle, so that makes him my nephew."

Wang Yao was surprised, but her face quickly returned to its habitual sneer.

Yang had an unpleasant look on his face as he got the child's attention. "Little Jingjing, I heard you failed your final exams."

"I woulda passed…" she murmured, moving to hide behind her father.

"You should learn from your older brother here. He got the best scores in his whole school," Yang said, suggesting Chaoyang was a good role model.

Wang Yao pulled her daughter towards her. "That's right, Jingjing, you need to study hard to *beat your brother*," she urged, emphasizing the last three words.

"OK, OK!" the girl whined, not liking the kind of attention everyone was paying. She was oblivious of the fact that she had a half-brother—nobody had told her.

"My poor nephew, his clothes have been washed so much that they've faded. Yongping, would you take him to buy some new clothes? Just tell me how much I owe you later," Fang said to the room. He gave a wink to Chaoyang, who did not know what to do.

"Um—" Zhu began.

"Go on, A-Jie will take your place," Yang urged. "This boy's clothes are in tatters. Make sure to buy him plenty of new things. Don't you agree, Mrs Wang?" Yang said, looking at her.

It would have been unseemly to disagree, so she said, "Of course. We were planning on buying clothes anyway. Yongping, we should take Chaoyang shopping. Jingjing and I will wait for you in the car."

The girl's face brightened. "Yay! Daddy, take me to Jinguang Department Store!"

The woman shot a look at Zhu Chaoyang, smiled theatrically and led her daughter away.

Once they had left, the teasing resumed in earnest. Zhu finally looked at his son and said, "Come on, I'm going to take you to buy some new clothes."

Chaoyang stood up, but then faltered. "Dad? Maybe I should just go home."

But the other men were not having any of it. "You already agreed, so you can't back out now! It won't take long and your father can drop you off afterwards."

Chaoyang nodded, still wishing there was a way to get out of this.

Zhu Yongping stepped away from the table, out of earshot of the others. He leaned towards his son. "Your sister doesn't know that she has a half-brother; she's only nine years old, and we didn't want to confuse her about my previous marriage. So you're Uncle Fang's nephew for today and eventually I'll tell her the truth. Got it?"

"OK," Chaoyang said in a small voice. He was utterly shocked that Jingjing did not even know he existed.

Zhu counted out 5,000 yuan of his winnings and handed it over. "Put this in your bag, and don't let anyone see. I don't want her knowing that I gave you money," he said. He didn't have to explain who "she" was.

"OK."

Zhu Yongping patted his son on the shoulder in an apologetic way. He tried to appear casual as he picked up the camera, "I should probably get rid of this old thing."

Chaoyang suddenly remembered that Pupu wanted to take a photo, and said, "Dad! You really don't want the camera?"

"Of course not. It's useless."

"Um, can I have it?"

"Oh, I'll get you a new one sometime."

Chaoyang knew there was zero chance that his father would buy him a new camera. "If you don't want it, I could just take some pictures for fun," he said.

Zhu was easily persuaded. "You're still in school anyway, so you don't need a fancy camera. Take it."

Zhu Chaoyang was uncomfortable throughout the ride in the BMW.

He was sitting in the front passenger seat and he kept his head bowed to avoid interacting with his father or his step-family. They laughed and talked like he wasn't even there. Every time he raised his head and looked in the rear-view mirror, he saw Mrs Wang smirking at him, and he quickly looked down again. He felt completely excluded.

When they arrived at the shopping centre, Zhu Yongping walked alongside Zhu Chaoyang and the other two followed behind. The mother and daughter seemed to be sharing a secret.

Chaoyang stopped in front of a sportswear shop.

"Do you want to buy some sports clothes?" Zhu Yongping asked.

"I... want to look at trainers," Zhu Chaoyang stammered.

Trainers from one of the big brands were extremely popular, as all of the kids were aware. Chaoyang had never owned a proper pair in his life.

He spotted a brand that a lot of his classmates talked about. "Dad—" he exclaimed. It wasn't until his dad coughed that he remembered he was supposed to call him Uncle.

"Uncle, I would like to try on this pair," Chaoyang said.

An employee appeared and asked for his size. Zhu Chaoyang took the shoes and tried them on. Zhu Yongping watched. The boy had barely tightened the laces when a young voice cried for attention. "Daddy! Come quickly, I want to buy something!"

"Just a minute, let's wait until Chaoyang has tried on his shoes."

"No! You have to come now! Come right NOW!" the girl screeched.

Zhu sighed. "You're a lot of work, sweetie! I'll be right there."

Chaoyang looked up and saw the woman next to her spoiled daughter. He couldn't stand the victorious expression on her face and quickly looked down again.

"Daddy! Hurry! Hurry!" the girl said, in a tone that her father never refused.

"OK, I'm coming," Zhu called. "All set? Are they the right size?" he asked Chaoyang impatiently.

"Yeah, just right."

"Then you don't need to try any others on," Zhu said. He looked to the salesperson. "We'll take these. How much?"

Chaoyang stood up as his father pulled out his wallet. He couldn't believe that the mere suggestion of a tantrum from Jingjing was enough to make his father impatient. Zhu Chaoyang pursed his lips and said, "Thanks for the shoes. We can buy clothes some other time. I should go."

"I can drive you home in a little while," Zhu said.

"I can take the bus. It's fine."

"Well, all right." Zhu Yongping looked relieved. The sooner he could put this awkward situation behind him, the better.

Chaoyang took the box with his old shoes under one arm as he stood up. He walked slowly to the shopping centre exit as Zhu told his wife and daughter that something came up and the boy had to go home. Chaoyang took a last look at them. Wang Yao gave him another smug smile, while little Jingjing stuck out her tongue. Chaoyang gripped the shoebox tightly, gritted his teeth and left without a backward glance.

9

When Zhu Chaoyang arrived home, he saw Ding Hao and Pupu leaning against a wall and chatting. Ding Hao looked dejected while Pupu was cool and detached. Ding Hao smiled at the sight of Chaoyang and pulled Pupu along to meet him.

"Back already?" Ding Hao said.

"Ahh, there was nothing to do," Chaoyang said.

Pupu observed him carefully. "You look sad."

"I'm fine," Chaoyang said, forcing a smile.

"He's sad? How can you tell?" Ding Hao asked curiously.

Pupu looked right into Chaoyang's eyes. "Have you been crying?" she asked him.

"Me? Crying? No way!"

Now it was Ding Hao's turn to look. "Chaoyang, you were crying, weren't you?"

"If it's because we came out of the blue, you can tell us. We won't hold it against you," Pupu said, her voice level.

That had not occurred to Ding Hao and he decided an apology was in order. "Sorry, I didn't tell you I was coming. I just showed up at your house with Pupu. We make trouble everywhere we go. Come on, Pupu, we should leave."

Just like that, the two turned to go. Chaoyang felt lost. "Wait!" he called. "You don't understand. It's not because of you at all."

Pupu looked doubtful. "It's not because of us? If someone else is bullying you, just tell Ding Hao; he fights like a pro. Nobody could beat him at the orphanage."

"Yeah, I'm a good fighter. If they wanna mess with you, they have to get through me first!" Ding Hao went on to boast about all the times he bested someone in a fight. He then promised

39

that anyone who was mean to Chaoyang would hear from Ding Hao. He would give those bullies a taste of his fists.

Chaoyang was introverted and only had one person he might call a friend since Ding Hao moved away. But he never expected these two to care about him, and warmth flooded him. So he told them everything, everything except the fact that his dad had given him 5,000 in cash. He did not trust them fully and the money would just be a temptation.

"You're his son. Why does he care about his daughter and not you?" Ding Hao asked. He corrected himself when he saw the look on Pupu's face. "I mean, boys and girls should be treated the same, but most adults care more about boys. How come it's the other way around with your dad?"

"People play favourites all the time. That's why he ignores you even though you're both his children," Pupu said scornfully.

Chaoyang sighed. He hated his stepmother so much that even talking about her put him in a sour mood. "My mum says that my dad is afraid of my stepmother; that's she's a witch. As soon as he sees her, he is completely under her spell. And then whatever that witch says, my dad does. It's no surprise that the girl is a spoiled brat, when you see how they dote on her. She always gets her way. My dad used to visit me more and give me money when I was younger, but then the visits stopped, because that witch kept fighting with him about it. So now I don't hear from him at all."

Ding Hao clenched his fist. "I can't believe that big bitch and her little bitch would treat you that way. If they weren't in the way, your dad would still be living with your mum. But... I don't see how I can help you."

Chaoyang gave him a friendly pat on the shoulder. "Never mind. I just have to live with it. Oh, yeah, Pupu, I got a camera from my dad. It doesn't take a charge very well, but it should do if we just want to take a few pictures. Then we can go to a shop and get them printed."

"Thank you, Brother Chaoyang," she murmured.

"Isn't he the best?" Ding Hao said.

"Mm-hmm," Pupu said.

Chaoyang felt a little embarrassed at their kind words.

"Hey, Chaoyang," Pupu said. "We can't take down Big Bitch because she's a grown-up, but if you knew what school Little Bitch went to…"

"I just know she's in second grade."

"Aww, if we knew what school she went to, we could beat her up there. That would show her!" Pupu said.

"Yeah," Ding Hao chimed in. "You could point her out to us and we would teach her a lesson. You wouldn't even have to show your face. We could throw her in a rubbish bin and close the lid. She'd cry like a little baby."

Chaoyang laughed at the image.

"Why stop there? I would take all of her clothes and put them in a dirty toilet," Pupu said, a malevolent expression on her face.

Chaoyang was surprised at her vehemence. Still, he had to admit that their plans sounded wonderful.

Pupu clearly wasn't joking. "I had a little brother. My mum loved him and completely ignored me. Only my dad was nice to me. Brother Chaoyang, your situation is like mine, but in reverse—your dad ignores you and your mum is nice to you."

"Are you still in touch with your brother?" Chaoyang asked.

"He's dead, just like my mum, I told you. And later on, I found out that he wasn't really my brother. My mum slept with some other guy and got pregnant. That's why Dad was framed for their deaths and shot in the head. I hate my mum! I hate my brother! I wish they could die again!"

Chaoyang nodded in sympathy. He realized that his situation was similar to Pupu's. Given what had happened to her dad, he could see why she was keen on exacting revenge on others.

He felt a tinge of regret that it wouldn't be possible to carry out this fantasy.

41

10

After they ate dinner, Ding Hao and Pupu both had showers. They told Chaoyang that when they ran away from the orphanage, they couldn't find a permanent place to stay, so neither had had a proper shower in months. Afterwards, the three chatted all evening.

"Why did you two want to run away from the orphanage, Ding Hao?" Chaoyang asked.

"Because," Ding Hao glanced at Pupu, "because the people were bad and we couldn't take it any longer."

"Bad? What do you mean?"

"It wasn't always that way. An old lady used to run the place; she was nice to everyone. Then she retired and a man showed up. A fat slob."

"He was a pervert," Pupu added.

"A pervert? Seriously?"

"He touched Pupu," Ding Hao said.

"What do you mean?" Chaoyang asked nervously.

Chaoyang spent little time with his classmates and his knowledge of sex was limited to what he saw on television—holding hands and kissing.

Pupu had no reason to be bashful and didn't mince words. "He took me to an empty room, took off all my clothes and touched me."

"But… but… how could he do that?"

"It happened a lot. He would take his trousers off sometimes and then put his dick in my mouth. It was so gross and hairy. I wanted to puke." She retched at the memory.

"Why would he put his dick in your mouth?" Chaoyang asked.

"Dunno."

"Do you know why?" Chaoyang asked Ding Hao.

"Me? Uhhh…" Seeing their ignorance, Ding Hao snickered and shook his head. "Anyway, it's bad," he continued. "Pupu told me about what that filthy man did to her, so the next time he went looking for her, I burst into the room before he had the chance to take his clothes off. He was real angry and locked me in a tiny closet for a whole day, without giving me anything to eat. When I grow up, I'm going to beat him to a pulp!"

"It wasn't just me, he did that to loads of girls," Pupu explained.

"Yeah, but Li Hong liked it! She said he was nice to her and bought her snacks. She wanted to marry him!" Ding Hao said.

"She can do as she likes! I'm never going back. Ever!" Pupu said.

"Same here. Once I snuck out to the internet café and the fat slob found out and hit me. He said I stole money from the orphanage."

"Why would he say that?" Chaoyang was mystified.

"I went to play computer games and he said I took the money that was meant for the support workers. He said I couldn't possibly have money otherwise."

"So… where did the money come from?"

"Lots of people would come visit us and would give us cash. The greedy bastard told us to hand it over to him so he could buy us snacks. But he never gave us any, even when we gave him hundreds. So I hid the money the visitors gave me and used it to play games."

"Is the orphanage looking for you?" Chaoyang asked.

The two nodded at the same time.

"The nice lady told us every child at the orphanage has an ID number," Ding Hao explained. "You gotta use it to buy train tickets, get a place to stay, all kinds of stuff. Someone can find out where we've been just by using that number. Right after we left, we were staying in a crummy hotel and saw our pictures on the news. That bastard was being interviewed, begging for us to come back. The worst thing would be if he caught us. I… stole his wallet right before we ran away. I had to though—if we didn't have his four thousand yuan, we wouldn't have made it this far. So, yeah, we can't go back. The director definitely wants to kill me."

"If you didn't run away, would you have to stay in that orphanage for life?" Chaoyang asked.

"No, they kick you out at eighteen. But it'll be like forever before we turn eighteen, so we couldn't possibly stay that long. It was like a prison. We couldn't go out. It was the strictest orphanage ever," Ding Hao said.

"That's because all of our parents were murderers," Pupu said. "They treated us as if murdering was in our DNA. As if we were a menace to society."

Poot.

The accompanying smell made it clear that the little sound was a fart. "Come on, Ding Hao, can't you give us a heads up before you float an air biscuit?" Chaoyang complained.

Ding Hao glanced at Pupu, who turned her head. He made a face and said, "Fine, next time I will tell you three minutes beforehand."

The three giggled uncontrollably.

When the laughter subsided, Ding Hao grew serious. "You're so lucky. I know your parents are divorced, but at least you have a home, you can go to school, and you have classmates. Nobody wants us. We have nowhere to go."

The mood had darkened, but Zhu Chaoyang did his best to save it. "Don't be jealous of me. I get bullied at school all the time."

"Who's bullying you? I'll skin them alive!" Ding Hao said, ready to be a hero again.

"Do you fight girls?" Chaoyang said.

"Girls?" Ding Hao smiled a lopsided grin. "Guys shouldn't fight girls, that's not right. Pupu can take her though. Although, she's only eleven, she might not win."

Pupu frowned at him.

"It's no use," Chaoyang sighed. "Her dad is a cop, so nobody would pick a fight with her. It's not the kind of problem that fighting can solve."

He told them how Ye Chimin had gotten him in trouble for things he didn't do. Just because he was the best in their class, she did everything she could to make him suffer!

"The teacher didn't believe you?" Ding Hao asked.

"Adults only listen to one side of the story—usually it's the girl's side. They're so stupid!" Chaoyang exhaled sharply. "Adults think that children are simple, and that their lies are easily uncovered. They have no idea how wicked some kids can be!"

Ding Hao and Pupu agreed.

"Adults think that kids from the ages of one to eighteen are all the same. A five-year-old might tell a clumsy lie, but once he is a teenager, he can tell really convincing lies. Adults underestimate us," Chaoyang added.

"You think that's bad. Grown-ups are the worst," Pupu agreed. "You were burned by your classmate, but adults let me and Ding Hao down all the time."

"Really?"

Ding Hao nodded, fuming.

"After my dad died," she continued, "my uncle said he would adopt me. But just a few weeks later, one of my classmates called me a murderer's daughter, so I hit her. She asked me to stop, but I just had to let it all out. I kept hitting her until she cried and ran away. Then that night her family found her drowned in a reservoir. They said I pushed her in! The cops took me to the station and I stayed there for two whole days. I told them I didn't do it, but nobody believed me. They let me go because they didn't have evidence, but that stupid family kept bringing

45

it up, and my aunt didn't want me any more. So she dumped me at the orphanage and my family never spoke to me again."

"So…" Chaoyang said slowly, desperate to know, but also a little scared, "… did you push her?"

Pupu looked deeply disappointed. "Of course not. I just beat her up and went home. I don't know how she fell in the reservoir."

"When my parents were arrested, I wanted to stay with my family but nobody wanted me," Ding Hao said. "I was on the streets all by myself, and some shop owner said I stole things. It wasn't me, and they didn't find anything on me, but the stupid guy wouldn't let up. He got his son to box my ears, so that night I found out where he lived and smashed his window with a rock. I got caught and they put me in with Pupu."

The three were quiet for a moment, their faces filled with frustration and anger. All the injustice of the world seemed to have landed on their shoulders.

Chaoyang changed the subject. "Hey, let's check out the camera. If we charge it tonight, we can take photos tomorrow."

"Do you know how to use it?" Pupu looked expectantly at him.

"No, but I think I can figure it out. There's a computer under my bed. The government gave it to my mum for job training but she never used it much. Let's see if it'll turn on."

They pulled out the computer and tried everything, but eventually they had to ask a neighbour for help. He managed to boot the computer and showed them how to use the camera.

Chaoyang was a quick study. He opened a folder to see the photos. They were all of his father with his second wife and daughter. They looked incredibly happy. His dad was always kissing his wife or hugging his daughter. Chaoyang started deleting files.

"Wait," Pupu said. "Leave a couple of photos so I can remember Little Bitch's face. If I ever meet her, I'll rough her up for you."

Chaoyang gazed at the happy family and remembered how terrible they had been to him that afternoon. He wasn't happy about it, but he left a few photos as Pupu asked.

"So you want a photo for your dad. Where do you want to take it?" Chaoyang asked.

"Somewhere pretty?" Pupu ventured.

Chaoyang thought about it. "Let's go to Sanmingshan. My mum checks tickets there so we can probably get in for free. It's a nature park, and there are a few places on the mountain that are good for photos."

"Yeah! I've never been on a mountain before," Ding Hao said.

"Yeah," Pupu said, looking out the window. "I think my dad would like to see me hiking on a mountain."

11

The next morning Zhu Chaoyang and his friends woke up early. There weren't any buses that would go there directly, so they took one into the city and then a two-hour bus ride to the nature park.

When they arrived, Zhu Chaoyang pointed out his overweight mother to his friends. Zhou Chunhong's bottom-heavy physique was emphasized by her short stature. "Wait here. I'll go see if Mum can get us in for free." He ran over to her.

"What are you doing here?" Zhou asked.

"I wanted to take my friends to see Sanmingshan." Chaoyang pointed at Ding Hao and Pupu. "See? That guy was my classmate in primary school, but he then moved to Hangzhou. And the girl is his sister. I want to show them around today. Oh, and Mum—" He pulled out the 5,000 yuan from his backpack. "I saw Dad yesterday and he gave me money! You should take it."

"That's a lot! When did he get a heart?" Zhou said, stuffing the money into her pocket.

"He was playing cards with Uncle Fang and some other people. They made him give it to me. And then his new wife and their daughter showed up," Chaoyang said.

His mother saw that he was still upset by the meeting. "What did they say?"

"Not much, but his daughter asked about me, and Dad lied and said I was Fang Jianping's nephew."

"I can't believe he would say something like that!" Zhou said, distressed at her son's obvious pain. "That is completely out of order. It would be better if he didn't even exist."

Chaoyang didn't say anything.

After her outburst, Zhou Chunhong tried to move on. "Your clothes are dirty, Chaoyang. I was supposed to go home tomorrow but I'm switching shifts with Auntie Li. I won't be back for a few more days so you will need to do the laundry yourself. Don't forget!"

"OK. I'm going to go hang out with my friends now."

"Have fun and be a good host. You should take them out to dinner tonight—do you need money?"

"It's OK, I still have a few hundred yuan. Um, can my friends stay at our house for a couple of days?"

"Of course," Zhou said. She didn't feel the need to set too many limits for Chaoyang: he followed all the rules and always did his homework.

Chaoyang waved his friends over and they greeted Zhou Chunhong politely. Then they went to the enormous staircase that snaked up the mountain.

Soon the three friends were inventing games and had forgotten their troubles. It was mid-week and they virtually had the park to themselves. After climbing halfway up the mountain, they took a break at a pavilion.

"Wow! I want to come here every day!" Ding Hao said, stretching his arms over his head.

Pupu stood next to him and took in the view. She spun around with a smile on her face. "Brother Chaoyang, do you think this is a good place to take a picture?"

"Sure," he said.

Ding Hao moved out of the frame. Pupu made a peace sign and gave a brilliant smile. Chaoyang showed her the picture on the tiny monitor and they all agreed that it looked good. They took a few more from another angle.

Now there was a man and an older couple in the background, but far enough away that the scenery was still good. Chaoyang took more photos.

"What do you think?" he asked, showing Pupu the screen.

"These are great!" she said.

"You should be in some photos, Ding Hao," Chaoyang suggested.

"No, thanks," Ding said.

"How about a video?"

"You can take videos?" Pupu's curiosity was piqued.

"Yeah, I've hit record already, say something!"

"What should I say?" she asked.

"Watch this." Ding put his hands together in the style of a newscaster. "Hello. You're watching the news report, hosted by me, Ding Hao, a super-famous host. The top news today is that three genius kids visited Sanmingshan. Uh, then…"

"Then what?" Chaoyang asked with a grin.

"Mr Ding? Anything else?" Pupu added.

"Then… then…" He gave up.

Suddenly they heard terrible screams. In the distance the man was still there, but the couple had disappeared. Seconds later, they saw the man lean over the low wall, screaming, "Mum! Dad!" He turned to the people at the shops. "Help! Help! There's been an accident!"

The three kids ran to the edge of the pavilion.

12

Everyone who heard the screams came running. Soon park staff were frantically shouting into their walkie-talkies. The three friends leaned over the wall to try to get a better look.

"I can't even see them! Do you think they're dead?" Ding Hao asked.

"Yeah." Chaoyang moved instinctively away from the wall.

"Why did they fall?" Pupu wondered aloud.

The wall was nearly two feet wide and people were able to sit comfortably without losing their balance. As far as Chaoyang knew, there had never been an accident here before.

"Maybe one of them had a heart attack and lost consciousness, and the other one fell trying to help them?" he suggested.

Ding Hao spotted the search team looking for the bodies below. "Let's go down there!"

"No way," Pupu said.

"But I've never seen a dead body before!"

"Oh, come on. It's going to be gross," Chaoyang said, giving him a look.

"I don't want to see all that blood," Pupu said.

"Please?" Ding Hao wheedled. "You can keep your distance. I wanna see."

"Fine. I want to go down and check that my mum's OK." Chaoyang sighed as they went down the long staircase.

Chaoyang spotted his mother speaking with several colleagues. "Mum, did you find those two people that fell a few minutes ago?"

"Oh, you came back down! You should go home. I have a lot to do, I can't talk right now," Zhou answered. She didn't think this was a good place for Chaoyang or his friends.

"Did they find them?"

Zhou pursed her lips. "Yes. The security guards are carrying the bodies away now."

"What did they look like?" Ding Hao asked earnestly.

Zhou was too shocked to answer.

The man who had shouted after the old couple appeared, crying miserably. He followed the security guards. "Mum! Dad!" he repeated over and over. The onlookers felt sorry for him.

Chaoyang and his friends waited until the commotion died down and then said goodbye to Chaoyang's mother. As they left the park, they saw the man again, speaking to police, security guards and other staff members. He was saying something about cremation. Guards picked up the two body bags and put them in the back of a pickup, followed by a police car. The man walked slowly to his car, which was parked by the entrance.

"Look, he drives a red BMW," Chaoyang whispered.

But he did not know much about cars and failed to note that it was the cheapest model available in China. Still, any BMW was a rarity in his life and it represented wealth to him. Pupu stared intently at the car until it disappeared.

13

Xu Jing entered the interview room, clearly distraught. She tripped and almost fell but Zhang Dongsheng was ready to catch her. Xu wrenched her arm away as if she did not want him to touch her.

Zhang had not expected this reaction. "I'm sorry, Jing, it's all my fault. I didn't take care of them," he said in a low voice. Now they were both crying.

Xu turned her head away, bit her lip and tried to stop her sobbing. The police officers invited them both to take a seat and offered them tissues and glasses of water.

"Thank you," Zhang said, accepting some tissues and drying his eyes.

"Thank you for coming. I know this is a difficult time. Xu Jing, your parents are in the crematorium now, I take it?" The interviewing officer's kind face was filled with sympathy.

She did not answer.

"We need to register this accident and in the next few days we will invite you to talk to the staff at the nature park. Is that OK?"

Zhang turned to her. "What do you think, Jing?"

She was in too much pain to respond.

"Can you please explain what happened on the mountain-side, Mr Zhang?" the officer asked.

"Everything was going just fine. I am a teacher and our summer break just started. I wanted to take my parents-in-law to Sanmingshan to get some fresh air. My plan was to visit the mountain in the morning and then take them home in the afternoon. My father-in-law has—had diabetes and high blood pressure, and I think the hike was a little too much for him. But he kept saying he needed the exercise. I never thought that... Oh, it's all my fault!"

Zhang buried his head in his hands.

The officer took notes. "Did they both have high blood pressure?"

"No, just my father-in-law. My mother-in-law was healthy for her age."

"How did they fall?" the other officer asked.

"We reached the platform and were going to take a little break. My mother-in-law asked me to take a few photos and the wall blocked the view a bit, so they both sat on it. They said a picture with them on the wall would look better. I was fiddling with the camera and in those few seconds when I was distracted, I heard them scream. When I looked up they were falling backwards down the mountain. I should have... I should have..." Zhang trailed off.

"I can't believe you let my parents sit on that wall! At their age! You did this!" Xu cried.

"You're right! It's all my fault!" he interrupted. "I never thought anything would happen, the wall looked sturdy enough. I just don't understand how they fell."

He looked to the police officer for help.

"Don't be too hard on him, Mrs Xu. Nobody has ever had an accident like this at Sanmingshan before. There are warning signs, but so many people take photos there that nobody would ever think that something so terrible could happen."

"If nobody has ever had an accident there before, *how* did it happen?" Xu Jing demanded.

"I don't know! It was all over so quickly," Zhang cried.

"All the evidence points to this being an accident. It is a sturdy wall; it's not dangerous at all. Maybe your father had a heart attack or fainted and then fell. Then he would instinctively grab for his wife and they fell together. We found medication in his pocket. Was your father taking medication for his blood pressure, Mrs Xu?"

"I don't know, you'd have to ask Dongsheng," she stammered.

"She's very busy at work. I usually take care of those things," he explained.

The officer was impressed at how well Zhang looked after his in-laws.

"I always reminded my father-in-law to take his blood pressure medication, but he didn't want to take it unless he felt like he needed it. Maybe if he had taken it regularly, this would not have happened," Zhang continued.

Before long, the interview was over. The officers recorded the deaths as an accident. Stopping to rest after intense activity was known to cause cardiac arrest in people with high blood pressure. The report suggested that the man fainted and took the woman down with him.

The officers did their best to comfort the bereaved and reminded them to take care of themselves. The nature park could not be held at fault since there was a warning sign on the platform. Xu Jing and Zhang Dongsheng would receive a small sum from the park as a token of sympathy. For all intents and purposes, the case was closed.

This is exactly what Zhang had expected. He had carefully planned the murders. He was pleased with his acting skills at the police station and didn't think that anyone suspected him—apart from Xu Jing, that is.

14

CHAOYANG'S APARTMENT

"What colour do you think mashed-up brains are—yellow or white?" Ding Hao was still jazzed from the day's events.

Pupu rolled her eyes and Chaoyang told him to lay off the death talk. Neither of them wanted to go over it again.

At the orphanage, Ding Hao's nickname was Blabber Mouth. Nobody trusted him with their secrets, because they knew that by the next day everyone would know them.

The gruesome deaths did not seem to dampen the friends' moods. As soon as they arrived at Chaoyang's place, they went to the computer to check out the photos. They were pleased with how old they looked in the serious ones and how funny they looked in the wacky ones. Even Pupu was laughing along. They clicked on the video where Ding Hao had pretended to be a newscaster.

"You actually sound like you're from Beijing! Impressive," Chaoyang laughed.

"When I grow up, I want to be a reporter," Ding Hao answered.

"Sounds like a good plan for someone who likes to share juicy stories," Chaoyang teased.

"That'll never happen. You'd have to go to school for that," Pupu said.

"You're right, my grades are awful, and I'm not going back to school," Ding Hao agreed glumly.

"Hey, do you want to go to KFC tonight? My mum said I should treat my guests," Chaoyang suggested in an attempt to distract them.

"All right!" Ding Hao was excited. "I've never tasted KFC! I can't wait."

Chaoyang was about to close the video and shut down the computer when Pupu stopped him.

"Hang on." She sat perfectly still as she stared at the screen.

"What's wrong?" he asked.

"Can we watch the video one more time?"

"Of course," he said.

"There it is," she whispered.

"What?" The boys asked simultaneously.

Pupu waited for the video to end. Her voice was cold. "He *murdered* them."

"Huh?"

"Those two old people didn't fall. That guy with the fancy BMW shoved them off the cliff!" Pupu exclaimed, taking the mouse from Chaoyang.

"What?" The boys couldn't understand what she had seen.

Pupu pressed play and they all watched the video again. This time, they all saw, far in the background, the man grabbing the legs of the couple and pushing them over the wall. The victims reached out for him, but he did not help them. The whole incident only lasted seconds, but it was clear to all three what had happened.

"He murdered them," Pupu repeated slowly.

"That's impossible!" Chaoyang said. His heart was racing.

Even Ding Hao was speechless. Chaoyang was terrified— nothing like this had ever happened to him before. Hearing about a murder on the news was totally different from knowing you were at the scene of the crime when it happened! The video was the scariest thing he had ever seen.

"I don't think anybody at the park suspected murder, which means we might be the only ones who know. We have to report this," Chaoyang said, trying to sound determined.

"Yeah, OK, let's report it," Ding Hao said, his head bobbing up and down.

Chaoyang hurried to the phone in his mother's room and picked up the receiver. He didn't know what to say to the police. Would they believe that three kids had witnessed a murder? Would they think it was a prank call?

He looked at his friends. "What should I say?"

They didn't say anything.

Chaoyang handed the phone to Ding Hao. "You do the talking, you're better at it."

"No, I can't," Ding Hao said, backing away. "Pupu, why don't you do it?"

She shook her head.

"Then… I'll just tell the truth? Do you think they will believe a thirteen-year-old?"

"If they don't, we can go to the police station and show them the video," Ding Hao said.

"Yeah, OK. I'm going to call them now." Chaoyang screwed up his courage, picked up the receiver and dialled 1-1-0. "Hello, my name is—"

The line went dead. Pupu had pressed the button to end the call. She looked solemnly at him and shook her head. "Don't report it, we have to sort things out."

"Sort what out? This is a major crime!"

"Would you give the camera to the police?" Pupu asked softly.

"Of course!"

"What about me and Ding Hao?"

"What about you and Ding Hao?" Chaoyang was still confused.

"They'll ask about all the people in the video, then they'll make us give a statement and find out that Ding Hao and I are runaways. Next thing you know, we're back at the orphanage."

Ding Hao inhaled sharply in surprise. "Yeah, Chaoyang, you better wait, we gotta think about this. We swore never to go back to the orphanage. We can't… we just can't…"

"So what do we *do*?"

The phone rang. Chaoyang hesitated, looked at his friends and wrung his hands anxiously. Pupu grabbed the phone and spoke in her sweetest voice. "Hello? Sorry, I dialled the wrong number. It was an accident."

The call handler chewed her out for wasting their valuable time and Pupu said "sorry" at least a dozen times. Finally she hung up. "I'm hungry. Maybe we should get food and talk about this afterwards?"

15

The three kids sat at a table, sharing a bargain bucket and plenty of sides. Normally Chaoyang loved corn on the cob, but today it was tasteless. "But if we don't report that man, he'll get off scot-free."

"Ding Hao and I are in the video. As soon as they know who we are, they will contact the orphanage and it's game over," Pupu said.

"But we can't just stand by and let him get away with murder!" Chaoyang exclaimed.

Pupu arched her eyebrows. "Maybe they were bad people."

"Bad people? They were an old couple!"

"You don't know," she retorted.

Chaoyang looked to Ding Hao. "What do you think?"

Ding Hao stuffed a piece of chicken in his mouth to avoid answering, but then realized there was no way to get out of it. "Chaoyang's right, we can't let the guy get away with it. But Pupu's right too: the police would definitely send us back to the orphanage. How about we report it once Pupu turns eighteen, so neither of us have to go back to that place?"

Chaoyang frowned, then shook his head. "That video would haunt me."

"What are you afraid of? We could say we didn't notice the murderer in the video earlier," Pupu argued.

"I am positive I would have nightmares about this," Chaoyang responded nervously.

They sat in silence.

Pupu finished her bread roll and then looked at them earnestly. "I have an idea."

"What is it?" Chaoyang asked.

She paused for effect. "We should make a deal."

"How?" he asked, confused.

"We give the video to the murderer, but before that, we make him give us money!" Pupu said, her eyes glinting.

"You mean, sell it to him?" Chaoyang gaped.

She nodded confidently. "He drives a BMW, doesn't he? We don't have a place to live and we need money. So the best thing is to sell the video and get money so we can live by ourselves for a few years. What do you think?"

"But…" Chaoyang protested.

"We'll split the money three ways. Come on, Brother Chaoyang, nobody knows about this but us. We can put your share in a bank account because if your mum found out we would have to explain," she said.

Chaoyang was so shocked it took him several seconds to answer. "Pupu, that's blackmail. That's a crime!"

"What about you, Ding Hao? Are you in?" Pupu asked.

Ding Hao played with his hair. "It would be good to have money. But… isn't it dangerous trying to make a deal with a murderer?"

"That video is life or death for him! He would definitely want to buy the video off us," Pupu argued. She gave her idea a little more thought. "Chaoyang doesn't need the money like we do. He would be taking a bigger risk by hiding the money and not telling anyone."

Chaoyang said nothing. He was not interested in negotiating with a murderer—what if he killed all three of them to eliminate them as witnesses? This was not only blackmail; it would be helping a murderer walk the streets. It didn't sound good. He had always been a good student. He avoided conflict; his experience with bullies had taught him that staying away, and keeping quiet, was the best option. Making contact with a murderer was ludicrous, let alone trying to strike a deal with one.

Chaoyang was starting to think he should secretly report his friends to the police so they would go back to where they came from. Then again, they would never forgive him—they might beat him up or worse. Even if he managed to get them sent to the orphanage, they might get out again, or they might take revenge when they turned eighteen. Chaoyang remembered how Ding Hao promised to get even with the director of the orphanage—he clearly didn't let go of a grudge.

Chaoyang realized that he was afraid of the murderer—and of his new friends. There didn't seem to be an easy solution. Ding Hao and Pupu's appearance was turning his life into a nightmare! How he wished he had not answered the door!

16

After finishing their KFC meal, the three kids still had not reached a consensus. They walked to the largest Xinhua Bookstore in Ningbo. It was three storeys tall and had air-conditioning, making it a great place for Chaoyang to hang out in the summer. The three separated, with Ding Hao making a beeline upstairs for the children's books, and Chaoyang going to the reference section. He felt relaxed the moment he entered this space. He wished he could buy all of the exam books that were arranged on a large table and go through the problems one by one. After half an hour of indecision, Chaoyang finally selected a book of problems from the International Mathematical Olympiad. He sat on the floor and started to read it, perfectly content.

Another half an hour passed. Pupu appeared holding a book. She sat down next to him. "Ding Hao is obsessed with a book he found—he doesn't want to leave."

Chaoyang did not want to leave either—the bookstore was much more interesting than his apartment. More importantly, he wanted to put off the conversation about blackmailing the murderer for as long as possible.

"We can stay. The store doesn't close until nine, and we can take the bus back. I come here all the time," he said.

"That sounds amazing," Pupu said enviously.

They left Ding Hao upstairs and kept on reading. Then Chaoyang heard a familiar voice: "Jingjing, what books are you supposed to get? We should ask someone to help us find them."

"It's the four classics, Dad. *Journey to the West, Water...* something, and two more," a young girl answered.

"*Water Margin, Dream of the Red Chamber* and *Romance of the Three Kingdoms*. Aren't those a little bit challenging for someone your age?"

"Our teacher said we wouldn't understand them but we would have to read them later. I want to see what they look like."

"Then I'll buy them for you. We can buy whatever books you want," the first voice replied magnanimously.

"Dad!" Chaoyang blurted out and immediately regretted.

Pupu looked up, her curiosity piqued. Zhu Yongping stepped into the aisle and saw his son on the floor. He glared and put a finger to his lips, a commandment to be silent.

"The four classics are upstairs, Jingjing. Let's go find them," he spoke loudly.

"Oh, and, Daddy, I need to get a calligraphy copybook. Our calligraphy teacher told us to buy one but I forgot last time," Jingjing carried on, not noticing her father's distraction.

"OK, we can get it after we find the classics."

Zhu Yongping took his daughter's hand and guided her up the stairs. He stole a glance at Chaoyang and was surprised to find him gazing back at him. Zhu Yongping coughed and looked straight ahead. Chaoyang felt trapped in his own thoughts.

"That's your dad?" Pupu asked.

The question brought him back to the present. He nodded and then buried himself in his book. He did not know if she would empathize with him or feel sorry for him. Maybe she was completely indifferent to his problems—indifference seemed to be her natural state.

"Careful, your book," Pupu said before turning back to her own.

Chaoyang looked down. He had bent back the pages of his book without even noticing.

★

64

When they finally decided to go home, Chaoyang said little. Pupu avoided talking about the murder but Ding Hao would not stop going on and on about it. The other two gave him noncommittal responses and hoped he would let it go for now.

17

The next day, Chaoyang suggested going to the Children's Palace, a six-storey building that offered classes and activities. It had been renovated a few times since its opening in the 1980s, but it still looked tired. Inside there was a free science museum, a sports hall for table tennis, a library, and dozens of classrooms.

When Chaoyang said there was an amusement park next to the Palace, Ding Hao was thrilled by the idea of lots of rides. Pupu thought the park sounded fun, but she was conscious of spending more of Chaoyang's money. He convinced her that it would be nice to do something while they still had the chance, because they would be leaving soon. Plus, he was happy to spend a hundred yuan if it meant he could delay the conversations about dealing with the murderer.

Even though it was a hot day, the amusement park would be pretty comfortable thanks to the shade provided by mature trees. There was a train ride, a carousel, bumper boats, a small roller coaster and a few other rides. The prices were reasonable, which made them popular, so they could expect a long line next to every ride.

The three kids got off the bus and headed in the direction of the amusement park. It was crowded. Ding Hao was already charging ahead when Pupu noticed a girl at the entrance and grabbed Chaoyang's arm. He looked to where Pupu was pointing and spotted Jingjing and her mother, Wang Yao. It was so strange that just last week he barely knew what his half-sister looked like, and now that they met he had seen her three days in a row! Wang Yao was handing a bookbag to Jingjing and reminding her to do something. The little girl waved her mother off impatiently.

Chaoyang watched as Jingjing walked into the Children's Palace by herself. Finally he said to Pupu, "Come on, let me show you the best rides."

"Don't you want to get revenge?" she asked.

"Yeah, but it's impossible," he said meekly.

Ding Hao had noticed that his friends weren't following him and came back. "Come on, guys! Don't you want to get on a ride?"

"We just saw Little Bitch!" Pupu said.

"Aww, don't let it ruin your day, Chaoyang," Ding Hao sympathized.

Chaoyang nodded.

Pupu scowled at Ding Hao. "Didn't you say you wanted to teach her a lesson? This is our chance."

"Yeah, I did," Ding Hao said awkwardly. "But… what do you want me to do?"

"Torment her until she begs for mercy," Pupu spat.

He gaped at her. "No way, there's too many people, someone would see us!"

"Her mother just left. Let's follow her; maybe she'll be alone at some point. Then we can show her who's boss."

Blood pumped hard through Chaoyang's veins, but still he wanted to convince them to give it up. "She would definitely tattle on us. If my dad found out, we'd be toast."

"Ding Hao can beat her up, and you can watch from a safe distance. Then you won't get into trouble," Pupu said, a smile spreading across her whole face.

"Pupu, it's unfair for me to beat up a little girl," Ding Hao protested.

"She's not a little girl, she's Little Bitch," Pupu corrected.

"Fine, fine. Little Bitch. Still! It's not the honourable thing to do."

"But you said you wanted to teach her a lesson."

"Yeah, but…"

"I see how it is. Even if nobody else sees you doing it, you're more concerned about your reputation than your friend. Then I'll do it, but you better have my back if things get ugly." Pupu's tiny hands curled into fists.

"Chaoyang?" Ding Hao looked towards him for the voice of reason.

"I think…" he began. He stopped and remembered all the unfair things that happened in his life. His parents divorced when he was only two. If that woman had not stolen his dad, he would have a happy family. Being a child of divorced parents had caused him to be the target of bullying at school, and there was nothing he could do about it. If his parents were still together, he would have had a normal upbringing—surely then Mrs Lu wouldn't assume that he was acting out. If his parents were still together, they wouldn't have to worry about money all the time. His mum had lost her job and it took her ages to get another one through a government scheme. But the new job at Sanmingshan meant that she was away from home much of the time because it was so far away. They had to count every last penny, while that evil woman had everything she wanted.

It was all his stepmother's fault. He deserved a good life, but she took it away. Suddenly the image of his father holding Jingjing's hand and looking down at him in the bookstore flashed before him. He made up his mind and said quickly, "Let's get her. But don't let Little Bitch see me—you go first."

Ding Hao led the way to the Children's Palace, Pupu followed, then Chaoyang.

"Thank you," Chaoyang said softly to Pupu.

"I'm the same as you, remember?" she said simply.

18

Chaoyang knew the Children's Palace well and guessed that Jingjing would not be doing any of the activities offered on the first two floors. He kept a good distance away from his friends and avoided looking at them. The three went to the second floor, and while Chaoyang loitered in the men's toilets, Pupu and Ding Hao looked for Jingjing. They entered each room pretending to be interested in checking out the class, took a quick look at the students and left as soon as they were sure Jingjing was not there. They combed the second floor. Nothing. Then they scanned the third and the fourth floors. Still nothing. They went to the fifth floor.

Compared to the other floors, this one was nearly deserted. Just when Chaoyang was ready to give up, Pupu said, "I think I hear kids in the classroom back there. You stay here, I'll check it out."

She poked her head in and came back quickly.

"Yup, it's her," Pupu said.

"Are there lots of people?" Chaoyang asked.

"Not that many. They're doing calligraphy, and there's only one teacher."

"We can't just grab her, the teacher would stop us. How will we get her out?"

"Let's just wait in the corridor. Maybe she'll come out, maybe we won't get a chance to get revenge today," Pupu said calmly.

"OK, let's wait by the stairs," Chaoyang said.

"What exactly are we gonna do?" Ding Hao sounded uncharacteristically apprehensive.

"We shouldn't hurt her. Let's just make her cry," Chaoyang suggested.

"Just make her cry?" Pupu scoffed. "We can't let her off that easy."

"Pupu…" he said.

"OK, how about we stick her head in a toilet. She'll cry but she won't get hurt!"

"Genius!" Ding Hao exclaimed.

"This is going to be awesome!" Chaoyang was so excited he almost clapped his hands.

"There's just one thing," Pupu said, her eyes glinting.

"What?" Chaoyang asked.

"We need a toilet with poop in it."

"I can take care of that!" Chaoyang said a little too eagerly. He dashed to the men's toilets while Ding Hao and Pupu watched the door to the classroom from their hiding spot by the stairs.

"I got eyes on Little Bitch," Pupu said in a low voice, moments later.

"She's coming this way! Looks like she's going to take a leak!" Ding Hao whispered.

"And she's by herself. Let's grab her and drag her to the men's loo," Pupu said.

Jingjing had to walk past the stairwell to get to the toilets. Pupu and Ding Hao were ready for her.

"Stop right there," Pupu said, grabbing Jingjing's ponytail.

Jingjing yelped in pain and surprise. She turned around to see older kids who meant business. "Hey! What are you doing?"

"What can I say? It's your unlucky day," Pupu sneered. She grabbed her ponytail again and yanked.

"Oww! Stop it!" Jingjing cried.

"Or what?" Pupu asked. She jerked the ponytail a third time.

"Ow! Who are you? What are you doing? Help!"

Ding Hao quickly covered her mouth, but Jingjing bit down ferociously. He shouted and pulled back his hand, which was bleeding. Jingjing struggled, trying to return to the classroom, but Pupu grabbed her firmly around the waist. The younger girl wasn't going anywhere. Tears streamed down Jingjing's face. She tried to spit on them but missed. She scratched Ding Hao's arms, leaving long marks, and he panicked, slapping her in the face. Jingjing cried for help, but the classroom was too far away. Her cries were indistinguishable from the general noise of children singing and playing—no one came.

Chaoyang walked out of the men's toilets without realizing that Jingjing was just outside.

"Pupu, Ding Hao, what—? Oh!"

Chaoyang never expected that his friends would catch her so quickly. He reacted too slowly and Jingjing recognized him.

"*You!* You're making them do this!" she shouted, anger replacing her fear.

"No, I'm not." Chaoyang sounded unconvincing as he tried to figure out how to get away.

Jingjing pointed a finger at him. "My mother told me who you are! She says my dad fooled around with a fat woman and they had a mistake. You're that mistake!"

Suddenly everything went quiet for Chaoyang. He pushed Jingjing's forehead with one finger. "*You're* the mistake! I'm Zhu Yongping's son!"

Jingjing gave as good as she got. "Mummy says you'll always be a shrimp because your mum is short and fat. She made Daddy promise that he'll never give you money ever again! She says you're… you're a bastard!"

Pupu let go of her and slapped her, hard. Jingjing wailed and Chaoyang dragged her to the men's toilets by the ponytail.

When they were inside, Chaoyang picked her up and put her on the ledge of the large open window that faced an inner courtyard. Suddenly he was no longer interested in just dunking her head in a toilet. Jingjing struggled with all her might, but he was older and stronger.

"Let me go! You're crazy! Let me go!" she shouted and stood up. She balanced her toes on the bottom of the windowsill and

71

held onto the top. Surprisingly, her precarious position did not prevent her from screaming at Chaoyang.

Ding Hao could see that it was all getting out of control. "Chaoyang, get her down. She could fall."

Chaoyang only wanted to scare her into submission. He reined in his emotions and held onto her to make sure she would not fall. Still, he had to win this argument, once and for all. "Call me a bastard one more time and I'll push you."

Jingjing was beyond reason at this point. "You're a bastard! Dirty bastard! Help! Help!"

Chaoyang did not want her to attract attention, especially not where people in the courtyard might see her. He reached his right hand up to try and cover her mouth. "You are so stubborn!"

Jingjing tried to bite him and he moved his hand away.

"I told you she was a bitch," Pupu said drily. "She bites just like a dog."

Ding Hao stretched out his hand for Chaoyang to see. "She drew blood, can you believe it?"

"I dare you to bite, Little Bitch!" Chaoyang raged.

"You're crazy!" Her face was wet with tears, but she wouldn't stop abusing him.

He slapped her and she shrieked and cried but she would not yield. Chaoyang was beside himself. He wasn't going to push her off the windowsill, but he didn't know how to bring this to a satisfactory end.

"I know! Ding Hao, come here!" Pupu shouted. He stepped towards her and she whispered in his ear.

Ding Hao listened to her, and his face showed displeasure. "Isn't that a little…?"

"We have to do something!" Pupu was firm and Ding Hao reluctantly agreed.

Chaoyang watched Ding Hao reach into his trousers and grab a few pubic hairs. He pushed them next to Jingjing's mouth.

"Open up! Who taught you to bite like that, huh?" Ding Hao feigned toughness as he forced the girl's mouth open and stuffed the hairs inside.

Chaoyang was horrified. He never would have thought to do something like that. Then he looked at Pupu, the one with the brilliant idea—never in a million years would he think that a girl could come up with something so vile.

Jingjing started coughing and then heaving, but Ding Hao had her mouth covered so she couldn't spit it out. Finally she was fully aware of the precariousness of her situation, so she stopped being aggressive and started to shiver as she pleaded, "Please, Big Brothers and Big Sister. Please, let me go. I won't do it again. I was wrong."

"You gonna bite me again, little doggie?" Ding Hao threatened.

"No, I promise." She shivered again.

"So now you know you were wrong," Pupu said with a smug look. "You have to say sorry."

Jingjing continued whimpering, "I'm sorry, I'm sorry. Let me go, please."

"Looks like she won't bother you again, Brother Chaoyang. Get her down," said Pupu.

"Yeah, we should probably quit now," Ding Hao said.

Chaoyang was still angry but had his emotions under control. "You know you were wrong? OK, I'll let you go."

"I was wrong, Big Brother. Please let me down," Jingjing said.

At the words "Big Brother", Chaoyang's heart softened. He was her half-brother, after all. He threatened her once more for good measure. "Remember, you're the bastard, not me! If you say anything out of line, I'll get you!" He gave her one more thump.

The last punch scared her, and Jingjing was back to crying in an instant. "Help! I said sorry and he still wants to hit me! Ahhh! I'm gonna tell my daddy!"

"You!" Chaoyang felt like a huge bucket of dirty cold water had been poured on his head. The world stopped. "I wish you would DIE!" he roared.

He pushed her with all of his might, and the girl fell backwards. Ding Hao tried to grab her but was too late. They heard a sickening sound as the body hit the concrete below.

19

Chaoyang couldn't stop shaking. His feet were rooted in place. Ding Hao and Pupu went to the window. They saw a large pool of blood and a twitching form. At that moment, screams and shouts of alarm erupted from the lower floors. People ran over to the body, then looked up to the windows. The two instinctively moved away out of sight.

"What do we do, what do we do?" Ding Hao asked Chaoyang.

Chaoyang stood stock still.

Pupu quickly assessed the situation and pulled him towards the door. "Run first! Talk later!"

They raced down the hallway and started running down the stairs. By the time they reached the first floor, people came out of the classrooms to see what the commotion was. Chaoyang stopped and looked at Pupu and Ding Hao. "This is all my fault. Clear out of here, I'll deal with this."

"What'll you do?" Ding Hao asked urgently.

Chaoyang tried to smile. "You two have nothing to do with this. You should leave before you get in trouble."

Ding Hao was ready to mix with the crowds and escape. He pulled Pupu's arm, but she did not budge, saying, "Are you scared?"

"Scared?" Suddenly Chaoyang looked much older than his years. "I knew she would tell my dad. I was going to die anyway if he found out, so my life is over. There's no point in being scared—it is what it is."

"What are you going to do now?" she persisted.

"Turn myself in."

Ding Hao spoke in a low voice. "Your mum will be all by herself." Chaoyang was dumbstruck. His eyes rimmed with tears and he hung his head.

"Maybe she didn't die. If she didn't die, she'll squeal, there's nothing we can do. If it looks like she fell to her death, and nobody saw us…" Pupu murmured.

"Let's go to the courtyard and see," Ding Hao suggested.

"If she's not dead and she sees us, we'll get caught!" she warned.

Chaoyang exhaled. "I'll go down and see. You aren't related to her and she doesn't know your names, so nobody will suspect you. You guys can watch me from that window. If I'm arrested, you both should get out of here. Just mingle with the crowds going out. If I get out OK, we'll meet behind the building."

They agreed to the plan, which seemed sensible enough. Pupu and Ding Hao squeezed in next to all the other children looking out the window and waited for Chaoyang's signal.

Staff members circled Jingjing's body in order to keep the other children away. Parents hurried away from the brutal scene, pulling their children with them. But the curious and morbid types approached the body to get a better look.

Chaoyang was small and couldn't see anything except backs. To try to get a closer look, he pushed against people until he reached an open space, but he still couldn't see. Then he looked up towards Pupu and Ding Hao, and she made an OK gesture. Chaoyang left the Children's Palace and went around to the back. Pupu and Ding Hao exited a minute later.

"Little Bitch is dead," Pupu said, once they were all together.

"You're sure?" Chaoyang was not sure whether he should be happy or not.

"Oh, yeah, we could see everything from the window. They picked her up and the whole back of her head was crushed. As we came out the police were coming up the stairs to investigate," Pupu said.

"I'm dead meat. The police are definitely going to arrest me," he wailed.

76

"Don't be afraid: nobody saw you except me and Ding Hao. I'm not telling. Ding Hao?"

"Me?" Ding Hao straightened. "I would never sell out a brother! Not even if they tortured me."

Pupu glanced at him and suppressed a smile. "OK, Blabber Mouth."

"Have a little faith, I know when to shut up! We're friends, Chaoyang, and I'll be loyal to the end." He clapped Chaoyang on the shoulder and puffed out his chest to make himself look more heroic.

Their show of support made Chaoyang try to give them a smile. But he was still in shock at the way his emotions had consumed him. "Well, whatever happens, happens. Come on, let's go home." At these words, a thunderbolt cracked, and huge raindrops pelted down. People ran for cover and the whole area emptied in minutes. The three kids ran to the bus stop.

Chaoyang stood on the crowded bus and looked out the window. Everything that happened today felt like a strange dream. He looked at Ding Hao, who was in his own world, and he understood then that Ding Hao made a big show of being loyal and generous, but really he was a timid mouse on the inside. Chaoyang could tell by looking at him that his heart was heavy and that he was a little afraid.

Pupu had resumed her poker face. She noticed Chaoyang looking at Ding Hao and smiled quickly, as if nothing was wrong. Chaoyang struggled to return her smile.

20

CHILDREN'S PALACE

The storm washed away the blood in the courtyard, and key evidence along with it.

It was clear that not even a miracle would bring the little girl back. Emergency workers pronounced her dead at the scene. The police were left to deal with the body. Based on the extent of her injuries, the police deduced that the victim had fallen from one of the top two floors. They checked the toilets and were unable to find any evidence in the women's toilets. That left the men's toilets on the fifth floor, where they found some suggestions of a struggle.

The officers on the scene had already been suspicious that this was not an accident, and what they found in that toilet was enough to call in the higher-ups. Captain Ye Jun arrived with several of the serious crime officers. He carried one of Jingjing's shoes to the fifth-floor windowsill where some footprints had been found and it was a match. It was chilling corroboration.

Dr Chen, the coroner, examined the body. Without bothering to take off his rain jacket, he sought out Captain Ye on the fifth floor and urgently pulled him aside. "Ye, the girl had four pubic hairs in her mouth."

"What?" Ye Jun's eyes widened. "Are you suggesting she was sexually assaulted at the Children's Palace?"

"I know, it's sickening. I have asked technicians from the District Public Security Bureau to drop what they're doing and process everything as quickly as possible. I think this is the first sexual assault of a minor our team has ever dealt with."

Ye Jun was enraged. His own daughter was only thirteen and frequently came to the Children's Palace. He wanted to make sure the case was solved quickly to protect the community and reassure the parents. Otherwise, no one would bring their kids here ever again. "I don't care what resources we have to use. We have to catch this monster."

Dr Chen took off his raincoat and opened his toolkit. Captain Ye and the other officers put on gloves and shoe covers belatedly before gathering evidence. But too many people had passed through the toilet that day and it was difficult to identify what might be important. The floor was concrete and it was nearly impossible to get any impressions of footprints, and some were from overeager officers who arrived on the scene and neglected to secure it.

The officers searched the urinal and all the stalls but found nothing. The massive shit found in one toilet was assumed to be irrelevant. They had a paltry amount of evidence, so placed their hopes on the windowsill. An officer had been holding an umbrella out of the window to protect the evidence from the relentless rain. Dr Chen took fingerprints from the sill and the window, working efficiently. The walls were untiled and there was no point trying to get prints from them. After one more careful sweep of the room, Dr Chen left.

There was a briefing at Ningbo Jiangdong Public Security Bureau that evening. Chen laid out the facts: the victim fell from the fifth floor of the building. Her eyes were puffy, presumably from crying; she had pubic hairs in her mouth; and she had been slapped and punched. It suggested foul play, possibly a case of child molestation and murder. Fingerprints and fibres belonging to Jingjing were found on the windowsill. The two prevailing theories were that she was carried to the windowsill and pushed, or that when she was being attacked, she climbed on the windowsill and jumped or fell. They had also found fingerprints belonging to at least ten other people—it was unclear whether any of them were relevant. Evidence from the autopsy led the officers to assume that the perpetrator forced Jingjing to give him oral sex.

The officers at the meeting were filled with righteous indignation—how could someone do that to a nine-year-old?

"Was there semen in the victim's mouth?" Captain Ye asked.

"No," Dr Chen answered.

"Was that because… the perpetrator did not ejaculate?"

"There should have been some kind of semen traces, even if he did not ejaculate. The expert I spoke to said Jingjing might have spat it out or swallowed it, but there should be traces somewhere at the crime scene. The other question that's been niggling me is how anyone would have the nerve to molest a child in such a public place."

"Must be a pervert!" a policeman said.

"Why didn't he pull the girl into a stall instead of molesting her by the window? The lack of evidence in the stalls is surprising. If it happened in the open, anyone could have walked in on them. It was incredibly brazen."

The investigators were unable to reach any conclusions. Perhaps the killer liked to take risks.

"Some blood and skin cells were found on Jingjing's teeth. They almost certainly belong to the killer. Our initial analysis suggests skin cells from the hand, rather than genitalia. It's possible that she bit the killer's hand and he pushed her in anger or humiliation. Our lab staff are working on getting a DNA sample now."

The DNA of the blood in Jingjing's mouth was a clue that could change the course of the investigation. Unfortunately, they would have to wait until they found a suspect to match it to.

After Dr Chen finished his report, the other officers shared the evidence they had found.

Zhu Jingjing was dropped off by her mother, Wang Yao, at about 9 a.m. The girl was used to going to the calligraphy class on her own. It was the only class on the fifth floor that day, and usually had about ten students. The calligraphy teacher remembered Jingjing asking to use the toilet and some of the students in the class had heard crying, but it was unclear if that was Jingjing or a student from another floor, because nobody had gone to check.

Since the Children's Palace was an old building, it only had one CCTV for the entrance and the main lobby. Surprisingly, nobody had witnessed her fall, meaning nobody would be able to identify the perpetrator.

The police grimaced—the evidence was scant at best. They would be relying on that CCTV camera because the murderer would have passed it at some point. Still, it would be a nightmare to try and find him in the crowd—a lot of people came to the Children's Palace in the summer.

Ye Jun looked thoughtful. He then sent a few officers to contact students, parents and teachers who had been at the Children's Palace to see if they could give any assistance. He would speak to his superior first thing tomorrow to see if they could offer a reward for information that led to an arrest. Finally, he designated a few officers to sift through the surveillance footage for any suspicious males, especially a man on his own.

21

The rain that had started in the morning continued straight into the evening without any sign of stopping. The weather report said it would stop tomorrow. The sound of the raindrops hitting the window waxed and waned. Zhu Chaoyang watched television with a vacant expression on his face. Ding Hao had discovered that the old computer had a few games on it, despite not being connected to the internet, so stopped moping and became totally fixated on the games. He seemed to have forgotten what happened that morning and he ignored the pain in his palm. Pupu read a book.

The three of them kept to themselves.

They stayed that way for hours, until Pupu looked up at the clock. It was eight. "Ding Hao, Brother Chaoyang, I'm going to make some noodles. You want some?"

"Yeah, thanks," Ding Hao said without looking at her.

"OK," Chaoyang said absentmindedly.

Pupu scoffed. "Brother Chaoyang, you need to stop thinking about it. If they know you did it, they will come and find you. If they don't know, they won't bother you. Worrying about it won't change the outcome. So let's just act like it didn't happen. You're a kid. Kids who commit crimes don't get executed."

(The only thing Pupu was afraid of was being killed by a firing squad.)

"Kids who commit crimes don't get executed," he repeated, his mind still wandering. Then he jumped up and sprinted to his bookshelf. He opened a textbook about government and flipped through to a page about serious crimes that he had read before. He read and reread the paragraph several times, then put down the book and hurried over to Pupu. "I'm not fourteen yet! I'm not fourteen yet!"

"So?" she asked.

"The age of criminal responsibility is fourteen, so I can't be held criminally liable for certain crimes," he said in a rush.

Ding Hao looked at the two of them. "What does that mean?"

"It means that even if the police figure out that I did it, it's not a big deal, because I don't turn fourteen until January. I won't be punished that severely because I'm not fourteen!"

Ding Hao shook his head. "I'm turning fourteen in a few months and Pupu's not turning fourteen for ages. You're saying we can just kill someone on the street and it's no big deal?"

"I mean, it's still a big deal. But at least I won't go to prison, just a juvenile rehabilitation centre."

"What's the difference between prison and juvenile rehabilitation?" Ding Hao asked.

"I don't know, but at least I won't go to prison. I assume I'd still go to school and then get out when I'm eighteen."

"So it's like living at the orphanage?" Ding Hao asked.

"I don't know exactly, but anyway, I won't be criminally liable." Chaoyang looked relieved.

Pupu smiled. "See? The worst thing that happens is you go to that juvie-whatever for a few years. You can relax."

"The only thing is, I still might get in trouble," Chaoyang said.

"What do you mean?" Ding Hao asked.

"If my dad ever found out that I was the one that pushed Little Bitch, he would turn me in and I'd go straight to the juvenile rehabilitation centre. My dad would disown me and my mum would be all by herself, and she'd be really sad."

"Don't worry. They won't find out," Ding Hao said. He turned his attention back to the computer.

Pupu said a few more comforting words before going to make noodles. When they were ready, Ding Hao ate in front of the computer, while Pupu and Chaoyang sat in front of the television. For a brief period, the atmosphere was less oppressive.

Then the phone rang. Everyone froze. It was already 8:40 p.m.: who would be calling at this hour? Chaoyang crept to the phone, his jaw set. Pupu stood close by and Ding Hao paused his game. The phone rang a second time.

Chaoyang made fists and relaxed his hands, and finally plucked up his courage. "Hello?"

"Chaoyang, I wanted to tell you something. You know the child that your father had with that witch? She fell to her death today." It was his mother. He was appalled to hear a trace of delight in her voice.

"Fell... to her death?" he said dumbly.

"My colleague told me about it. She said the little girl fell from the fifth floor of the Children's Palace and died. Your father never worried about you in the past and now that his daughter has died, he's crying as if his own father died, that's what everyone is saying," Zhou Chunhong said. She felt that passing on the gossip was a little unseemly, because Zhu Yongping's parents were actually quite nice to her and her son. Her father-in-law was unwell, and her words were a slight on him, so she added: "I mean, your grandfather is a good person; it's just your father who is a good-for-nothing. I think now that the little girl is gone, your father will treat you better."

"Uh-huh," Chaoyang said weakly.

Zhou could sense that her son was acting strangely. "What's wrong? Are your two friends still with you?"

"Yeah."

"Did you have an argument?"

"No, everything's fine."

"Then what is it?"

He didn't answer.

"Did you go anywhere fun today?" Zhou persisted.

Chaoyang hesitated before answering. "We went to the Children's Palace in the morning and we played games at home in the afternoon."

"You were at the Children's Palace? Did you see the accident?"

"We saw that somebody fell, but we didn't know it was her. We came straight home."

"Oh, that must have been upsetting for you," his mother said, quickly finding an excuse for her beloved son.

"Yeah… a little."

"It's OK. You're not alone tonight so you'll be OK. Chin up."

"We're going to play some games."

"I feel better knowing you're all together. I'll come back in a couple days. Be good."

"I will," he said. He hung up and exhaled loudly.

22

Professor Yan Liang had bought a new phone to replace the stolen one, but it took a day to load his contacts. He thought of the text messages Xu Jing had sent and called her. "Xu Jing, dear, I lost my phone two days ago. Is something wrong?"

"Oh, everything's fine, everything's fine. Yeah, I'll call you later," she replied and immediately hung up.

Yan Liang frowned. That wasn't like her at all. Half an hour later, his niece called back. Her voice sounded panicked. "Uncle Yan, I'm sorry I couldn't talk to you just then. I needed to find a private place because I want to tell you that my mother and my father had an accident."

"What kind of an accident?"

"They… they passed away."

"They passed away? But they were both healthy," Yan said.

"Dongsheng took them to Sanmingshan. They fell off the mountain and died." Xu Jing sounded like she was about to cry.

"Oh, my poor Xu Jing. Tell me when the funeral service is, I want to be there," Yan Liang said.

"Uncle Yan?" Xu Jing asked hesitantly. "Would you come and visit me as soon as you can? I know it's a big favour."

"What can I do for you?" Yan thought it was a little strange because he was only a cousin and usually closer family members would be expected to deal with funeral arrangements. Also he didn't consider himself qualified for such a task.

"I don't think that their deaths were an accident."

Yan spoke carefully. "What do you think happened?"

"They were murdered," Xu Jing whispered.

"Murdered? Who would want to kill your parents?"

"Zhang Dongsheng!"

"Zhang Dongsheng?" Yan coughed. "Have the two of you been fighting? I know when something so unexpected happens, your imagination tends to run wild. But you can't go around saying things like that; if Dongsheng found out, he would be really hurt. You're married, you still have to make things work."

"I don't have to make things work any more. I've already told him I want a divorce. He hates me for not wanting to stay together and I'm sure that he killed my parents!"

Yan had no idea that the marriage was at breaking point. He clearly remembered how they were determined to get married, despite the disapproval of her parents. Zhang Dongsheng was born in the countryside and he didn't have a great job—Xu Jing's parents thought their daughter could do better. But even though her parents thought they were in different leagues, the two had loved each other. Xu Jing was obstinate and quickly decided that Dongsheng was the one; she'd ask for forgiveness instead of permission. How had everything changed so drastically in just four years?

No matter what Xu Jing said, Yan could not believe that Zhang Dongsheng would kill his parents-in-law. "Xu Jing, what did the police say?"

"The police have already filed an accident report. But we're only hearing his version of events."

Yan grimaced. "You don't believe the police report? You only believe your flights of fancy?"

"Uncle Yan, I am afraid for my safety! I think Dongsheng is going to kill me next. I couldn't tell you all this on the phone earlier because he was sitting right next to me. You're the only one I can turn to. Can you meet me somewhere? Please? I'll drive to Hangzhou if you want." Xu Jing's voice quavered as she held back a sob.

"What can I possibly do?"

"You're the only one who could investigate what really happened at Sanmingshan."

"Xu Jing, you know I'm not a cop any more. You should trust the official investigators; they know what they're doing," he said awkwardly.

The other line was silent. Finally she sobbed, "I thought you would believe me, Uncle Yan! Nobody believes me!"

"Don't cry, dear. It will be OK. I'm going to come and see you. Is that all right?"

Xu Jing immediately restrained herself. "Thank you, Uncle Yan! I'll find a place for us to meet, but don't tell Dongsheng you're coming to see me, I don't know what he'll do if he finds out."

Yan reluctantly promised not to tell him and agreed to meet his niece at a café that afternoon.

23

"Uncle Yan!" Xu Jing threw her arms around Yan and sobbed noisily.

Yan was unsure how to react to all this emotion and patted her back. He spotted a waitress who was openly staring at them, but pretending that she didn't see, which only irritated him more. He tried not to think about the waitress imagining Xu Jing to be his coquettish mistress. Yan preferred to do things the proper way—calmly and rationally. He steadied Xu Jing, sat her down and whispered, "Get it together!" He then sat opposite her, trying to make their relationship look as platonic as possible.

After a few minutes, she settled down for them to order drinks. She took a few sips before she spoke. "Uncle Yan, I strongly suspect that Dongsheng killed my parents. You have to believe me."

"Have the police sent you their accident report?"

"Yes, it came out yesterday."

"And you've read it?"

"Yes, but they don't have any evidence besides Dongsheng's statement!" She pulled out a copy for him to read.

Yan skimmed the report. "Everything points to an accident."

"It's not that simple!" Xu Jing insisted. "I underestimated him before, but he has an agenda, I promise you. I brought up a divorce last September, and we fought about it a few times. But then he stopped arguing and did everything I asked him to do. It was like he was a totally different person. He did all the chores, and he was nice to my parents. When I brought up the divorce again, he invited my parents over so the three of them could dissuade me. Even my mother was on his side."

"Maybe he was angry when you wanted to divorce him, then he realized that fighting was not going to win you back, so he started being nice to you and your parents. You call that an agenda?" Yan scoffed.

"Listen, when we first got married, my parents didn't like him and he was lukewarm towards them. My mum never considered him to be part of the family. But the moment I mentioned divorce, he became a different person. He was so strong-willed before, why would he suddenly suck up to them? I didn't understand then why he would go out of his way to treat them so nicely. But now it makes sense to me, he was just waiting for the right moment to get rid of them," she explained.

"So all this was part of a grand plan? Did you tell the police your suspicions about him?"

"No, I didn't think they would believe me."

"You still seem to have some wits about you," Yan said coldly.

Xu Jing was shocked by his words. She spoke in a low, desperate voice. "Uncle Yan, I know that Dongsheng was your student and I'm accusing him of something very serious."

"Let's ignore that fact for a minute. You claim he pushed both of your parents down the mountain at Sanmingshan. Why didn't anybody see him do it? Surely, the police would have spoken to other visitors."

"Apparently, nobody saw him. It was a Wednesday morning, so the park wasn't busy."

"I don't know what to say." Yan paused. "He didn't want a divorce and your parents were also advising you against a divorce, but then he killed your parents. Do you think he has lost his mental faculties?"

His tone suggested that if Dongsheng had not lost his wits, then Xu Jing had.

Xu Jing pursed her lips. "He's going to kill me next."

"Oh, so now you're making him out to be a serial killer! Why would he want to kill you?" Yan asked derisively.

Xu Jing could see that her uncle believed in his former student and not her. More tears leaked down her face. "He... he hates me. Plus once I'm out of the way, he will inherit my family's money."

"He's killing three people to get at your money?" Yan gritted his teeth, his patience wearing thin.

"I knew nobody would believe me. But it's the truth! My parents were convinced he was a gold digger, and they forced us to sign an agreement before we got married that kept the Xu family money away from him. The money he earns goes into an account that only I have access to. If we divorced, he would have absolutely nothing."

"I know what Zhang Dongsheng is like. Once he gets an idea in his head, he never gives up. But if he didn't love you, why did he get a job instead of earning a postgraduate degree? If he didn't love you, why would he sign such an extortionate agreement? Why would he risk everything to be with you when we both know that he calculates the risks and benefits of every decision he makes?" Yan's voice had risen as he spoke.

Xu Jing was stunned into silence.

Yan looked at her and sighed. "Your parents died suddenly, that's a great blow for you. I can understand that you would feel unsteady right now. But you have to remember, you went against your family's wishes when you married Dongsheng. You promised to be with him for a lifetime. Every marriage has its rough patches. You should stay by his side."

"I can't," Xu Jing said, a bitter smile on her face.

"Why not?"

"I've fallen in love with someone else. I'm having an affair."

"Xu Jing!"

"Uncle Yan, I know you're angry. But love isn't something that can be controlled by reason. When I married Zhang Dongsheng, I thought I was head over heels in love, but—well—I wasn't really thinking straight. It was only after we married that I saw just how incompatible we were. He really *is* a country boy. Then I met my soulmate, the person I'm supposed to be with. I regret marrying Zhang Dongsheng and causing him pain, but I'm in pain, too."

"Does he know that you are having an affair?"

"I think he has figured it out," she answered.

"But he still wants to be with you, right?"

"He acts like he's forgiven me, but I'm not convinced." Her laugh was hollow. "Did you know that he pressured me to cremate my parents as soon as possible? I managed to put it off until yesterday, but now they've been cremated. He said the police recommended it!"

"How high was the platform that they fell from?"

"They said it was over three hundred fifty feet."

"In that case their bodies would have been terribly mangled. It would make sense to cremate them and let them rest in peace. Do you really think the police should have kept the remains in a freezer for loved ones to look at?" Yan asked.

"I know now that nothing I say will make you believe me," she said. "I don't have evidence. I just have a sense of foreboding. If I die in an accident, it will be Dongsheng's doing. Then you'll finally know that I was telling the truth."

Yan shook his head sadly. He disapproved of her actions, but he still pitied Xu Jing and her grief. Zhang Dongsheng was brilliant, and he might have been capable of carrying out such an attack, but she had no proof, and Yan did not think his niece had provided an adequate motive.

24

The rain kept pouring, dampening Chaoyang's already low mood. Ding Hao was glued to the computer while Pupu read books. Their fear had abated somewhat; none of them mentioned yesterday's accident.

After another dinner of noodles, Ding Hao headed back to the computer. Pupu stopped him. "Ding Hao, tomorrow Chaoyang's mother is returning and we'll have to sleep somewhere else. We need a plan!"

"One step at a time. I'll find a job and we'll try to get you enrolled in a school here," he said, plopping down on the couch.

"Just because you want a job, doesn't mean you'll find one," Pupu said.

"What do you want to do, then?" His tone was resentful.

"What will you do if you can't find a job?" she asked.

"That won't happen. Finding a job is easy, right, Chaoyang?" Ding Hao had an awkward smile on his face.

"I don't know, I've never worked," Chaoyang said.

"Employing someone under the age of sixteen is a crime, I read it right here," Pupu countered, pointing to Chaoyang's government textbook. "Nobody's going to hire you."

"But they won't know that I'm not sixteen, right? I'm tall for my age," Ding Hao protested.

"You don't have any ID," she continued.

Ding Hao stared at the ceiling, forcing down his resentment. "So what do you think we should do? Wait till I'm sixteen?"

Chaoyang was unsettled by this exchange. He was hoping his guests would leave as soon as possible. They couldn't stay at his place forever, could they? He didn't want them to go back to the orphanage either. He wanted them to find somewhere safe—but somewhere that wasn't his home.

Pupu pursed her lips. Finally, she looked at him. "Brother Chaoyang, I want to sell the camera to that man, the murderer. Are you OK with that?"

Not that again! Selling the camera was very risky, but if he refused her now, she might tell the police about what happened to Jingjing. After all, they had only spent a few days together, and Chaoyang was not sure how strong their friendship really was. When he had gone downstairs to buy noodles, he had seen a poster on the community noticeboard in the street—the police were offering a reward of 30,000 yuan for information leading to the capture of Zhu Jingjing's attacker. That kind of money might be enough for the two runaways to abandon their loyalty towards him. He didn't want to think about that.

Then again, if they were able to sell the camera to the murderer, Pupu and Ding Hao would have enough to live on for a few years, so they would be less likely to rat him out. At least they would all be guilty of committing blackmail, so all three would have an incentive not to blab.

After doing this calculation, Chaoyang said, "You do need a lot of money right now. I think maybe… selling the camera is the only way you can make some. But we still have a problem: how do we find him?"

The three racked their brains. How could they find the murderer without attracting the attention of the police?

25

The next morning they had a haphazard breakfast. They still needed a plan, but nobody had any bright ideas. Pupu went to the bathroom and didn't come out for at least ten minutes. Ding Hao's patience wore thin. "Pupu, are you done yet? I need to pee!"

"Uh, almost done," Pupu said through the door. "Chaoyang? Does your mum have any pads? I, uh, started my period."

"Let me check!" Chaoyang answered, going into problem-solving mode. He ran into his mother's room, noticing with relief that the little piece of yarn had not moved. He had replaced it every time after he had gone into the room, and although he felt bad for not trusting his friends, he still thought he had to take precautions. Chaoyang found the pads in a drawer and Pupu opened the door a tiny crack to take them.

A few minutes later, she came out of the bathroom looking a little bashful. She had never had her period before.

The two boys looked at their feet, not knowing what to say.

"How much money do we have left, Ding Hao?" Pupu asked.

"About two hundred."

"Will you give me some? I want to buy some pads and I want to replace the one I took from Chaoyang's mum."

"It's no big deal. She'll understand," Chaoyang interjected.

But Pupu was insistent. The boys couldn't think of anything better to do, so they went with her. The corner shop in the building did not have the right brand, so they kept walking until they reached a supermarket. Pupu went in while the boys waited outside.

Pupu was in the store for less than a minute before coming out again. "That man is in the store! He's the one from the mountain!"

"Seriously?" The boys stared at her.

"Yeah, he was buying some tissues and paper cups. He'll come out any minute."

"Are you sure you didn't mistake him for someone else?"

"I'm sure. I got a really good look at him in the car park," Pupu said.

A man walked out, but Chaoyang wasn't sure. "That's him?"

When the man opened the passenger door to a red BMW to put away his purchases, his question was answered—Pupu was right.

"Don't let him get away!" Pupu said as they all ran towards the car.

Zhang Dongsheng was surprised when a little girl pulled at his arm and he turned around to see two boys behind her: one tall, one short. "Can I help you?"

"Did someone in your family have an accident at Sanmingshan?" Pupu asked.

Zhang searched their faces with a frown. The boys were visibly frightened, but the girl stood her ground.

"What did you just say?"

Pupu did not mince her words. "You killed them."

"What are you talking about? Who told you that?" Zhang exclaimed.

The boys avoided the man's gaze, but Pupu was unrelenting. "We *saw* you push them."

"Nonsense!" Zhang hissed. He opened the driver's door with the intention of ignoring them.

"Know what else? We caught it on camera. If you drive away now, we'll hand it in to the police," she threatened.

Zhang turned to look carefully at the three of them. His gaze settled on the girl, who was the smallest. "Watch your tongue, demon child!"

"Don't believe us? We'll show you the camera. Chaoyang, run home and get it!" she ordered.

Zhang watched him gallop off and said nothing. He closed the car door and drummed his fingers on the roof. The two kids stared intently at him.

Ten minutes later, Chaoyang returned, breathless from running both ways. Pupu told him to stop when he was ten feet away from the man. "Does it still have a charge?" she whispered.

"Let me see," Chaoyang said. It had one bar left, which meant it could die at any moment.

Pupu let Zhang Dongsheng watch the video, but stood between him and Chaoyang so he couldn't snatch the camera. Chaoyang held it with the monitor facing Zhang. The man's lips pressed into a thin line. He couldn't believe it. He had checked his surroundings so carefully at Sanmingshan; there had been nobody nearby on the platform! He had thought that anyone in the pavilion would be too far away to give him any problem. But here were these meddling kids ambushing him at the supermarket of all places.

Zhang took two giant steps towards the camera. Chaoyang whisked it away and trotted a safe distance from him.

"What do you lot want?" Zhang growled.

"We want to sell you the camera," Pupu said.

"Sell the camera?" Zhang was taken aback.

"Yeah, you give us money, and we give you the camera," she explained.

The video on the camera was damning evidence; he had no idea why they would sell it to him. What was the catch? "There's too many people here. Let's talk about this somewhere else," Zhang said cautiously.

"Where?" Pupu asked.

"How about we go to a quiet café?"

"What do you guys think?" Pupu asked the boys.

"I dunno," Ding Hao said.

"We can go to a café. But I want to take the camera home first," Chaoyang said.

"Fine. You two can get in the car and wait, you look too noticeable standing around like this," Zhang said through clenched teeth.

Ding Hao drew his friends into a huddle. "If we get into his car, will he…?"

"Maybe," Pupu said.

"I don't think so," Chaoyang said. "He wouldn't do anything in broad daylight. Just stay in his car and I'll be right back. He won't hurt us if we still have the camera."

26

Pupu and Ding Hao climbed into the back seat of the BMW. Zhang Dongsheng smiled at them slowly. "What are your names?"

"Pupu," Pupu said warily.

"I'm Ding Hao," Ding Hao said.

"What about the other young man?"

"Zhu Chaoyang," Ding Hao said.

"OK. My name is Zhang Dongsheng. You're all middle school students, I take it?" He kept a smile on his face. Ding Hao nodded but Pupu stayed quiet.

"What school do you attend?"

Pupu was not going to answer that question, but Mr Blabber Mouth had other ideas.

"We don't have a school," he answered.

"You don't have a school?" Zhang laughed and assumed that the boy was just being cautious. "Well, where do you live?"

"We live…" Ding Hao began, but Pupu punched his arm and he shut up.

"None of your business!" she said with a glare.

"OK." Zhang suspected that the girl was going to cause him the most trouble.

He tried a few more times to get information from them but Pupu was on high alert, so he finally gave up. When Chaoyang returned, Zhang drove them to a café where they sat at a secluded table. "Order whatever you want, my treat."

"What's good here?" Ding Hao asked, perking up.

Zhang slid a menu towards him and watched as they ordered drinks and snacks. They were too young to pose a threat to him. He drew his lips into a smile. "Were you playing by the pavilion that day?"

"Yeah," Chaoyang said.

"When did you notice that part of the video?" Zhang asked.

"Later that day," he said.

"So, who knows about it besides the three of you?"

"No one."

"What about your parents?"

"They don't know," Chaoyang said.

Zhang tried to judge whether he was lying or not. "Why didn't you tell your parents?"

"My mum is away."

"And your dad?"

"Put it this way: he doesn't know," Chaoyang said a bit stiffly.

"Right." Zhang turned to the other two kids. "What about your parents?"

Ding Hao didn't respond.

"They're all dead," Pupu said, her face impassive.

"They're all dead?" Zhang said incredulously. "Who's taking care of you? How do you three know each other?"

"None of your business," she said coldly.

Zhang's eyes flashed with anger, but he quickly recovered his composure. "So why didn't you give the camera to the police?"

"Because we wanted to sell it to you," Pupu said.

"How can you be so sure that I'll buy it?" Zhang asked with a fake smile.

"You drive a BMW, so you have the money. If you don't want to buy it, we'll hand it over to the police, and you'll be on death row," she answered.

He was stunned—how could such a small person threaten him so openly? Though he looked ready to attack her now, Pupu did not flinch.

Chaoyang was encouraged by her bravery and spoke up. "So, do you want the camera or not?"

Zhang reined in his emotions and turned to Chaoyang. "I'll give each of you two thousand yuan for the camera."

"That's not enough," Chaoyang said, shaking his head.

"Then how much do you want?"

The three friends hadn't settled on a sum. "Just a minute," Chaoyang said to Zhang. They left the table and huddled. "What do you think?" Chaoyang asked.

"We need at least five thousand per person, then Pupu and I will have ten thousand. That ought to do it," Ding Hao suggested.

"I don't want the money, I don't have anywhere to put it. You can have it," Chaoyang said.

"You don't want it?" Ding Hao's eyes widened.

"If my mum finds out, she'll think I stole it. Plus I'd be happy if you're able to live off it."

"But if you give it all to us, that… I would feel bad." Ding Hao was visibly moved.

"I have a family, you don't," Chaoyang said. "We're friends, right?"

"Yeah, and we always will be," Pupu said, her eyes glistening.

Ding Hao slapped their shoulders as he took on the role of the big brother. "All right, let's tell him fifteen thousand."

"That's not enough, is it?" Chaoyang asked.

"It's a lot of money!" Ding Hao objected.

"It's a lot to us, but maybe it's not that much to him," Pupu said. "Brother Chaoyang, how much money do you think we need to live until we're eighteen?"

"If we assume Ding Hao can't find work, you'd need about five hundred a month, so about six thousand a year for monthly expenses, but I'd round up to ten thousand a year to cover other expenses. If you want to study at a university, you'd have to start saving now. You'd need like sixty thousand per person."

"We need to pay rent too," Pupu reminded him.

"Oh, yeah, rent, that's a lot of money."

"Let's tell him one hundred thousand per person," she said calmly.

"A hundred thousand per person! I've never even seen that much money before! Who would buy a camera from us for that much money?" Ding Hao exclaimed.

"I think he'll go for it. That car he drives is worth a couple hundred thousand yuan, you know," Chaoyang said.

"OK, that settles it," Pupu said. The three came back to the table and sat down.

"Have you made a decision?" Zhang asked sweetly, cradling his coffee in his hands.

"Yes," Pupu said.

"How much?" Zhang asked. He took a sip.

"One hundred thousand per person," Pupu said.

Zhang nearly spit his coffee out. "You've got to be kidding me. A hundred thousand? Per person?"

"That's right. One hundred thousand per person," she said.

"What are you going to do with all that money? What if your parents find out? Hell, what if anyone finds out you have that much money?"

"Relax. We won't tell anyone," Pupu said.

"We'll give you the camera as soon as we get the money, and we won't tell anyone about what you did," Chaoyang chimed in.

Zhang took another sip of coffee and studied them. They hadn't hit puberty yet, but they were negotiating like hardened criminals.

His wife controlled all of the money, meaning he couldn't withdraw 300,000 without her permission. And he didn't want to negotiate with these three little terrors in the first place. They'd probably go on a spending spree and someone would find out. If the money were to be traced back to him, he would be exposed.

Zhang was quiet. Then he took a deep breath and exhaled slowly. "How about ten thousand per person, and you can spend it how you like. Your family won't notice if you're careful."

"That'll do, right guys?" Ding Hao said to his friends.

Zhang smiled at Ding Hao, pleased at how malleable he was.

"One hundred thousand per person. Any less and we're going to the police," Pupu insisted.

Zhang wanted to kill the girl *now*, but not in such a public place. Chaoyang quaked at the sight of the man's anger. Pupu was unperturbed.

"If that's how you want to play, fine. I don't want the camera any more. You can hand it over to the police," Zhang said.

"You can afford it. Your car is worth several hundred thousand," Chaoyang protested.

"I don't own that car. The most I can give you is ten thousand per person. I don't have more than that."

"Ten thousand per person! It's a deal. Right, Pupu?" Ding Hao said.

"Shut up!" Pupu hissed. She was cross that he was not sticking to the plan. "Come on, Chaoyang, let's go to the station. Maybe the police will give us a reward for handing in evidence."

"Aw, come on. Thirty grand would be plenty. Guys?" Ding Hao hesitated, then followed them as they started to leave the café.

Chaoyang and Pupu did not look back.

"Wait. Come back. Sit down," Zhang hissed.

The three returned and sat back down.

"You don't have more than thirty thousand. We won't accept anything less than three hundred thousand. What's there to talk about?" Pupu sneered.

Zhang was incensed but knew they had the upper hand. "I still have to deal with the funeral service and I can't withdraw that much money right now. Can you wait a few days?"

"Yeah, but you gotta hurry," she said.

"Once I have the funeral out of the way, I'll scrape the money together. None of you have a bank account, do you? I'll have to get cash. Where do you live?"

"We live at—" Ding Hao began.

"Don't tell him!" Chaoyang interjected.

"Then how will I contact you? By phone?" Zhang asked.

"We'll contact you. Tell us your number and we'll call you in a few days," Chaoyang said, neatly preventing the murderer from learning his address.

Zhang hesitated before taking a slip of paper and scribbling his number on it. "We are holding the funeral service today and I have a lot of work to do. Call me the day after tomorrow."

"All right," Chaoyang said.

"But you can't tell anyone about the camera, not even your parents," Zhang warned.

"We won't," Chaoyang said firmly.

"Well, this is all I have time for now. Do you need me to drop you off?"

"No thanks. Come on, guys. Let's go." Chaoyang stood.

They hadn't even left the restaurant when Ding Hao wheeled around to ask Zhang a question. "Can you give us just a little cash, please?"

Zhang looked at Ding Hao. "How much?"

"A few hundred."

Zhang made a face and fished 600 yuan out of his wallet. Ding Hao thanked him and went on his merry way. Zhang sank wearily into the chair.

27

When they left the café, Chaoyang broke into a run. The other two followed and they sprinted down a narrow street, then turned again and again, until they finally ended up in an alley. Chaoyang stopped to catch his breath, and a few seconds later, his friends caught up with him.

"Why are we running?" Ding Hao complained.

"I thought he might follow us. If he knows where we live, we're toast," Chaoyang said.

"So what if he knows?"

"He is a killer," Chaoyang enunciated every word. "Aren't you afraid that he might kill us?"

"Like he would kill us."

Pupu gave him side-eye for his foolishness. "Ding Hao, you really are an idiot."

"What?" Ding Hao cried.

"We agreed on one hundred thousand per person. Then he offered ten thousand per person and you were tripping over yourself to say yes," she shouted at him.

"I was just… just trying to help. It didn't seem like he would give us three hundred thousand. Thirty thousand would still be good." Ding Hao looked hurt.

"You shouldn't try to decide how much is OK on your own. When you go looking for a job, I would not be surprised if you get paid a tenth of what you're supposed to," Pupu scoffed.

"That's not the same! He said he couldn't pay more than thirty thousand, and I believed him!" Ding Hao whined.

"Chaoyang just said that the murderer's car was worth a lot of money, weren't you listening? This is a life-or-death situation for him! Of course he's going to pay!"

"Ding Hao, you were too hasty back there," Chaoyang agreed. "Honestly, thirty thousand is not enough for you to live on until you can find a job. You need a place to live, food and clothes. And you have to pay for school fees. That requires a lot of money."

When he realized that Chaoyang was taking Pupu's side, Ding Hao gave up. "OK, I messed up. I'll let you guys do the talking next time."

Pupu sniffed contemptuously and looked away.

"Pupu, don't be like that. We need an action plan," Chaoyang said.

"Action plan! Sounds like we are in a TV show!" Ding Hao rubbed his hands together excitedly.

"Yeah, only this is real life. We're not kids any more, and if we make a mistake we won't get a second chance. Murderers are really dangerous," Chaoyang said earnestly.

"I'm not a kid any more," Ding Hao protested.

Pupu glared at him. "Like I just said, you really are an idiot."

Ding Hao hung his head.

"Were you afraid back there?" Chaoyang asked, switching the topic.

"I was at first, but then I thought there was nothing to be afraid of," Ding Hao boasted.

"That's because you're an idiot," Pupu said.

"Harsh!" He whined again.

Chaoyang looked at her. "Were you scared?"

They expected her to say she wasn't—she was the only one who looked Zhang Dongsheng in the eyes. She surprised them when she nodded, showing a tiny bit of vulnerability. "Yeah, I was."

"But you didn't act it," Ding Hao said.

Within seconds, Pupu's cold mask reappeared. "If you act afraid people will walk all over you. That's why I acted tough."

"Wow," Chaoyang couldn't help saying.

"When they executed my dad, everyone taunted me. Some kids even hit me. I never fought back until one day I gave them everything I had. Then nobody ever messed with me," she said.

"Were you afraid, Chaoyang?" Ding Hao asked.

"Yeah, but we still had to get the job done, didn't we?"

"Thanks for staying by our side, Brother Chaoyang," Pupu said.

"That's what friends are for," Chaoyang replied, his cheeks reddening.

"So, about this action plan…" Ding Hao said, clapping his hands.

"Let's go home first," Chaoyang advised. "We have two days to work this out. Be on the lookout, I don't want him to find out where my home is."

They went to a bus stop. They had to take a bus into the city centre and then a second bus to get to Chaoyang's building. He made them get off one stop early, so they could make sure nobody was following them.

28

According to local custom, people who died outside of the home should have a funeral service in a place other than the family home. The Xu family did not want to wait and opted to have the service just a few days after Xu Jing's parents died. Then the old couple could rest in peace.

The Xu family had rented a room in a community centre for older people. Everyone was preparing for the service and reception, when Zhang Dongsheng returned with the tissues and paper cups from the supermarket. He turned around and was surprised to spot Yan Liang sitting on his own.

Yan nodded to Zhang and waved him over. Zhang felt his heartbeat quicken, remembering how Yan used to work at the Zhejiang Criminal Investigation Division. He probably still had contacts with police officers in the Zhejiang area. Xu Jing always said that her uncle was a brilliant detective and had cracked every case he had ever worked on. Zhang also knew from his classes with Yan that he wasn't the kind of professor who was completely preoccupied with theory, that he always looked at the practical too. Yan enjoyed applied mathematics, which was why all the computer science students flocked to his mathematical logic class. There was no doubt that he had used his superior logical deduction to solve problems he encountered on the force. But then Zhang reminded himself that Yan was here as a family member, not as a detective. Zhang was still confident with how he handled the murders—nobody would be able to incriminate him. Unless, of course, those meddling kids let that camera fall into the wrong hands.

"It's been years, nearly four, Professor Yan! Xu Jing said she had asked you to come but I didn't think you would make it," Zhang said, shaking Yan's hand warmly and sitting next to him.

"Professors get long breaks over the summer, and I really wanted to come. When I arrived, they said you had gone to the store to buy some things. But you've been away for quite some time," Yan replied.

Zhang lied easily. "I had forgotten that I needed to speak to the driver of the funeral procession and to pay the florist. It all took longer than I expected."

Yan nodded, satisfied. "You must be incredibly busy."

Zhang sighed and lowered his voice. "Jing's still upset about the accident. As soon as she is alone, she starts crying. All the work is on my shoulders."

Yan felt sorry for him and almost didn't ask, but he couldn't help it. "Are you two going through a hard time together?"

Zhang looked down, then back at Yan. "Did she tell you?"

Yan nodded.

"We…" Zhang stopped, as if admitting this was difficult to say out loud, "… we might get divorced."

"I thought you two were perfect for each other."

"Maybe…" He sighed again and pulled a cigarette out of his pack. He didn't offer Yan one, knowing he wasn't a smoker.

"You've started smoking again?" Yan asked with concern.

"I don't smoke very much, only when I'm stressed." Zhang gave him a wry smile.

"Do you want to talk about it?" Yan asked gently.

"You're probably the only person I'm willing to talk to. There are few people I admire more than you," Zhang answered, blowing a cloud of smoke. "I think it all goes back to the fact that I'm a country boy. Country people and city people aren't the same."

"Things went well when you first got married, though…"

"We ignored a lot of problems when we were dating but when we got married they were harder to ignore. My parents have lived in the mountains all their lives and they don't know how

109

to behave sometimes. When they came to visit us, Jing resented them for not keeping their room and the rest of the apartment tidy. She wanted them to stay in a hotel whenever they came to Ningbo. My parents wouldn't hear of it—they believed that families should always be together. I promised Jing I'd clean up after them when they visited. We fought, and of course she won. I asked my parents to stay in a hotel, and they said it was fine, but it broke their hearts. All these little things kept adding up. I always make sure I'm getting value for my money, but she doesn't care about the price at all and says I'm stingy. She's becoming more and more distant. If I try to give her a hug, she pushes me away," he said, his eyes reddening.

"Do you still love her?"

"Yes," Zhang said with a smile. "It doesn't matter what she does, she'll always be the girl who defied her parents to be with me."

Yan was moved by these words and gave a little sigh. "What are you going to do next?"

"She brought up divorce last year, but I couldn't bear to let everything fall apart. I am trying to make things right, but nothing has really changed. She doesn't know what she really wants in life. And, honestly, her parents were so disparaging to me, I felt like an outsider in my own family. So I tried to do something positive about it by spending more time with them. It was a little selfish maybe, because I thought they would help me talk Jing out of divorce. Sure enough, they helped us put it off, and if... if they hadn't had the accident... maybe they would have convinced her. It's all my fault because I knew that Xu Jing's father had high blood pressure, but he didn't like talking about it and rarely took his medicine. The police suspect that going up the steep hill and then stopping to take a photo caused him to have a stroke. I worry that I'll never be able to make it up to Jing." Zhang extinguished his cigarette and put his head in his hands, hiding his face.

"Don't blame yourself for the accident. You didn't want it to happen. Accidents happen all the time," Yan reassured him.

They sat in silence for a while. Zhang raised his head and finally said, "As long as she's happy. I'll try to be a good husband, but if she doesn't want to be together, I'll respect her wishes."

Yan was touched by Zhang's selflessness. "Don't be so negative. I'll talk to her, she'll come around."

"Thank you, Professor Yan!" Zhang still looked depressed, but his heart was jubilant. Yan had bought the act.

29

Chaoyang emerged from under his bed followed by a cloud of dust. He shoved two large boxes under the bed and rubbed his hands. "The camera's way in the back now, and we're the only ones that know. Don't get tricked into telling that man where it is. Got it?"

Pupu nodded earnestly and glanced at Ding Hao. She didn't have to say what she was thinking.

"Relax, I won't tell Zhang Dongsheng," he said, visibly annoyed.

"We need to think of a safe way to collect the money," Chaoyang said.

"You think... he might kill us so we don't tell the police?" Ding Hao frowned.

"He might," Chaoyang said gravely.

"What do you think?" Ding Hao asked Pupu.

"I don't know for sure, but we should be ready for anything," she said.

"But we have the camera!"

"Yeah, and as long as we do, he won't lay a finger on us. Did you see his expression when I said I was going to put the camera away before we talked? At the café, he controlled his anger because he knew it was in his best interests," Chaoyang replied.

"But once we take his money, we'll have to give the camera to him," Ding Hao said.

"Or maybe we don't have to," Pupu smirked.

"What do you mean?" he asked.

"What I said. We get the money and we don't give him the camera."

Ding Hao gaped at her. "He's really clever. How could we possibly get him to do that?"

"We tell him to give us the money first. You think he's going to go to the police and say we duped him? If we keep the camera, we'll always have protection," Pupu said.

"Then we'd always have enough money. I like that. But isn't that something that bad guys would do?" Ding Hao said hesitantly.

"We're not in a TV show!" Pupu cried in exasperation.

"Blackmailing him wouldn't work forever," Chaoyang said.

"Why not?" she said.

"The first couple of times, he would comply because you're threatening him with something that is extremely important to him. But by the third or fourth time, he'd be pushed to his limit. He'd do whatever it takes to make the threats stop. Think about it: if you were him, would you let three kids threaten you for years?"

"Then what do we do?" Ding Hao asked.

"We can only ask for money once. Then we give him the camera and we never speak to him again."

"But then we always live with the risk that he might try to kill us. We still know what he did," Pupu protested.

Chaoyang nodded. "True."

"We can't give it to him, but we can't *not* give it to him. What do we do?" Ding Hao frowned.

"When he gives us the money, we need to be in a well-lit place with lots of people. He won't hurt us if there are witnesses. And he can't know where we live. If he doesn't know where to find us, after a few years, he'll be sure that we aren't going to double-cross him and he won't try and kill us," Chaoyang reasoned. He wasn't sure if he trusted his own judgement on this.

The other two thought about that, then nodded, confident in his assessment.

"The thing is, we haven't worked out the specifics. I think we should leave the camera at home, take the money and then give the camera to him in a public place. And one of us should

113

stay at home so if anything happens to the two people doing the deal, the third person can call the police," Chaoyang continued.

"Then he won't try to hurt us. That's good," Pupu said.

"I told you Chaoyang was smart," Ding Hao beamed. "So who's going to stay here?"

"You will," Chaoyang answered.

"Why me? You two are so small! I would do the best in a fight," he protested.

Pupu rolled her eyes. "You always won fights at the orphanage but he's an adult, and he's strong, and … he … he might bring a weapon or something. Besides, you're a liability, you might let something slip."

"Pupu, if you weren't my sister, I would smack you for that!" he complained.

Chaoyang quickly smoothed things over. "It's OK, you can play games while you wait. Just remember one thing: if someone knocks on the door, you have to check who it is. Don't open the door unless it's us."

"Fine," grumbled Ding Hao.

30

The funeral service was in the morning, the reception was at noon, and clean-up and payments were scheduled for the afternoon.

Xu Jing was acting rudely towards Zhang Dongsheng and his parents. His parents disliked her so much that they had booked an overnight train to return home the same day. Zhang dropped his parents off at the station and came back home, where Xu Jing was waiting for him. He reached out to touch her shoulder and she jumped. "Don't touch me!"

His hand hung in the air for a few seconds. "I'm really sorry for not taking better care of your parents."

She looked coldly at him. "What are you going to do next?"

"What do you mean?"

"You heard me! What are you going to do next?"

"I don't know what you're talking about," he said, shaking his head.

Xu Jing walked away from him and sat on a sofa. She looked listlessly into the middle of the room. "Let's get a divorce," she said.

"Divorce?" Zhang sat on the sofa opposite her and lit a cigarette. He took a puff. "Your parents passed away only a few days ago. Are you sure you want to go through with this... right now?"

"Yes. You can have the new apartment. If that's not enough, tell me how much money you want and I'll give it to you. I can't keep living like this."

Zhang shook his head, a pained expression on his face. "Jing, I didn't marry you for money. You knew I was poor and you didn't resent me for that before. What has changed?"

She did not answer.

"I guess people change when they get older," he continued. "I'm not good at anything. I'm not like those guys who study abroad, rise in the ranks and build a stellar career for themselves. Your family has five properties and you work at a huge tobacco company. Maybe we shouldn't have married in the first place. I'm idealistic—I thought we could make a go of it."

She covered her face and sobbed quietly.

"Jing, I hate to see you cry. I was hoping you would reconsider, but if you want a divorce, let's do it. I only have one request. Can you buy a house for my parents? It doesn't have to be big."

Xu Jing looked at him with red-rimmed eyes.

He smiled wistfully, then said, "I'm still happy that you came into my life."

"I'm… I'm sorry," she choked out.

"Don't be sorry. You'll always be my princess."

"Let me give you the new place, or let's sell it and I'll split the money with you. I'll still buy a house for your parents," she said, after a pause.

"You really do want to go through with this," he muttered, extinguishing his cigarette. "If we divorce now, your relatives will talk. Don't you want to wait a few months?"

Xu Jing thought for a moment. "I… I want to move out," she stammered.

"Why?"

"No reason."

"You don't even want to live with me for just another couple of months to prevent gossip?"

Xu Jing hung her head.

"So you want a separation?"

She did not reply.

Zhang sighed loudly. "Fine. When are you planning on moving?"

"Today," she whispered.

Her answer made him reel. "You don't have to leave! This is your home. How's this? I'll move into the new apartment tomorrow and live there for a while. After the divorce, I'll find somewhere else."

"I'm sorry," Xu Jing repeated.

Zhang stood and patted her on the shoulder. She flinched.

"Are you afraid of me?" he asked, sounding surprised.

"No, no, I'm just jumpy," she answered quickly.

"OK." As Zhang went to the bedroom to pack, he made a mental note that Xu Jing would have to be dealt with as soon as possible.

31

Today was the day that Chaoyang and Pupu were going to call the murderer.

Fearing the call might be traced, they called him from a payphone. Not the one in the local shop, because the owner there would recognize Chaoyang. Instead, they took a bus to an area where he was sure nobody would know him. They dialled and heard a familiar voice.

"Hello?"

"It's us," Chaoyang said.

"Oh, hello!" Zhang sounded different, friendlier, putting Chaoyang on edge.

"Where are we going to meet today?" he asked.

"You could come to my apartment," Zhang offered.

"We should meet in a public place."

"You're a smart kiddo. But you should know I can't carry such a big bag of money without attracting attention. And after today, we're strangers, we'll never talk about this again."

Chaoyang covered the receiver with one hand and relayed what Zhang had said.

"What do you think?" Pupu asked.

"We don't have the camera so he won't try any funny business," he whispered.

"OK, then."

"Are you still there?" Chaoyang asked.

"Yes. So what's it going to be?"

118

"We'll go to your place," Chaoyang said.

"Make sure to bring the item I'm going to buy," Zhang said. "And don't tell *anyone*."

"OK."

"You can take a taxi to get here. I'm at the Prosperity Bay Luxury Apartments, Building 5, Unit 1, Apartment 301. Have you written down the address?"

Chaoyang had already memorized it, so said goodbye and hung up. The two children looked at each other and started on the next step.

Chaoyang and Pupu arrived at the entrance to the apartment complex after taking the bus. Chaoyang had brought a big backpack for the money. They could tell just by looking that the building was the kind of place where rich people lived.

They quickly found Unit 1 but were stumped by the door security. Neither had ever seen a number pad outside a door before. Chaoyang hesitantly pressed 3-0-1 and heard a ringing sound. "Come in, it's open," a voice said.

The door opened and they went to the third floor. Pupu tugged gently on Chaoyang's shirt. She looked nervous.

"It's OK, we'll just follow our plan."

Pupu nodded and quickly steadied herself for the meeting.

They saw that the door to 301 was open. Zhang appeared with a smile on his face. "Hello." Then his face fell. "Why is it just the two of you?"

"Ding Hao's not coming," Chaoyang answered.

"If we don't meet him in a few hours, he'll contact the police," Pupu said calmly.

Zhang's mouth dropped open. Then he remembered to smile again. "Please, come in."

He closed the door behind them and both Chaoyang and Pupu felt a chill. They stood just inside the door, not sure what to do next.

"You don't need to take off your shoes, just sit down," Zhang said, moving towards the living room.

Chaoyang took in his surroundings. The entryway was tiled and the living room boasted a fancy wooden floor and nice furniture. Chaoyang knew nothing about houses, but this was fancier than his home. The open-plan kitchen looked new, and all the appliances were shiny, but something was missing. Then it came to him. The house was too clean. There was nothing on the tables or shelves and only one pair of shoes on the shoe rack.

"Do you live here?" he asked.

"Yes," Zhang answered quickly.

"Then why does it look like nobody lives here?"

Zhang's eyebrows shot up briefly. "I just moved in yesterday."

Alarm bells were ringing in his head, but Chaoyang kept his cool.

"Have a seat, let's get down to business," Zhang said.

The two children sat on a sofa. The low tabletop in front of them was made of clear glass with a steel shelf underneath for storage. Glass tumblers and an opened bottle of juice were arranged on their side of the table. Several copies of *Shu Li Tian Di*, a popular science magazine for children, were set out on the other side.

"I'm thirsty," Pupu announced, her eyes on the juice.

Zhang smacked his head theatrically. "I'm a terrible host, you must be thirsty in this heat. I'll get you some soda."

"Juice is fine," Pupu said, reaching for the bottle.

Zhang snatched it away. "This bottle has been open for a few days; it's not fresh. I'll get you some soda."

"I don't drink soda," Chaoyang said, remembering the tips in *Home Remedies to Increase Height*.

"Then I'll boil some water for you," Zhang said, frowning.

"OK." (Like most Chinese, Chaoyang preferred his water warm rather than cold.)

Zhang took away the juice and returned with an unopened

bottle of soda, which he poured for Pupu, and a glass of warm water for Chaoyang, who watched all of his actions carefully.

Zhang sat down. "Do any of your parents know you're here?"

"You have asked us that a million times! We haven't told anyone," Chaoyang said.

"You really are clever. So... did you bring the camera?"

"No," Chaoyang said.

"No?" Zhang looked surprised.

"First you give us the money, then we'll give you the camera," Pupu chimed in.

"OK."

"Do you have the money?" Chaoyang asked.

"Not at the moment, no," Zhang said, smiling apologetically.

The lack of trust was plain on the boy's face. "You have an expensive car and this nice house, what's the problem?"

"They're not *mine*," Zhang said emphatically.

"Who do they belong to?"

"My wife."

"But whatever she owns is yours too, right?" Pupu said.

"I married a very wealthy lady, but her parents were protective of their wealth. I don't have access to my wife's money," he said awkwardly. "She has everything."

"If you don't have the money, why'd you tell us to bring the camera?" Pupu asked coldly.

"I don't think it's safe in your house. I was planning to give you ten thousand for now and give you the rest later."

"The camera is perfectly fine where it is. We won't tell anyone about it—unless the deal is off."

Pupu was provoking him again, but this time Zhang was unperturbed. "Well, there's nothing I can do about the money right now. I'll think of something. I'll have it all soon."

"How long will it take?"

"About a month, I think," Zhang aimed for another friendly smile, but missed.

"Why will you have the money in a month?" Pupu pressed.

"I'm an adult, and I'll find a way to get money in a month. OK, little lady?"

"Don't call me little lady!" Pupu snapped.

"OK, then." Zhang's tone was blasé.

Pupu looked at Chaoyang. "What do you think? Should we go home?"

He didn't answer at first—he was too focused on the copies of *Shu Li Tian Di* fanned across the table. "Do you have kids in high school?" he asked Zhang.

"I'm not old enough to have kids in high school," Zhang said.

"This is the latest issue... Oh, you're a teacher, aren't you?" Chaoyang said.

"Yes," Zhang admitted reluctantly.

"Do you teach maths or physics?"

"Mathematics." He hated revealing even this much information about himself.

"That's my favourite subject," Chaoyang said.

Zhang could not care less what the boy's favourite subject was. He was tired of these troublesome kids—they were a waste of his time.

"You're a teacher? I thought teachers were good people," Pupu said.

The room went quiet. Zhang pressed his lips into a sharp line. Chaoyang thought the question was enough to make the murderer explode in fury, but he didn't say anything. Pupu took another sip of her soda.

Chaoyang coughed, hoping he could move past the awkwardness. He leaned over and picked up the issues of *Shu Li Tian Di*, noticing more magazines below the glass. "Oh, look, you have *Mathematics Monthly* too!"

Zhang wanted to stop him from touching the magazines, but it was too late. "Ah, did you want to read one?"

"These are for high schoolers; that might be too difficult for me," Chaoyang said. He was so engrossed that he did not notice Pupu panicking.

She took a big gulp of soda and surreptitiously poked him in the ribs. He followed her gaze and saw a long knife that had been underneath the magazines he had just lifted up. The handle was positioned so that Zhang could grab it easily.

With lightning speed, Chaoyang snatched the knife and removed it from its cover, noting how sharp it was. "Why were you hiding a knife under the table!" he yelled. The two kids moved towards the door.

Zhang stood up slowly. "That's just a knife. We just renovated the apartment, so things are not in their proper place. The knife was a gift from my wife's uncle from his trip to Germany."

"Why did you make us meet at your house? Was it so you could knock us off?" Pupu asked.

"No, that's ludicrous! There's two of you and one of me: how could I possibly get away with it? All I want is to buy the camera and never see you again. Killing three people to save three hundred thousand is not worth it. Trust me, I've thought about it," Zhang snarled.

"So why did you move here all of a sudden?" Pupu asked.

Zhang sighed and sat down again. "My wife and I had a fight. She wants to get a divorce. So I have to live here until we sort things out. When we first bought the place, I thought we would be living here together." He clenched his teeth and tried to hide how upset he was.

Pupu looked at him, not sure if she should believe him.

Chaoyang carefully tucked the knife in his backpack, wanting to leave as soon as possible. "There's no point in us staying since you don't have the money. We'll contact you in a while. Next time, no funny business."

He reached for the door handle. Pupu touched his arm and

whispered to him. "Your mum's coming back today. Where are me and Ding Hao going to live?"

"Oh yeah…" Chaoyang was faced with a dilemma.

Pupu turned to Zhang. "You said you could give us ten thousand before. Could you give that to us now?"

"Do you need money that badly?" Zhang asked.

"Never mind the reason."

"But I'm worried you'll go on a spending spree. If you attract attention…"

"We won't!" Pupu said.

"Well then, what do you need so much money for?"

"We need somewhere to live," she finally said.

"Why don't you have a place to live…" Zhang asked, his eyebrows furrowed.

"None of your business," Pupu said.

"Will you be living with other adults, or just you three?"

"We won't be living with adults and we won't tell other people about the money."

"Why aren't you living at home? Did you run away from home?" Zhang guessed.

"No," Pupu said.

"You don't have a home?"

"None of your business."

Zhang looked genuinely sympathetic. "You should be going to school at this age, not worrying about where you're going to sleep."

The girl scowled at him.

"You remind me of my own students," he continued. "I can't stand the thought of you not having a roof over your heads. Tell you what, we have a little studio apartment that's completely empty right now. I'll clean it up so you can live there, and I'll give you some money for food."

Pupu looked to Chaoyang for guidance. He thought for a moment. "Do you really have another empty place?"

"Yeah, it's a studio; it's small. Normally we have tenants but it's free now. I'm the one who finds tenants; my wife won't know."

Chaoyang looked back at Pupu. Her eyes were desperate, and she had said that they could neither afford a hotel nor risk registering at one because the orphanage would probably be contacted. For his part, Chaoyang wanted Pupu and Ding Hao to leave his home asap. It was a difficult situation, but they needed to do something.

"Sounds OK," Chaoyang said to her.

Zhang smiled. "Good, then I'll take you there now. You can move in today."

32

Doctor Chen walked into Captain Ye Jun's office and dropped a bunch of documents on his desk to get his attention. "The City Criminal Technical Department performed a full autopsy on Zhu Jingjing; these are the results. No semen. It's possible it was swallowed and broke down before we could detect it. We have the DNA from the hair and blood, but it's not in the system."

Ye Jun frowned irritably and lit a cigarette. "Were we able to get any prints from the victim's clothes?"

"No, not after all the rain," Chen said.

"You're telling me we don't have anything besides the DNA and the prints on the window?"

There were so many fingerprints that the process of eliminating those that were not relevant would be incredibly time-consuming.

"The only reliable evidence we have is the DNA of the perpetrator from the skin cells found in Jingjing's mouth."

"We have such a small team, and we don't have the equipment or experience that other PSBs would have. Are there any cases that we could refer to?"

Doctor Chen considered the question for a moment. "There's one from ten years ago, but…"

"But what?"

"That case had a top-notch special task force, headed by Yan Liang," Chen replied.

"Yan Liang? That's a name I haven't heard in a long time."

"You're old enough to have been trained by Yan. You went to his lectures, didn't you?"

"Of course. I remember he was the most intellectual person on the force. I had assumed that he would be all talk and no action, but actually he had an excellent record of cracking cases. He was even recognized by the Ministry of Public Security. He wasn't like those criminal psychology types; he was practical," Ye Jun said.

"Their task force had over 100 people. But I'm not sure that case will be relevant."

"Tell me more about it anyway." Ye Jun took a puff.

"Two girls from different families were found in a shed on an abandoned construction site; they had been raped and killed. The perpetrator used a condom and destroyed the rest of the evidence by setting fire to the whole site. The provincial government was nervous about all the attention the case was receiving and assembled a large task force. Once they narrowed down the suspects to thirty men, Yan used criminal logic to identify a man who didn't have an alibi, but whose motive seemed pretty weak. The suspect was interrogated for hours but would not admit to anything. Yan was sure he had the right man, and when a colleague found physical evidence that linked him to the site, they finally arrested and convicted him."

"That sounds a lot trickier than the case we're dealing with," Ye Jun said thoughtfully.

"It certainly was," Chen agreed. "That criminal was careful about covering his tracks. This time the main problem is that we don't have enough resources."

Ye Jun nodded. So many people had been in and out of the crime scene that day that it would take many hours just to rule people out. They needed a breakthrough to solve the case quickly. Otherwise they might never solve it.

It was a big case for Ye Jun, but wouldn't be considered very important elsewhere. Even if the city bureau sent technicians to help sift through surveillance footage, they would still have to rely on their own team. It was the fourth day of knocking on doors and they still had no leads.

The team was focusing on the people on the sole CCTV camera at the Children's Palace. One at a time, they investigated anyone who seemed at all suspicious. They were confident that the perpetrator would be an adult male or perhaps a teenage male. The team also believed that the perpetrator would be alone on the assumption that a man who brought his children to the Children's Palace would not be so rash as to attack a girl while they were there. These assumptions gave them potential targets, which they had to track down in order to get DNA samples. The job was challenging because they only had the faces and no way of knowing their names or addresses. It took ages to identify individuals just from the CCTV, not to mention collecting their DNA and fingerprints. There were only twenty or thirty officers in the police station and they had other cases to deal with—only a couple of officers could work on the case full time. To make matters worse, some of the footage was fuzzy and no clear features could be identified. How would they be able to investigate them in a reasonable time frame? What if the perpetrator wasn't a local, or what if he had already skipped town? Ye Jun knew that was a real possibility, but hoped they would be lucky.

A knock on the door. "Captain Ye, Zhu Jingjing's father is here. He wants an update on the investigation."

"Cases aren't solved that quickly," he grumbled. "Tell him we are making progress and we will be in touch as soon as we have something to report."

As the officer turned to leave, Ye changed his mind. "Hang on, stay right there."

Ye Jun looked at Doctor Chen. "Hey, in Yan Liang's old case, you said the offender was holding a grudge, right?"

"That's right. It seemed unimportant to police at the time, but it had been simmering away in his mind for years. His wife had had affairs with two men. When he learned about them, he didn't say anything. Then as the child grew up, he looked less and less like his 'father'. He arranged a paternity test that confirmed that the boy was not his. He was determined to take revenge, so he carefully planned the crime: abducting the daughters of the two men that his wife had affairs with, and raping and killing them."

"Zhu Jingjing's family is wealthy, right?" Ye Jun asked thoughtfully.

"Yes, her father, Zhu Yongping, runs a seafood factory, I've heard it is pretty big."

"People who have successful businesses are likely to step on other people's toes. Maybe our guy is someone who has a problem with the victim's father?"

"It's possible," Chen said.

Ye Jun turned to the waiting officer. "Have Zhu Yongping and Wang Yao review the CCTV footage, to see if they can recognize any faces. If revenge is the motive, they might actually know the killer."

33

"Do you think he actually wanted to kill us?" Pupu whispered to Chaoyang once they were on the bus home.

Chaoyang nodded and kept his voice so low that Pupu had to lean in to hear him. "If all three of us were there, he would have taken the camera and killed us."

"Why wouldn't he just take the camera? Why would he want to kill us?"

"I think just the fact that other people know he's a murderer is too much. There's always the possibility that we would tell someone about what he did. He probably can't sleep at night," Chaoyang reasoned.

"But he's just one person. How would he kill all three of us?"

"He might have managed it with that knife. Or maybe it was just there for backup," he answered.

"What do you mean, backup?"

"Do you know, I think he put poison in the juice. He said it was bad because it had been open for a few days, but nobody brings old juice to a new place. I think he wanted to kill us but when you said that Ding Hao would call the police if anything happened to us, he had to change his plan."

"So… if all three of us had gone to his place today, he would've poisoned us with the juice and finished us off with the knife?"

"Yeah, basically."

"That was close," Pupu gulped.

Chaoyang nodded again. "He told us on the phone that he had the money. It is so unlikely that he just happened to move in yesterday! That place is so new and he doesn't have neighbours; nobody would hear us scream. You know what else? He smiled a lot today, but that was just an act. He hates all three of us."

"You're really smart, Brother Chaoyang. You see right through him," Pupu said admiringly.

"I'm not that smart, he's just underestimating us."

"But you think we should still try to make a deal with him?"

"Definitely. As long as we split up and keep the camera safe like we did today, he won't be able to hurt us. Once we have the money, we won't ever talk to him again."

Pupu frowned. "Yeah, but what about me and Ding Hao going to move into his little apartment? Isn't that dangerous?"

"It's OK. He still doesn't know where my house is and that means he doesn't know where the camera is. You've got to live somewhere, and my mother wouldn't let you stay with me. So you'll need to live there. But we all need to be careful and not let him extract information out of us."

Pupu smiled. "You don't have to worry about me! It's Ding Hao that we have to remind—he's not the sharpest tool in the shed."

Chaoyang laughed. "Let's not mention the whole we-almost-got-killed thing to him. I don't think he would dare live in that studio if he found out."

"OK. Let's tell him that the man's giving us a little bit of money to live on, but he doesn't have the rest of it ready yet."

"You should probably get some new clothes and some nice food. You deserve it, after everything that's happened," he said.

"You deserve new clothes! You're the one that has been letting us live at your house all this time," she said appreciatively.

"Thanks, but I'd better not. My mum would want to know where I got them. It would just cause problems."

"Oh, OK."

"One more thing. When you stay at Zhang Dongsheng's apartment, I would find a short piece of string and jam it in the closet door of the room where you'll be sleeping. Every time you open your closet door, make sure you put it back. If the string isn't in its usual place, that means that man went into your room

131

without telling you. If he's snooping around, we know we need to keep our guard up. The more we know, the better."

"You mean like the yarn in the door to your mum's room?" Pupu asked.

Chaoyang looked at her in shock but she did not seem to be angry with him. He stuttered through an apology, "I'm sorry... when you first arrived, I... I—"

"I know. Anyone in your situation would take precautions. Ding Hao never noticed and I won't tell him," she said.

"Thanks," Chaoyang mumbled.

They got off the bus one stop early and took a circuitous route home. Chaoyang knocked instead of using the key to see how Ding Hao would respond. They were pleased when he checked that it was them before opening the door.

They filled Ding Hao in on what happened, omitting the knife discovery. Ding Hao was slightly disappointed that they didn't have all the cash, but when he heard that they had found a place to live and 1,000 yuan of spending money, he was elated. Soon after, Ding Hao and Pupu gathered their stuff and said goodbye to Chaoyang. Apart from the fact that he wouldn't be able to play computer games, Ding Hao seemed to be happy to be going to a new home.

34

Zhu Chaoyang's mother returned home that evening. She cooked a simple meal and they ate at their tiny table while the ceiling fan squeaked overhead. Chaoyang concentrated on eating to avoid talking.

"Mum, can I be excused? I want to read in my room," he said when he finished.

"Just a minute," Zhou Chunhong said before he could escape. "You've barely spoken to me since I've come home. What's bothering you?"

"Nothing. Everything's fine."

She searched his face. "Did your two friends go home?"

"They left today."

"Did you have a good time?"

"Yeah, we went to a bunch of places."

"So… did your father call you recently?"

"No," Chaoyang said, looking down.

"You should visit your grandparents tomorrow. Your grandpa isn't doing well after his stroke and he may not have that much longer. They have always been good to you, and the last thing we want is for Zhu Yongping to use your failure to visit them to claim that you weren't filial to them. We don't want him to have an excuse not to allow you to receive your rightful inheritance," Zhou said with a sigh.

"OK, I'll go tomorrow. I'm a little worried though, what if I see Big B—, I mean, the witch? The last time that happened, Grandma told me to come back another time."

His mother huffed. "You are their grandson, you're one of the family! It's perfectly natural for you to visit them! That witch only had a daughter—she does not have the right to tell the family what to do! I think her daughter's death is a sign from heaven."

"Mum! Don't say things like that," Chaoyang interjected.

"What? I have the right to speak my mind, don't I?"

"Is Dad arranging Jingjing's funeral?" Chaoyang said, not meeting his mother's gaze.

"Of course he is!" Zhou said, her voice rising. "That hypocrite has been comforting that witch every single day. I've known Zhu Yongping for so many years and I've never seen him cry before. Now this happens and he acts as if his whole world is falling apart. If he gave you a tenth of the love that he gave to that little girl, you wouldn't be suffering the way you are now."

"OK... maybe Dad will give us a little more money now," Chaoyang said quietly.

"I'll believe it when I see it! Your father and that woman are perfect for each other—selfish, uncaring and oblivious."

"Do you know anything else about how the little girl died?" he asked hesitantly.

"She fell. You knew that, didn't you?"

"I did, but I didn't know it was her when I was there. How did she fall?"

"I heard that she was ra—" Zhou was about to say "raped" but thought her son was too young to hear something so vile. "I heard that a man had his way with her and pushed her from the top floor of the Children's Palace. The police are still investigating. There was a wanted poster at the corner shop."

Chaoyang sat in silence.

"Chaoyang, don't go to the Children's Palace ever again," she said.

"Why?"

"Because dirty old men hang around there. None of the parents I know are letting their kids go back."

"Dirty old men don't target boys, do they?"

She ignored this. "Don't visit any unfamiliar or secluded places. The world is a scary place and bad people can trick you when you least expect it."

"Don't worry so much, Mum, I'm going to be fine." Chaoyang smiled at her in an attempt to ease her worry. Secretly he was very concerned that she would find out what he had done. Or worse: that he would be questioned by the police.

35

Captain Ye Jun had just arrived back at the station after his lunch break when an officer rushed to speak to him. "Zhu Jingjing's mother is here. She said she knows who the killer is and she won't tell anyone but you."

"Bring her to my office!" Ye Jun said.

"Officer Ye!" Wang Yao burst in, her eyes bloodshot. An officer followed her, his efforts to stop her completely ineffective. "You have to get the killer! Don't let him get away with this!" she raved.

Ye Jun was stern. "Please calm down, we will do everything in our power to catch the killer. Do you know who he is?"

"My husband had a child in his first marriage, before he met me. It's him! Zhu Chaoyang! We watched all of the CCTV footage twice: nobody else could be the killer."

"Zhu Chaoyang?" Ye Jun asked quizzically. The name sounded familiar. Then he recalled that his daughter had a classmate with that name, a boy with excellent exam scores.

Ye opened the file of the footage, and Wang Yao gave the time stamp where the boy could be seen.

The screen showed the entrance to the Children's Palace and the main lobby. Children chased each other and frolicked. Zhu Jingjing appeared on the screen along with several waves of young children. One minute later, two youngsters appeared, a tall male and a petite female. Neither Wang Yao nor Ye Jun took any notice of them. Soon after, a boy wearing a dull yellow T-shirt appeared. He stopped and looked left and right, then continued walking in the same direction.

Wang Yao pointed at the short, scrawny boy and shouted wildly, "That's Zhu Chaoyang! He's the one who killed my daughter!"

Ye Jun exchanged a look with the other officer. "How old is he?"

"Fourteen."

"Why do you think he's the one who killed your daughter?"

"I looked at every face, and he is the only one I recognize," Wang Yao said gravely.

Ye Jun coughed politely. "Is there… any other reason?"

"He hates me and Jingjing. He killed her to get revenge."

Ye Jun had seen plenty of families with complicated relationships. The children of the first wife tended to resent the second wife and any half-siblings. What boy wouldn't hate the person who took his father away? He had been hopeful that Wang Yao would lead him to the killer but this accusation seemed most unlikely. Zhu Chaoyang looked nothing like the powerful perpetrator they were expecting. A note of disappointment was detectable in Ye Jun's voice. "Apart from the fact that he hates you… is there any reason why you suspect him?"

"Is that not enough?" Her eyes widened, as if she thought he would bend the law for the boy.

Ye Jun shifted in his chair. "Of course it's not enough. We need evidence. What you've given me is just a possibility."

"Oh, you want evidence? He entered the Children's Palace less than a minute after Jingjing—" Wang Yao reached over and fast-forwarded the video, "—and he leaves just a few minutes after Jingjing falls."

"Everyone at the Children's Palace knew about the fall— dozens of people left just minutes afterwards. It would be strange if Zhu Chaoyang stayed there after a big accident like that," Ye Jun argued.

"Go back to the beginning! Don't you see the way he looks around, like he has a secret? He was looking for Jingjing! That can't possibly be a coincidence!"

Ye Jun considered her argument. The thing that niggled him was how small Chaoyang looked. It seemed highly unlikely that

137

a short fourteen-year-old would force Zhu Jingjing to perform oral sex on him.

At that moment, Zhu Yongping burst into the office and took Wang Yao by the arm. "Why did you come here when I told you not to? We need to go home!"

She freed herself in one swift movement and shrieked, "You won't admit that your own son killed our daughter!"

"Chaoyang couldn't possibly be the killer, don't be stupid. We're going home," Zhu Yongping said to Wang Yao. He apologized to the officers for the scene as he pushed his wife towards the door.

Ye Jun and the other officers did their best to assuage her as her husband continued to try to guide her away, but Wang Yao was hysterical. She kept shouting at the top of her voice, "You have to arrest him! Zhu Chaoyang is the killer! He's the killer!"

Despite Ye's initial reaction that Zhu Chaoyang was not likely to be the killer, he couldn't send Wang Yao away without reassuring her that the police would take her accusation seriously. He asked Zhu Yongping to provide more information. Zhu Yongping told them Zhu Chaoyang's age, his current address and his distant relationship with the new family. Ye promised again to investigate the boy and Wang Yao finally agreed to leave.

"What a strange lady. There's no way that shrimp did it," one officer sighed as the couple left.

Ye Jun frowned. "I think her suspicions are not totally unreasonable. The timing of the boy's entry and the way he looked around does suggest that he was looking for someone."

"He's not even five feet tall. He probably hasn't hit puberty yet," the officer continued.

"Zhu Chaoyang is only thirteen and a half, and he's studying at Qiushi Middle School. How could he be involved in a rape and murder case?" another officer added.

Ye scanned his notes.

"Captain Ye, doesn't your daughter go to the same school?"

"Yes, she does. I think Zhu Chaoyang is in her class. Every time they have an exam, he is at the top of the class. I keep telling Chimin to study harder but she doesn't listen."

"Top of the class? Doesn't seem like the type who would murder someone. Dammit, I thought Wang Yao was going to blow this case wide open," the first officer grumbled.

"Either way, we need to investigate this. He might not have done it, but he might have some information. After all, she was his sister," Ye Jun said.

His fellow officers nodded.

36

Zhu Chaoyang was worried sick about Pupu and Ding Hao now they had left for Zhang Dongsheng's studio apartment. The murderer claimed he was being a good Samaritan, but Chaoyang didn't trust him one bit.

Unfortunately, with his mum now at home, Pupu and Ding Hao did not have much choice. It was unlikely that anyone would rent a room to two minors. Most landlords would suspect that they were runaways and call the police. Then they would be dragged back to the orphanage and Chaoyang's secret might be revealed in the process. It would have been easier if he could have kept them at his apartment, but his mother would have thought it was strange that they never went home. Without mobiles or a way of contacting them, Chaoyang had no way of knowing how they were getting on other than visiting them. But he didn't want to go—it was risky.

His mother had left to buy food, while Chaoyang continued to toy with the idea of going to see Pupu and Ding Hao when he heard a knock on the door. He crept to the peephole and shrunk back in fear. Two police officers! In uniform! He had hoped that the investigation into Jingjing's death would not uncover his connection. A knot formed in his stomach and his heart thumped as he hid behind the door. How much did the police know? What should he say? He would have to deny everything.

"This is the address, isn't it?" one officer said.

"Maybe they're not home. Should we come back in the afternoon?" the other said.

"Shit. We came all the way out here on a hot day and nobody is home," the first one complained.

Just as they were turning to leave, Chaoyang opened the door. He tried to remain calm as he spoke through the security door. "Are you looking for someone?"

"Are you Zhu Chaoyang?" A heavyset, muscular man in his thirties flashed his badge and looked seriously at him. "I'm Officer Li Lu."

"Uhh… is something wrong, Officers?" Chaoyang asked, avoiding their gaze.

"We need to ask you some questions. Open the door."

Chaoyang put his hand on the lock, hesitating. "What is this about?"

"This is part of an investigation," the second officer said. He kept his voice kind, trying not to frighten the child.

Chaoyang looked at the two policemen for another moment, but had no choice. He opened the door and invited them in. "Let me get you some water," he said, turning his back to them.

"Thank you, but we don't need anything," Li Lu said, watching the boy. "Is your mother home?"

"She just left. Did you want to ask her some questions?"

"We want to verify a few things, that's all," the kind officer said. "You went to the Children's Palace on Thursday, the 4th of July, didn't you?" Technically a parent or guardian needed to be present in order for them to conduct an interrogation, but they didn't really suspect Zhu Chaoyang—they merely wanted to go over what he had done that morning.

"The Children's Palace…" He froze, his hand momentarily unable to pour steadily. His back was still turned and the police could not see his expression.

"You remember, don't you?" the kind officer prompted.

Chaoyang inhaled deeply, quietly. They were going to ask him about the Children's Palace after all.

After Jingjing died, he had thought a lot about what he was

141

going to do. The best case scenario was that the police never investigated him. The next best was that they did, but that he denied killing her, no matter what. If he admitted to his crime, his father would know and he would be in so much trouble he would wish he were dead. The worst case scenario was if he flatly denied everything but the police found out the truth anyway. At that point, he would have to rely on the law he had read about which protected offenders under the age of fourteen. That was how he came to the conclusion that he would lie to the police— if the plan failed, he wouldn't be worse off.

He was nervous, but not really afraid. The only thing that *really* scared him was his father.

Chaoyang turned around. "I remember now. I was at the Children's Palace then."

"Were you alone?"

"I… was alone." Chaoyang turned back to grab the two glasses and carefully handed them to the officers.

Both said thank you, but neither took a drink, setting the glasses on the table instead. "So what did you do at the Children's Palace, all by yourself?"

"I read books."

"Were you reading books the whole time?"

"Yes." Chaoyang was becoming less nervous.

"Do you frequently visit the Children's Palace?"

"That's how I spend my whole summer. If I'm not at the Children's Palace, I'm at Xinhua Bookstore," he said.

Officer Li Lu moved into the living area and looked at a wall covered with multiple awards for Chaoyang's academic achievement. He nodded. "When did you leave the Children's Palace that day?"

"Before lunchtime."

"Did anything happen before you left?"

Chaoyang paused. "You're talking about Zhu Jingjing's death, aren't you?"

"So you know it was her? Did you see her fall?"

"No, I only found out that it was Zhu Jingjing when my mum told me on the phone, after I got home."

"Did you speak to her when you were at the Children's Palace that day?"

Chaoyang shook his head. "No. I barely know—knew her."

The heavyset officer frowned. "You didn't know her?"

"I had only seen her once or twice."

"How is that possible?"

"My father didn't want me to have anything to do with her. She never knew that my father had been married before meeting her mother. She didn't even know that my father had me before she was born," Chaoyang said, his head bowed.

"Is that so?" The kind officer looked at him with concern. He felt sorry for the boy, but he still had his job to do. "We looked at the CCTV footage of the Children's Palace and you entered shortly after Zhu Jingjing. You were also seen looking around, as if searching for something. What were you doing when you first entered the Children's Palace?"

Chaoyang's heart skipped a beat. He had never expected security cameras to record his movements and he wasn't ready for so many questions. But he had to stick to his plan and deny everything. "I wasn't following her, I didn't even recognize her. I went to read some books and then I heard someone say that someone fell, so I went to look. There were a lot of people around the body and I could not see who fell. In the evening, my mother called and told me it was Zhu Jingjing."

The officers exchanged a look. There didn't seem to be any gaps in this story. They both discreetly examined Chaoyang's hands and forearms, looking for scratches. Dr Chen had said the skin cells in the victim's mouth probably came from a hand. Chaoyang did not have any marks, reducing their suspicion of him further. They tried to get more details by taking the boy through his account again, but he stuck to his version.

Then the kind officer asked to take Chaoyang's fingerprints and a blood sample.

"A blood sample? What for?" he asked.

The officers simply asked him to cooperate. With a sinking heart, he knew he didn't have a choice.

Finally it was over. The officers were on their way out when Zhou Chunhong returned. When she saw the police officers she demanded an explanation. When they told her why they were at her home, she lost her temper. "You think that my son is responsible for the *death* of Zhu Jingjing?"

The officers were calm. "No, we were just asking routine questions as part of the investigation."

"Why are you investigating my son?" Zhou demanded. The answer came to her in a flash. "Zhu Yongping told you to investigate him, didn't he? He's despicable! His daughter dies and he suspects his own son! He's not fit to be a father!" she screamed.

The officers knew they couldn't confirm or deny her allegation. It would be unprofessional to confirm it and denying it would be lying. They did their best to reassure her and departed as quickly as possible. Chaoyang stood for a moment, then retreated to his room and softly closed the door. Zhou looked after him in despair. She wondered what her son was thinking and felt guilty for her outburst, deciding that her son did not want to talk as she had called his father names. She walked into the kitchen and started cooking.

Chaoyang was not worried about what his mother had said. He was going over the questions he was asked, trying to work out what the police knew. They seemed to accept the fact that he went to the Children's Palace alone. But they kept mentioning the security footage, so they must have examined it closely. Did Pupu and Ding Hao avoid the camera somehow? Why didn't the police ask about them?

The boy reviewed everything again and suddenly remembered that he was afraid Jingjing would recognize him, so had made Pupu and Ding Hao go ahead of him. That was why it looked like he came in alone. When the police saw him looking around, it was because he was looking for them! Chaoyang's new priority was making sure that the police did not find out about his two friends. He decided not to visit them. He hoped that they would not come to see him, because if the police saw the three of them together, they could probably put two and two together very easily.

37

Chaoyang was sent downstairs to buy some cooking wine in the afternoon and saw Pupu sitting by herself on a concrete bench outside his apartment block. She stood up and was about to rush over to him but he put his finger to his lips. She immediately understood. Chaoyang then ducked into a tiny residential alley. Pupu followed him.

After they entered the first alley, Chaoyang started running again into a small street, another small street and another alley. Finally he stopped on a large, busy street that was far enough from his house for him to relax a little. He slumped against a tree trunk to catch his breath.

"What's going on? Why are you running so fast?" Pupu panted. Her cheeks were slightly pink.

"The police came to my house this morning."

"The police came to your house?" she repeated loudly.

Chaoyang coughed to cover her question. He lowered his voice and signalled that they should walk and talk. "Yeah, they were asking questions about Little Bitch."

"Do they know that you pushed her?" Her voice was quiet now.

"I dunno. I am pretty sure that they don't know, otherwise they would have arrested me by now," Chaoyang said.

"So basically, you're a suspect?"

"Basically."

Pupu stopped abruptly. "Brother Chaoyang, I promise, I didn't tell anyone about this and neither did Ding Hao. I swear."

He gave a mirthless laugh. "I know you didn't tell anyone."

"But why do the police suspect you, if nobody saw you push her?"

"The police said they have CCTV footage of Little Bitch entering the Children's Palace and me coming in soon after her. Maybe Big Bitch saw the video and told the police to investigate me." He then told her all about his interview.

"Whoa. Are you worried?"

Chaoyang shook his head, then nodded, a strange smile on his face. "I'm not afraid of the police. Remember I'll still be protected by the Law on the Protection of Minors. I am a little terrified of what my dad will do when he finds out though."

"What do you think he'd do?"

"I don't know, but I can't think of anything more awful." He didn't want to go into the fact that he had been desperate to please his father his whole life, but nothing seemed to work.

Pupu nodded sympathetically.

Chaoyang sniffed and then sighed. "We'll just have to see if the police arrest me or not."

"What do you think will happen if you get arrested?"

"It's hard to say. Nobody saw me do it, but I lied to the police and said I went to the Children's Palace alone. You went in before me, so the police don't know about you. But if they find out that the three of us entered the Children's Palace together, I think we'll get caught."

"Don't worry, Brother Chaoyang, even if we have to go back to Beijing, we won't sell you out," she promised.

"The point is, kids can't trick the police. If they find out that you were at the Children's Palace with me, they will get to the bottom of things somehow. That's why I want to make sure that the police don't know that you and Ding Hao are my friends. Don't contact me for a while. We need to wait until we find a safe way to meet," he explained.

"How do we do that?"

Chaoyang considered the possibilities. "How about I hang out at Xinhua Bookstore every afternoon from about 1 p.m., and if you need to talk to me, you can find me there?"

"Sounds like a plan," Pupu said.

"The police took my fingerprints and a blood sample. I'm a little worried about that, though," Chaoyang admitted.

"What do they need that for?" Pupu asked.

"In TV shows the cops always use fingerprints to connect a killer to the crime scene. I'm not sure if I left any fingerprints at the Children's Palace."

Pupu shook her head. "All you did was touch her clothes. You can't leave fingerprints on clothes."

"I didn't know that!" Chaoyang said. "How did you know that?"

Pupu shrugged nonchalantly. "But what's the blood for?"

"They'll probably use it to get my DNA."

"Your DNA, really?"

"We learned about it in biology. All kinds of tissues in the human body contain DNA. I have been going over everything that happened and I can't work it out: Little Bitch never scratched me, so it doesn't make sense that the police would want my DNA."

Pupu squinted in concentration. Then her eyes widened suddenly.

"What is it, Pupu?" Chaoyang asked.

"*You* didn't leave anything that has your DNA, but Ding Hao did. Little Bitch bit his hand, remember? She bit off a chunk of skin and it started bleeding. And his hair…"

Chaoyang's eyes widened too. "We can't let anyone find him! We can't afford to mess things up with the murderer, so we can't let him figure out that we don't want to report him to the police. That could lead to problems for us."

"That's what I said to Ding Hao! We can't let him find out any of our weaknesses."

148

Chaoyang nodded. "By the way, why were you hanging around outside my house? Is something wrong?"

Pupu's face clouded. "I think the murderer went through our stuff when we left the house today and I wanted to tell you."

"How could you tell?"

"The piece of string in the door."

"Was it on the floor?"

"No, but it was put back in a different place. I had placed the string where there was a little splatter of paint on the edge of the door. When I came back, it was just a little bit higher than before."

"Where did you guys go?"

"He came over in the morning and gave us money and a handful of coupons to KFC. He said we should go there for lunch. Then he said he wouldn't be back until tomorrow and asked us a bunch of questions, but we didn't fall for his tricks. He left and we went to the KFC across the road, but when we got back, the string on the door had been moved just a little. Nothing else looked different. Ding Hao said he didn't touch anything in the room all day. I'm pretty sure the murderer was looking for the camera. I wanted to tell you about it, but I knew that your mum would be at home so I didn't knock on the door. It only took a couple of hours for you to show up," Pupu finished with a sardonic smile.

"Sorry to make you wait so long," Chaoyang said.

"It's fine. You couldn't know I was here anyway. I'm not sure if the murderer plans to buy the camera from us or if he is going to keep playing tricks on us."

"We really have to be careful around him," Chaoyang said with a frown. "He clearly went through your stuff, and he might have been looking for the camera or for clues as to who you are."

"So... what do we do next?"

"I think you should pretend nothing happened; just see what he does next. You don't have the camera, so he won't hurt you.

He'll have to pay up if he wants the reassurance that nobody will tell the police."

"You're amazing. We'll do that then."

"OK, that's settled. I need to hurry. My mum sent me to buy cooking wine and I've already been gone for ages."

38

"Captain Ye, an update: Zhu Chaoyang gave us prints and a blood sample but they don't match," Officer Li Lu grumbled. He tossed the forensic report on the desk. "He's so small and he doesn't even have any peach fuzz on his upper lip, so I don't think he has hit puberty. He couldn't possibly be the killer."

Ye Jun scanned the report and flicked some ash from his cigarette into an ashtray. "What was he like when you questioned him?"

"Nervous, but not more than is to be expected. He was well mannered. With all those awards on the wall, it's no surprise that he's the best in his class."

"Hmm." Ye Jun looked away, thinking. "So was it a coincidence that he entered the Children's Palace less than a minute after Jingjing did?"

Li was confident. "Jingjing's mother is grieving; she is not thinking straight, that's my opinion. She needs someone to blame. You know what was odd though? Zhu Chaoyang's place was cramped and run-down. They don't even have air-conditioning! You would never guess that his father is a successful businessman."

"That's ridiculous," Ye Jun huffed.

The officer nodded. "We went to Zhu Yongping's factory to speak to his business associates and staff, and apparently Wang Yao handles all of the finances. She doesn't let him give any money to his first wife or his son. Zhu used to secretly give them some but even that led to too many arguments. Zhu Chaoyang's mother has a low-wage job selling tickets at Sanmingshan. She can barely put food on the table."

Ye Jun reflected on this information. "If we ignore the fingerprints and DNA for a minute... Zhu Chaoyang and Zhu Jingjing live completely different lives, despite both having Zhu Yongping for a father. Chaoyang has every reason to hate his stepmother and half-sister. Do you think he would get a classmate to do the job for him?"

"Unlikely. He doesn't hang out with the rough kids at his school and he seems to have barely even known Zhu Jingjing."

"He barely knew her?" Ye Jun repeated, still incredulous about this.

"When I interviewed Zhu Yongping, he said that his wife is inconsolable and that she is taking out her anger on Zhu Chaoyang. He said that Zhu Chaoyang and Zhu Jingjing met for the first time last week. That was corroborated by Zhu's friends— apparently Wang Yao took her daughter for a day out and came back early to her husband's office, where she discovered Zhu Chaoyang and made a big deal out of it. That was how the boy met Zhu Jingjing. Zhu tried to claim that Chaoyang was his nephew."

"Why would he do that?"

"I gather that the little girl was raised to believe that Zhu Yongping had never been married before and that she was his only child. He clearly doesn't give any thought to Zhu Chaoyang."

"Zhu Yongping is not the first father to treat his children unequally. At least he gave the kid money from time to time. But in the end, the children suffer the most. Poor Zhu Chaoyang," Ye Jun sighed.

"It's depressing but every time we pick up a young person for petty crime, they have an unhappy childhood or divorced parents. It's incredible to have someone like Zhu Chaoyang doing well despite the odds. I almost regret going there to question him," Li said.

Ye nodded. As his suspicion gradually evaporated, his sympathy for Zhu Chaoyang only grew.

39

The day after he was interviewed by the police, Zhu Chaoyang was reading in his room when he heard angry voices outside. One was his mother's.

Chaoyang sat bolt upright, pulled on a shirt and flew down the stairs. At the bottom of the stairs, he saw his mother carrying a plastic bag from the butcher's. Then he clocked Wang Yao—they recognized each other in the same instant.

"It was you!" she exclaimed, charging at him.

"No, no, it wasn't me," Chaoyang stammered. He saw a strange glint in her eye and couldn't help but shrink away from her.

Wang Yao saw his fear and immediately read it as guilt. "You bastard! You killed Jingjing! You'll pay for this!" As she advanced on him, Chaoyang turned sharply to go back up the stairs, but she threw her phone and hit him square in the shoulders, causing him to shout in pain.

"Don't you lay a finger on my son!" Zhou Chunhong thundered. She smacked the back of Wang Yao's head with the piece of raw pork in her bag.

The neighbours, alerted by all the noise, hurried to pull the two women apart. Wang Yao surprised them with the strength that sprang out of her grief. She flung her head back and took the opportunity to bash Zhou on the head with both fists. (Zhou, being a head shorter, was at a disadvantage.) The neighbours had trouble separating them.

Chaoyang couldn't bear to watch his mother humiliated like that. He pushed his fear aside and charged at Wang Yao, "Ahhh!"

Chaoyang yanked her hair and she kicked him with her high heels. He ignored the shooting pain in his legs and fought back.

Finally, they were all restrained by the neighbours. Chaoyang glared at Wang Yao, his face covered in bright red scratches. She had scratches on her face and her hair was dishevelled. Zhou Chunhong had fared the worst—a large lump was forming on her head, clumps of her hair were missing, and she was bleeding.

It devastated Chaoyang to see how badly his mother was hurt. "Are you OK, Mum? I won't let her hurt you again!" He looked at Wang Yao and hissed, "Go to hell, bitch!" The neighbours did not let him get near her again, but he kicked his legs at her anyway.

"Come and get me, you little bastard! If the police won't do their jobs, I will take the law into my own hands." Wang Yao smiled ominously.

Chaoyang shot back, without even thinking about it, "I'm glad that Little Bitch died. I wish you were dead too!"

They were still itching to fight. If it were not for the people firmly holding them apart, there would have been more damage. Suddenly a Mercedes SUV pulled up outside the apartment block and Zhu Yongping jumped out. He ran over and tore Wang Yao away as he reprimanded her. "Come on! We're leaving. Don't make a fool of yourself, not in public."

"You think I'm making a fool of myself?" Wang Yao spat as she struggled. "Who would laugh at such a thing as my daughter's death? *Your* son killed my daughter and the police are doing nothing about it. Did you pay them off?"

"How many times do they have to tell you? He wasn't involved!"

The woman gave a demented laugh. "Wasn't involved? I swear, that little bastard killed her. Look, he hurt me! Teach him a lesson, Yongping! It hurts."

Zhu stroked her hair, a look of compassion in his eyes, and she finally quietened. He turned to give a reproving look to his son and his ex-wife, and then manoeuvred Wang Yao towards the SUV.

"Dad!" Zhu Chaoyang shouted. "Big Bitch hit us first! Look at what she did to Mum!"

Zhu stopped short and turned to look at his son. "Did you just call your own stepmother a bitch? How can you be so disrespectful?"

Chaoyang was stung by the words, but said nothing. Then his mother, who was bleeding heavily, screamed, "You're a poor excuse of a human being, Zhu Yongping! She hurt your son and you're still protecting her!"

The neighbours started taking sides. Zhu Yongping was not about to apologize, so he let Zhou Chunhong hurl abuse at him as they stood outside the Mercedes. At that moment, two police cars showed up. Neighbours had called 110 as soon as the fight started and Ye Jun had insisted on coming along when he heard that the quarrel involved Zhu Chaoyang and Wang Yao. But Wang Yao did not seem to appreciate his appearance for she started screaming at Zhu Chaoyang again moments after Ye Jun arrived.

Zhou was so angry at her ex-husband for disrespecting them that she freed herself from her neighbour's grasp and ran over to kick Wang Yao, and then tried to slap her in the face, but Zhu grabbed hold of his ex-wife's wrist with his left hand and slapped her with his right.

The sound rang out in the air.

Chaoyang felt everything go quiet. He couldn't hear anything. His voice was barely a whisper. "Dad…"

The police quickly pulled the women and Zhu Yongping apart. Ye Jun escorted Zhu to the police car, cursing as he went. "You slapped your ex-wife in front of your son! What the hell is wrong with you? Get in, we're going to the police station!" Zhu pressed his lips together and allowed the officer to push him into the car.

After that, Ye Jun interviewed the witnesses who had stayed, and they all agreed that Zhu Yongping had protected his wife despite her overly aggressive behaviour. It was obvious that Wang Yao had struck Zhu Chaoyang first, but that was unimportant to Zhu Yongping. Rather than consoling his son, he had reprimanded him and slapped his mother.

Ye noted the lifeless look in Zhu Chaoyang's eyes and sighed. "We made things perfectly clear when we last spoke," he told Wang Yao contemptuously.

He then set the record straight for the neighbours. "We have investigated Zhu Chaoyang and found no evidence to connect him to the crime. There are many people who can vouch for his character, including my own daughter. He is not involved in this case! Anyone who harasses Zhu Chaoyang will get a free trip to the police station!"

Wang Yao laughed again. "Lock me up, I don't care!" She then turned her gaze to Chaoyang. "Watch your back. I'll bury you!"

The crowd began to curse and jeer at her.

Ye Jun pointed a finger at his chest. "Are you kidding me? Do you not see the uniform? Threaten him again and I'll charge you with harassment. If you so much as lay a finger on him, I'll make you wish you had never been born."

Ye Jun was known for being a hard arse. He had arrested countless small-time crooks and was famous for cursing people as if he were still in the military. The baddies threatened that when they were released, they were going to show Ye Jun who was boss. But when they actually faced him again, they were meek as mice. No one dared to cross the line. Still, under the gruff exterior he had a good heart and the local community liked him. Watching the way he dealt with Wang Yao made the crowd clap with delight.

After Wang Yao and Zhu Yongping were driven away in a police car for questioning, Ye Jun looked at Zhou Chunhong. He suggested that she come to the station so that everyone could resolve their differences under the watchful eye of the police—otherwise poor Chaoyang might be scarred by the experience. He reassured her that her son would not be asked to accompany her there and that he, Ye Jun, would keep the situation under control if tempers flared again. Zhou agreed. She wanted to tell Chaoyang she was leaving but he was in such a daze that she had to shout at him to get his attention. She told him to go inside and make himself something to eat while she went to the station.

When Zhou clambered into the second police car, the crowd dispersed, the entertainment over for the day. Ye Jun spoke to Chaoyang for a few minutes and offered him his personal number, saying he could call if he ever felt threatened. As the police car drove off, Chaoyang slowly turned towards the stairs and took a deep breath. He felt surprisingly calm. He wasn't thinking about the quarrel and he wasn't thinking about his mother's injuries or his own scratched face. He was thinking about killing people.

He had never meant to kill Zhu Jingjing. But this time, he had actually wanted to kill Wang Yao. He bit his lip and trudged up the stairs.

40

The next day Chaoyang went to Xinhua Bookstore at 1 p.m. as he had arranged with Pupu. She was already there, reading a book from the children's section. He stood in front of her, reluctant to interrupt her.

"What are you reading?" he finally asked, examining the cover.

"*Krabat*. It's a German folktale, it's really good. Krabat lost both of his parents and he goes to a mill to work as an apprentice. The master teaches dark magic to the boys, but every year he sacrifices one of them, so they are afraid to work there but they can't leave. Then Krabat fights back."

"Sounds creepy, but good."

"You should read it," Pupu said.

"OK." He took a copy off the shelf and sat down next to her.

"I have something big to tell you," she said.

Chaoyang raised his eyebrows. "So do I."

"You go first."

"Big Bitch came to my house, looking for a fight. She hurt my mum badly and she kicked and scratched me too. Then my dad came and defended Big Bitch even though she started it. Then the police came and took them both away! They made my mum go to the police station too, when she didn't do anything wrong!"

"Chaoyang, that's awful," Pupu murmured.

"My dad agreed to give my mum a thousand yuan to cover her medical expenses. Then the police said that settled everything."

"That's it? They didn't lock up Big Bitch?"

He shook his head. "No, the police don't lock people up for getting into a fight. They told Wang Yao that they understood why it happened but if she did it again, they would have to charge her. My dad defended her the whole time."

"Why would he do that?"

"He's not my dad any more," Chaoyang replied quietly but firmly.

Pupu decided to drop it.

"What did you want to tell me?" he asked.

"The murderer said he was going on a trip for two or three weeks and we shouldn't do anything stupid while he was away. Then he gave us some money and said he would pay us the rest in exchange for the camera when he got back! That's fishy, isn't it? What do you think he is up to?"

"He's going on a trip?" Chaoyang frowned as he thought. "He's not even worried about the camera and what we might do with it! That means he must have something really important to do. You don't think he found out where I live, do you?"

"No, he doesn't know. We haven't told him anything," Pupu assured him.

"But what could be more important to him than that camera?" Chaoyang scratched his head. "Maybe he does need to go on some kind of trip for work. The camera is at my house, so as long as he doesn't know where I live he can't surprise us."

"I think that man is really devious, Chaoyang. We need to watch out."

"What do you mean, devious?"

"He figured out how to get on Ding Hao's good side: computer games. All it took was one old computer and Ding Hao was licking his hand like a dumb dog. He is going round calling him Uncle now!"

"I was worried that might happen. The murderer might trick him into revealing information," Chaoyang said.

159

"I told Ding Hao a thousand times! But he promised me that he wouldn't say anything."

Chaoyang nodded. "Just keep reminding him. That man might act all friendly, but we know his true nature!"

41

Things were quiet for Chaoyang after Zhang Dongsheng went on his trip.

The police did not ask him any further questions. Wang Yao did not send anyone to harass him, either. Then again, his dad didn't call to check on him, which was disappointing. Zhou Chunhong noticed that Chaoyang was talking less and less and she tried to hide how sad it made her. When he saw her crying, he did his best to comfort her.

Every day after lunch, Chaoyang went to Xinhua Bookstore. Pupu went too, so they read and talked every afternoon. Pupu said Ding Hao was parked in front of the computer, but Chaoyang did not mind spending time with her. Every day Chaoyang read reference books and she read fun books. It would be nice to spend the whole summer like this, without a care in the world. He tried not to think about the future, about Zhu Jingjing, about his father who never called. He tried not to worry about Pupu and Ding Hao, or the camera, or what would happen once school started again.

It was strange, but this summer was the most troubled one of his life and also the most wonderful. Pupu made him happy. She made him feel like he wasn't alone.

Two weeks later, Chaoyang was eating noodles and watching the news on television. He was home alone and had turned on the local news channel for company, which was describing a car accident.

The newscaster looked serious. "At 8 o'clock this morning, a red BMW lost control on Xinhua Road, hitting the barrier and causing a multi-vehicle accident. The traffic police have blocked Xinhua Road. The female driver in the BMW was declared dead at the scene. According to the investigation by the traffic police, the young woman died suddenly, causing her to lose control of the vehicle…"

On the screen, the red BMW was partway on the barrier, but it did not look seriously damaged. Strangely, the news report seemed to be suggesting that the car accident had not caused her death, but the driver's sudden death had caused the accident.

The report cut to a shot of a hospital. "Just over three weeks ago, the woman had lost both of her parents in an accident at a nature park. One person close to her said that she was not taking the death of her parents well, and that she was regularly drinking and using sedatives. One theory is that she suffered a mental breakdown that contributed to her losing control of the vehicle. The woman's husband was away but has returned to Ningbo on news of the tragic accident. The husband is reported to be distraught. Our thoughts and wishes are with the husband and the victim's family at this time."

The newscaster said more uplifting words, but Chaoyang had stopped paying attention to her words. His eyes were glued to the screen, where a man was crying bitterly. It was the man who was supposed to buy a camera from them. Chaoyang shuddered involuntarily. It seemed like Zhang really did have something more important to do—killing someone else! The report had claimed that the sudden death was caused by the sedatives, alcohol and the woman's poor mental health, but Chaoyang did not believe that for a second. Zhang had killed his wife.

But how did he manage to do it while he was out of the area? How did she die while she was driving by herself? Chaoyang was determined to find out, otherwise the triple murderer would likely try to use the same tactics on him and his friends.

42

The next day, Chaoyang hurried to Xinhua Bookstore right after lunch. He was looking forward to seeing Pupu and telling her what he had discovered. When Ding Hao arrived on his own, Chaoyang was crestfallen. Ding Hao playfully locked his arm around Chaoyang's neck as if wrestling him. "Long time no see, Chaoyang!"

He wasn't amused. "I thought you couldn't leave your computer for more than five minutes."

Ding Hao beamed a goofy smile and hugged Chaoyang's shoulder, then sat on the floor next to him. "Listen, I know when to stop. I know when it's time to play and when it's time to be serious. Pupu's been slandering me."

"Maybe it's a good thing that you're spending all your time indoors," Chaoyang said.

"What's that supposed to mean?" Ding Hao asked.

Chaoyang was thinking about how he didn't want the police to link the DNA evidence found at the Children's Palace to Ding Hao. But he and Pupu had agreed not to tell him their fears about the evidence, so he quickly switched the subject. "Where's Pupu?"

"She…" Ding Hao smiled again, then lowered his voice. "Guess why I'm here and Pupu's not."

Chaoyang didn't answer.

Ding Hao coughed and put on his serious face. "Pupu asked me to do something for her."

"What?" Chaoyang looked confused.

"Uh... Pupu... likes you." Ding Hao blurted out the sentence and smiled a genuine smile.

"Oh, you mean, Pupu told you to tell me that she likes *me*?"

The boy nodded enthusiastically, then shook his head. "She didn't want me to tell you directly. She wanted me to test the waters. You know, see how you feel."

"I don't think what you said counts as testing the waters. You just told me outright," Chaoyang said.

"I wasn't subtle, was I?" Ding Hao looked awkward. "Well, don't tell Pupu that I was so direct."

"Ding Hao, what is going on?"

"It's..." He faltered and started again. "So Pupu wanted me to come and test the waters, and see if you are interested in her, in that way. She didn't say that she likes you. But I can tell that she does, she definitely does. That's why she wanted me to talk to you. Does that make sense?"

Chaoyang was quiet for a moment. "Are you messing with me?"

"Why would I do that? Come on, tell me. Do you want to be Pupu's boyfriend?"

"Be her boyfriend?" Chaoyang's head was swimming. He was expecting to talk about the murderer and how he had killed his wife, now he was talking about girls! He would be lying if he said he didn't have feelings for Pupu. She was cute, like a porcelain doll. Chaoyang had not hit puberty yet, but he had already started looking at girls differently. He had had crushes on some of the girls in his class, but he was never bold enough to do anything about it. The girls in his class liked tall, handsome guys, not puny nerds like him.

"Come on, spit it out! Do you like Pupu or not?" Ding Hao pressed.

"Uh..." Chaoyang didn't know what to say. "What about you? Do you like her?"

"Me?" Ding Hao looked a little grossed out. "She's my sister, how could I like her like that?"

"But you've known each other for a long time and you've been through a lot."

"No seriously, I think of her as a sister. Plus," he lowered his voice again, "I like somebody else."

"Who?"

Ding Hao lifted a sleeve and revealed a crude tattoo. "See that?"

Chaoyang looked at the characters. "What does it say? Person king?"

"It's Quan!" Ding Hao pouted at him.

"Why Quan?"

"There's a girl in my hometown, I've known her for like, forever. Her name is Li Quanquan. After I was sent to the orphanage, she wrote me letters. I dipped a pen in blue ink and scratched Quan into my arm. When we escaped, I really wanted to go to my hometown to see her but I was afraid someone would recognize me. I wonder what she looks like now." Ding Hao realized he had said a lot about his crush. "But listen, Chaoyang, you have to keep what I said about Quanquan a secret. If Pupu finds out she'll laugh at me."

"Does Quanquan like you back?" Chaoyang asked.

"I dunno. She never mentioned it in any of the letters and I was afraid to ask. I haven't received any letters since last year. Maybe… maybe she has a boyfriend." He sat quietly for a brief moment and then smiled. "Let's talk about something else. Do you like Pupu or not?"

All thoughts of murderers went out of his mind and Chaoyang hung his head bashfully. "Why does Pupu like me?"

"She likes smart people, and she thinks you're smart. Stop beating around the bush. Just tell me if you like her or not, and I'll be your messenger."

"I… I don't know what to say," Chaoyang said, blushing.

Ding Hao laughed. "Pupu is really nice, and she's pretty. She's frosty with most people but she actually talks to you. Am I right?"

"Yeah."

"So what are you worrying about? All you have to do is tell me if you like her or not. I'll support you, no matter what."

"Well…" Chaoyang swallowed. "Maybe she doesn't really *like me* like me, I'm not sure what she means…"

Ding Hao laughed and clapped his friend on the shoulder. "I know what you're getting at. I'll toast you when the day comes. I'm going to go back now."

He stood up to leave. Chaoyang knew his friend was eager to get back to the computer, but had to ask one more question. "Wait, Ding Hao. Did Mr Zhang come back?"

"Nope. He said he was going on a trip for work for two or three weeks and he would talk to us as soon as he got back. It's only been two weeks."

"Oh… right. OK, see you later." Chaoyang didn't bring up the murder of Zhang Dongsheng's wife, thinking it wouldn't do any good to tell a numbskull like Ding Hao. He would tell Pupu tomorrow.

Ding Hao's message was surprising, but it gave him a warm feeling inside. He would have to think about it for a while. How was it possible that a girl liked him?

43

Ding Hao headed home and Chaoyang tried to read for a while. It was strange not having Pupu there with him, even a little boring. It was better to be bored at home than bored at the bookstore.

He got off the bus and was almost home when he heard his name: "Zhu Chaoyang."

He turned as a plastic washbasin full of something smelly came flying towards his face. He tried to duck, but the bowl hit him on the shoulder. Chaoyang came to the horrible realization that he was now covered in urine and excrement. He froze, not comprehending what was happening, and when he tried to locate his assailant, it was too late—two young men were already getting into a van down the street. Chaoyang grabbed a rock from a nearby flower bed and threw it in their direction. He stood motionless in the street.

He was quickly surrounded by sympathetic passers-by. "Oh, how awful!" they clucked. "Who did that to you, you poor thing?" One of them handed him a packet of tissues, but it was hopeless. Chaoyang's eyes were stinging. He accepted the tissues, carefully trying to avoid coming into contact with anyone, and wiped his face and then ran for home, head bowed. After a few steps, he burst into tears. He tried to shake the shit off his clothes and continued on his way.

He encountered a few neighbours at the foot of the main stairwell. One woman stopped him. "Chaoyang, what's happened to you? You should call your mother and tell her to come home. Someone has written awful messages in the hallway outside your apartment."

Chaoyang rushed upstairs. They started in the corridor on

the floor below his floor: big red crosses, daubed all over the walls. On either side of his door was scrawled: "An eye for an eye. Everyone must repay their debt."

The neighbours followed close behind him. "Chaoyang, get your mother. Does she owe money to anyone?" one asked.

"Chaoyang, what are you covered in? What is that smell?" another questioned. It was clear that some people were worried for him and others were simply worried that they would be caught in the crossfire.

"Chunhong is trustworthy—she would never borrow money from someone without paying them back. I bet it was Zhu Yongping's crazy wife, getting revenge," a man concluded.

"Most likely," another neighbour agreed.

Chaoyang felt like the whole world was spinning.

A neighbour ran up the stairs, her voice frantic. "I called Chunhong," she cried, "and she said someone attacked her earlier on, the same as Chaoyang. The attackers ran away before anyone could catch them."

"They got her too?" Chaoyang was filled with rage. He wanted to scream at the world, but instead fished his key out of his pocket and opened the door. He went straight to the telephone to call Ye Jun. To hell with the filth on his fingers.

Captain Ye Jun arrived with another officer within ten minutes. When Ye saw the red paint, he banged his fist against the wall. Without waiting to hear what the neighbours had to say, he shouted to his colleague, "Li, I want you to arrest Wang Yao immediately. She'll probably be at work, at Zhu Yongping's seafood factory."

He turned to Chaoyang. "Don't be afraid, we'll take care of this. Take a shower and put on some fresh clothes. I'll take you to your dad's work."

Chaoyang nodded gratefully. After a quick clean-up, he hopped into Ye Jun's car. They soon arrived at the seafood factory. Several officers were arguing with Zhu Yongping outside the entrance. When he saw the owner, Ye Jun leapt into action. "Where's Wang Yao?"

"Zhu Yongping says she's not here and he can't reach her," an officer explained.

Ye Jun glared. "Mr Zhu, we need to take Wang Yao with us to the station for questioning. Hand her over."

Zhu Yongping started giving out cigarettes but Ye Jun smacked them away. "Don't try that shit with me!"

Zhu was trying to smooth things over. "Officer Ye, please don't take her away. I had no idea that she was going to do… whatever it is she's done. My wife is incredibly stubborn, she doesn't think that the law applies to her—"

"Don't make excuses! I warned her not to harm Chaoyang!" Ye grabbed Zhu Yongping's chin and forced him to look up. "Look at your son. They threw piss and shit all over him and did the same to your ex-wife. Their apartment was vandalized. Despicable! Can you stop and think about your poor son instead of your second wife for just one second?"

Zhu Yongping looked pained but he kept babbling about Wang Yao. His friends, who had shown up when he called them in for support, had intended to use their influence to convince the police not to press charges. But when they heard what happened, they shook their heads disapprovingly. None of them were willing to side with someone who vandalized property and dumped shit on people, especially a young boy. They told Zhu to find Wang Yao quickly and do right by his son.

Attacked on all sides, Zhu sighed and slumped to his knees, covering his head with his hands. Seeing her husband's plight through an office window, Wang Yao suddenly appeared, yelling, "What do you want from me?"

Zhu Yongping dashed over to her. "Go back inside! I'll take care of this."

"I'm glad you had the sense to come outside, Wang Yao. Take her away, boys," Ye Jun said.

The officers were about to handcuff her when she wrested her arms free and whipped her hair around. "Hey! What are you arresting me for?"

"Do you really need to ask? You dumped excrement on two people, and you vandalized property."

"I never did that! I've been here at the seafood business all day."

"I don't have time to listen to you play dumb," Ye Jun said.

"You need evidence before you can arrest someone, right? You said you couldn't arrest that bastard Chaoyang because you didn't have the evidence, so why is it different for me? My daughter is dead, and you still haven't managed to catch the killer. But arresting me is easy, isn't it?"

"So that's how you want to play it," said Ye Jun, gritting his teeth. "We were going to chalk this up to public disorder. But don't think that you can get away with this simply because you instructed some hooligans to carry out the crime. If you'd rather have me drag them into the station first, I'll do it. By the time their arses are in the station, this case will be far more serious. Just you wait!"

Ye Jun led his men away. Zhu Yongping looked agitated as he scampered after them. "Please, Officers, my wife is being silly. Please forgive her. Please forgive her!" He then turned to her. "If you did it, just admit it! Don't be so foolish!"

Wang Yao walked reluctantly after the police. But when she noticed Zhu Chaoyang standing behind Ye Jun, she went ballistic. "You little bastard!"

Chaoyang had already been seething since she stepped outside, and he lost control. "You bitch! You dirty slut! I'll get you for this and what you did to my mother!"

Zhu Yongping held out an arm, blocking him from getting any closer to Wang Yao. "Stay out of this. This is a matter for adults."

"Dad, are you really taking her side, after all this?" Chaoyang staggered backwards, giving his father a strange look.

Zhu looked chagrined. He pulled his son aside, and whispered, "Chaoyang, your stepmother did a bad thing. She has always been prejudiced against you, and since Jingjing's death, she has let her feelings run wild. I promise you, this won't happen again. Talk to your mother, please. Convince her not to press charges. I really don't want your stepmother to be arrested."

Chaoyang's voice cracked. "But I was covered in shit."

His father pursed his lips. "In a few days I'll send you ten thousand yuan. You can get someone to paint over the writing. That should settle it."

Chaoyang looked tearfully at his father in disbelief. He was unable to speak.

"That's settled then," Zhu concluded. He patted his son's shoulder apologetically. He was secure in the knowledge that his son would never disobey him. Still hurt, Chaoyang stepped back, nodded and walked over to Ye Jun. He whispered something in the officer's ear.

Ye Jun frowned in disapproval, but eventually sighed and approached Zhu Yongping. "If the victim is not willing to press charges, we will not investigate the attacks on Chaoyang and his mother. But painting threatening messages in a public place affects the entire community, and that crime must be investigated. Wang Yao still needs to accompany us to the station."

"OK, I understand," Zhu said. "Officer Ye, I'll go with her to the station."

Ye Jun curled his lips. "I suggest that you drive your son home. He's been through a traumatic experience and could use some support."

"Well…" Zhu glanced at Wang Yao, but his friends stepped in and shouted, "Use your brain, Yongping, take your son home!"

"OK, Chaoyang, I'm going to take you home." His reluctance was obvious in his voice.

He reached for his son's hand but Chaoyang pulled back. "No thanks, I can take care of myself." And with that, he turned and sprinted away.

44

Yan Liang hung up and stared at his phone in shock. A Xu relative had informed him that his niece died when she was driving and it was lucky that other people were not hurt. He was told that her husband was distraught at the news, especially as he had been in a remote village at the time, teaching underprivileged students. The day after the accident, the traffic police had written their report, the hospital completed the death certification, and Zhang Dongsheng had arranged for the immediate cremation of the body. But according to local custom, the family should wait seven days before cremating and burying the dead. That Xu Jing's parents were cremated so quickly was understandable due to the horrible nature of their accident. But why was Xu Jing cremated so soon after her death? It didn't make sense. Yan Liang's eyebrows knitted, remembering how his niece had warned him that if she died it would be Zhang's doing. *Did he have the capacity to kill his wife?*

Yan Liang was vexed. He sat in his desk chair for a good half hour, rubbing his eyes. Finally he left for the police station.

Captain Ye Jun was reading some documents when he heard footsteps and looked up to see Yan.

"Hello, Captain Ye."

Ye saw a man in his forties, wearing delicate glasses with gold frames. His expression changed from surprise to excitement. "Yan! What brings you here?"

Yan gave a hesitant smile. "I, uh, happened to be in the area. I wanted to see if you were still working here, so thought I would call by. I'm surprised that you're still at the same PSB."

Ye Jun laughed. "Ever since I took your class I've been passed over for promotion! No, I'm only kidding. I wouldn't want to be working anywhere else. Have a seat. Do you have a meeting to attend today?"

Yan remembered Ye Jun from the criminal logic classes he had taught and trusted him. While it was a short course, Ye had asked a few questions in private, so Yan was confident that he could cut straight to the chase. He cleared his throat, "Actually, I wanted to speak to you about a recent death."

"A murder, you mean?"

"Well, I don't want to jump to conclusions."

"You're… ah…" Ye Jun was worried about where the conversation would lead. Yan had quit the force and an ex-cop couldn't investigate cases because he would need access to confidential information.

"It's OK, I spoke to Gao Dong at the Zhejiang Public Security Department. He said he would send a fax giving you authority to share confidential information with me."

Ye Jun was surprised. Gao Dong was the deputy director of the Zhejiang Public Security Department and was in charge of all criminal investigations across the province. He must have worked with Yan on some important cases—Yan had friends in high places. Ye picked up the phone and started to dial a number. Just at that moment, a junior officer came in. "Ye, this fax is for you. Public Security Department."

Ye read:

Professor Yan Liang needs to borrow documents for personal use. Ningbo Jiangdong Public Security Bureau is to comply with his requests, under the condition that the documents are not sensitive or strictly confidential.

An official stamp was affixed to the bottom.

"Deputy Director Gao just called Director Ma and said that if we have any cases that are problematic, we should ask Professor Yan for assistance," the officer added before exiting.

Ye Jun brightened. "Professor Yan, did Deputy Director Gao invite you to help us on the Children's Palace case?"

"What case?" Yan asked.

Ye Jun briefly described the facts and explained how Yan had closed a somewhat similar case in the province, so he might have the best chance at sorting this one.

Yan smiled awkwardly. "I asked old Gao for a letter of introduction, but the matter I am interested in is not particularly sensitive. Old Gao certainly knows how to get things done, slipping another case in like that!"

That reminded Ye Jun that Gao Dong had been pushing to get the Children's Palace case resolved quickly. Allowing Yan Liang to read the files might lead to new approaches; rumour had it that Yan Liang always got his man. Ye Jun decided on a direct approach and asked Yan outright to join the Children's Palace case. But Yan was only interested in finding out why three members of the Xu family had died recently. Seeing the captain's enthusiasm, the professor explained the situation as tactfully as possible: he only wanted to borrow a few files from a traffic accident, and Ye Jun's case was strictly confidential since it involved a child.

Ye Jun was deflated, but agreed to give Yan what he wanted. In turn, Yan apologized for not being able to help and said modestly that he was far too rusty to be helpful on the Children's Palace case.

Finally, Yan began: "There was a traffic accident on Xinhua Road on the 28th. A woman died suddenly while she was driving. Did you hear about it?"

"No, I didn't. It would have been handled by the traffic police. What do you need to know?"

"I'd like to contact the case officer and review the police record, the accident report, any video footage of Xinhua Road and reports from the hospital."

"You think it wasn't an accident?" Ye questioned.

"I can't be sure. The woman was my niece so I want to have a better understanding of what happened."

Ye called up the CCTV footage of the accident on his computer and invited Yan to review it with him. There was a line of cars stuck in the morning rush hour. Yan focused on the red BMW, which he recognized as his niece's car. When the traffic light turned green, the cars slowly advanced, but the BMW moved erratically, veering left and right and then headed straight for the barrier, denting the left bumper.

"According to the report, there were traffic police on duty at that junction so they were able to reach her car in a matter of minutes," Ye said. "The report says Xu Jing was unresponsive and her mouth was flecked with foam. They broke the car window and took her straight to the hospital, but she was already dead. Sedatives were found in the car. Her husband and close friends explained that Xu Jing's parents had died recently and she was mentally unstable. She regularly took alcohol and sedatives to help her sleep. The cause of death was recorded as neurotic disorders due to alcohol and sedative misuse."

"No complete autopsy, no chemical analysis, no physical analysis," Yan noted.

"It was a run-of-the-mill death, not a criminal case. It wasn't necessary."

"That's true, the traffic police did everything according to the rules," Yan conceded.

"Do you think there was foul play?"

Yan said nothing.

"But Xu Jing was alone in the car."

Yan gave a wry smile. "There are many ways to kill a person."

Ye thought carefully. "But, Professor Yan, this looks like an ordinary accident to me. She's not the first person to die like this. It is a little surprising because of her age, but she was under a lot of pressure, and even a young woman can die suddenly. What do you see that I don't?"

"There isn't anything particularly obvious, but..." Yan paused. "Can you look someone up for me?"

"Who?"

Yan pursed his lips. "Xu Jing's husband, Zhang Dongsheng."

"Surely you don't think he did it!"

"You must *not* tell anyone I've asked. I don't have any evidence and my suspicions could turn out to be wrong. He is family, and there would be major repercussions after a false accusation."

"All right. What do you need to know?"

"I want to check what Zhang Dongsheng was doing on the day of Xu Jing's death," Yan said.

45

Zhang Dongsheng returned to the new apartment at 10 a.m. He was completely exhausted. He had kept a vigil for two nights, so he only had a short time to rest during the day. Despite his fatigue, he was feeling good.

Xu Jing died on her way to work, which was probably the best possible outcome—it cast the least suspicion on him. He had had her cremated the next day, destroying all evidence. With no heirs or close relatives, the Xu family assets, including all five properties, now belonged to him.

Xu Jing's infidelity was unimportant now. He had once loved her very much—the happiest day of his life was his wedding day. But that feeling had eroded and she had become a stranger to him.

There might be a few people who suspected him or who would gossip about how lucky he was to inherit the entire Xu fortune. But that did not matter. Two accidents occurred in the family, that was all. If anyone suspected him, there was no way of proving they were not accidents. Unless he confessed, the deaths could not be linked to him.

Except for that one bit of evidence, that truly damning evidence… those little brats. They were a pain in the neck. Zhang was generally good at solving problems, but had been unable to get the camera footage so far. The three little blackmailers were proving surprisingly crafty and vigilant. He still had not had an opportunity to kill them all at once. Obviously, he could torture two of them until they revealed where the third one was, and then kill them separately, but that was too complicated, too risky. He was certain that if he made one wrong step, those kids would inform the police. He just needed to wait until their vigilance wore down, then find a way to destroy them. He stretched and got ready to take a nap. The doorbell rang. Frustrated, Zhang went to the intercom to see who it was: Zhu Chaoyang.

Zhang assumed the shrimp wanted more money. His finger hovered over the button that would allow entry. "Uncle, I know you're in there, your car is here."

Zhang pulled a face and pressed the button. "Come on in, kiddo."

Zhang played the role of gracious host. "Would you like some soda? Oh, that's right, you don't drink soda. Juice then."

Zhang handed him a glass and Chaoyang took a huge gulp without a trace of worry. "Thanks."

"It's been a while since I've seen you, how are you doing? Do you need money? I can give you some more spending money but I'm not able to give you the three hundred thousand yet," Zhang said.

"That's OK. I didn't come here to ask for money," Chaoyang said, pulling up a chair and sitting down.

"This is not about money?" Zhang looked surprised. "What then?"

"I want to know how your wife died."

Zhang's face creased as he sat down. "How do you know my wife died?"

"I saw it on the news," Chaoyang said.

"Right." Zhang arranged his face to look sad. "The doctor said that her nerves were weak so she had a sudden death. I don't know what to tell you."

"I thought you would be happy about this."

"How dare you say that!" he spat out.

There was no sign of fear on Chaoyang's face. "Your parents-in-law died, and now your wife is dead. You were the one who said you married into a wealthy family and you didn't own the car you drove or the house you lived in. Now it's all yours. Why wouldn't you be happy?"

Zhang exhaled through his nose. "I killed my in-laws, you saw that. But I did not kill my wife. I loved her and my heart is broken. It's not the same without her. You'll understand when you get older."

Chaoyang nodded, playing along. "So did you really go on a trip?"

"I went to a mountain village near Lishui to teach poor children. I was supposed to stay for a few weeks, but, of course, as soon as I heard that my wife had died, I came straight back."

Chaoyang lifted an eyebrow. "Really?"

"Yes, really! Why do you ask?"

"I want to know how you killed someone without being in Ningbo. You made your wife's death look like an accident."

Zhang gnashed his teeth. "It *was* an accident. Not like Sanmingshan. I went to that mountain village with colleagues, and they can verify my whereabouts. Honestly, how could I possibly kill her when I had not been in Ningbo for the two weeks before her death?"

"That's exactly what I want to know. Otherwise, you could use the same tactic to kill us."

"How many times do I have to tell you! It. Was. An. Accident!" Zhang cried. He reached for a cigarette and lit it. There was no way he was letting the little fiend in on his secret. His doorbell rang again, and Zhang left Chaoyang sitting there and went to the intercom: Yan Liang. Why was he visiting now? And why was he coming to his new apartment? How had Yan learned about this address? He wouldn't have been so nervous if Chaoyang weren't there. What if the little devil let his secret slip? The tiniest clue would be enough for Yan to figure everything out. Zhang briefly considered not answering the door, but then remembered how the boy had deduced that he was at home. Yan would surely do the same.

Zhang quickly spoke to Chaoyang, a threatening look in his eye. "I have a friend coming up. Don't tell him anything. Understand?"

Chaoyang smiled sweetly and shook his head at the threat. "I'm not making any promises, unless you tell me how you killed your wife."

"It was an accident!" This time, Zhang's voice was panicky.

"Don't expect me to help you out," Chaoyang said, sensing he had the upper hand.

The doorbell rang again and again. "Dongsheng, open the door," Yan said through the intercom.

Zhang's head whipped back to the intercom screen, then back to Chaoyang. He cracked. "OK, OK, I did it. Now, when my friend arrives, are you going to cooperate?"

"How'd you kill her?"

"Poison! No more questions!" Zhang hissed.

"OK, I'll play along… for now," Chaoyang said cheerfully.

Zhang pressed the button and said, "Hi, Professor Yan. The door's unlocked. Come on up."

"Should I hide somewhere?" Chaoyang asked.

"No, if he found you, I would have a hard time explaining why. Just say you're my student…" Zhang quickly expanded on what Chaoyang should say. "Call me Teacher Zhang. If Yan asks, tell him you're getting extra lessons from me over the summer, and you were just stopping by to borrow some books. Then leave. Got it?"

Chaoyang made a face but did not argue. He scooped up a few copies of *Shu Li Tian Di*. "OK."

Chaoyang looked incredibly pleased with himself. Zhang frowned again. The boy wasn't so brazen when they had first met. He was becoming more and more like Pupu.

46

They heard the knock, and Zhang tapped the boy's forehead. "Remember what I told you."

"I got it," Chaoyang said.

"Coming!" Zhang put on a tired but welcoming face as he opened the door. "I didn't expect to see you here!"

"A relative told me that you were holding a vigil every night and it was causing a strain, so I wanted to check that you were OK. They told me I could find you at the new apartment. Oh, who is this?" Yan looked at the boy with surprise.

"This is a student I'm helping over the summer break. I told him he could take some books home to study since I'm too tired to help him this week."

"I'm so sorry for your loss, Teacher Zhang. I'll see myself out," Chaoyang chirped right on cue.

"I'll contact you in a few days. Don't be lazy, you still need to study!"

"OK." Chaoyang was heading for the door when Yan showed an interest in him.

"What grade are you in?" he asked.

"I'm starting my second year of high school next year," Chaoyang fibbed.

"You're a high school student?" Yan was deeply surprised— the boy looked much too small. Technically teachers were not allowed to tutor their students privately over the summer, but a lot did to earn extra cash, and parents would do anything to help their children get ahead. Yan was not concerned about private tutoring, but thought there was something odd about the young boy holding a stack of advanced maths magazines and he couldn't help asking.

Zhang was nervous but pleased to see that Chaoyang was quick on the uptake. Their charade would be plainly obvious if he had said he was in middle school while holding the high school version of *Shu Li Tian Di*. Fortunately, Chaoyang had answered calmly and had not attracted undue attention. Zhang's relief was short-lived.

Yan took a copy of the magazine from the boy with a gentle smile. He sized up the child, flipped the pages and found a differential equations problem. Yan pointed at it. "Can you solve this problem?"

Zhang swallowed: a clever high schooler could handle it, but not someone in middle school. Chaoyang was doomed to fail.

But the boy smiled confidently. "This problem has no solution."

Zhang silently cursed the boy. Yan would surely call his bluff.

Yan looked at it, chuckled and returned the magazine to Chaoyang. "You're right. I think it's a printing error, the 22 here should just be 2. Dongsheng, you have some very clever students this year! Finding that mistake in less than a minute, that's impressive."

"Oh," Zhang said tonelessly. He was shocked but hid it well. He had assumed that all three of the imps were idiots—he had never taken time to discover that Chaoyang was far cleverer than the other two. Chaoyang was going to compete in the China Mathematics Competition that autumn and had a good chance of winning. He just wanted Chaoyang to leave.

The boy remembered his manners. "I'm not that clever. It is even more impressive that you discovered the printing error so quickly."

Zhang started to shout at him in his head. Now was *not* the time to gush over a mathematics problem! Still, the exchange had put Yan in a good mood. His eyes twinkled at the compliment—he knew he was a genius but it was still nice to hear other people say it.

Fortunately, Chaoyang left then. Zhang breathed a quick sigh of relief as he closed the door and gathered his strength to deal with his favourite professor.

47

Yan began by giving his condolences, since he was visiting as a relative, not a detective. "Xu Jing was such a lovely young woman. You must be devastated."

Zhang nodded, a pained expression on his face. He removed a cigarette from his pack and lit it, looking vacantly ahead. Yan watched him for a good while, then moved to the living room. "This is the place that you and Xu Jing were going to renovate together, if I recall correctly."

Zhang nodded.

"It's sad. You're going to live alone now," Yan sighed. Zhang's little finger twitched but Yan could not see it from where he was standing. "Would you give me a tour?" Yan asked.

Right then, Zhang was certain that Yan suspected him. Perhaps this ex-cop thought he could discover clues in the new apartment. Well, he could snoop around as much as he liked—he wouldn't find anything! Zhang told Yan he was too tired for a tour, but Yan could show himself around. Zhang sat and smoked, silently congratulating himself on having the boy pretend to be his student, while Yan slowly combed each room. Like Chaoyang before him, Yan noted the everyday clutter was missing. He returned to his host and sat down. "Seems like you've been here for some time. You're living on your own?"

Zhang nodded. "Soon after Xu Jing's parents died, she asked for a divorce again. I agreed but was worried that people would talk if we went through with it immediately after the bereavement. She said she wanted to move out so she didn't have to live with me. But I decided it would be best if I moved out instead, and came here the day after her parents' funeral."

"The relationship did break down then," Yan said. He regretted not providing more help to his niece.

"I had an ulterior motive for moving out."

"Oh?" Yan tilted his head, indicating interest.

"I wanted her to have some space because I thought that would make her less stubborn. Soon after I moved here, I went to Lishui to teach in a mountain village. I sent her photos every day and hoped that she'd change her mind. She replied to me, see?" He had a bittersweet smile on his face as he handed his phone to Yan.

Yan saw that the couple had sent photos and voice messages to each other.

"May I listen to the messages?" he asked politely.

"Of course."

It was clear that Zhang was trying to win Xu Jing back by making her laugh and talking about the funny things that had happened in the village. She did seem genuinely interested and could even be heard laughing at his jokes. She seemed nothing like the distraught woman that Yan had spoken to in private. He noted the frequency of Zhang's texts. It would be relatively straightforward to confirm his location at the time of Jing's death through cell tower analysis. There were group photos of Zhang and the other teachers, who could corroborate his whereabouts. That was enough evidence to establish that Zhang was nowhere near Ningbo in the days leading up to Xu's death. It would take a minimum of six hours to drive from the tiny mountain village to Ningbo, meaning twelve hours round trip, and there were no flights that would get him there and back in a short time frame.

Was it really possible that Xu's death was an accident after all?

"It's a shame you couldn't get back together, but then you couldn't have predicted this accident. But what if her death was not an accident?"

"Wasn't an accident…?" Zhang murmured, shocked.

"The likelihood of a sudden death is extremely low for someone so young. You know that I used to be a cop. Do you think that getting back together with Xu Jing might have caused someone to become jealous? Jealous enough to hurt her?"

"Are you suggesting that Jing's lover did this?"

"Possibly. Do you know who he is?"

"I only know that she met him at work. I don't know his name or what he looks like."

"If an extensive autopsy had been performed, it would have been possible to find out if she really had a physical breakdown. The coroner at the traffic police only does a superficial job, checking the blood alcohol levels and so on. The crime division would be much more thorough: why didn't you wait seven days to cremate the body? It seems odd not to follow custom in this instance," Yan said, looking at Zhang with his penetrating gaze.

Zhang's reaction was nothing like what Yan expected. He set his teeth and gripped the ashtray until his knuckles whitened and then extinguished his cigarette.

"What's wrong?" Yan asked.

"Professor Yan, do you think I was responsible for Xu Jing's death?"

"No, why would I possibly think that?" He met Zhang's gaze.

"I can read the subtext of your question. Besides, other people are probably wondering the same thing. Xu Jing's parents died and then she died. All the property owned by the Xu family suddenly belongs to me. That's convenient, isn't it?"

"Well…" His reaction had put Yan on the back foot.

"It seems suspicious that I was so eager to cremate my wife, when other people were telling me to wait. Doesn't it?"

"Hmm…"

"I don't have to explain myself, but I'll tell you because I don't want any misunderstandings between us. I was eager to cremate my wife because on the day when I rushed back to Ningbo,

I found a box of condoms in our home. And, well… Jing and I… we haven't made love in a long time." His eyes filled with humiliation and grief. "I knew that she probably had sex with that colleague from work, but I never would have dreamed that she would be with him when I was still trying to save our relationship. She brought that man into our home! At that moment, I just wanted to get her cremation over with, so I could be done with the whole thing."

Yan observed Zhang quietly and again said nothing. After a moment he stood. "You should rest, you have been under a great deal of stress. If you need anything at all, you can call me."

Yan left with a nagging feeling that he still did not have a clear picture of the whole scenario; it left him with a compulsion to clean his glasses. He was reminded that Xu Jing had said that if she died it would be Zhang's doing. And yet, logically speaking, he appeared innocent. He had an excellent alibi, his answers were perfectly reasonable, and his emotional responses seemed acceptable.

Then why was his gut telling him that Zhang was guilty?

48

Later that afternoon, Chaoyang sat in Xinhua Bookstore with an air of expectation. "*There* you are!" he said when Pupu arrived.

"We see each other every day, don't we?" she asked.

"I have something to tell you," he said with a serious air.

"Go ahead." Her cheeks turned a delicate shade of pink.

"That man, Mr Zhang? He killed his wife."

"What?" She looked up, her eyes widening. She had been hoping to hear something else, and she certainly wasn't expecting news of another murder.

"He killed her!" Chaoyang had not noticed her brief look of disappointment.

"How did you find out? Has he been arrested? Do we need to leave the apartment? And what about you—"

"He hasn't been arrested. The death looked like an accident, but I kept asking questions until he told me the truth." The boy explained what he saw on the news and what happened at Zhang's apartment.

"You confronted him all by yourself? You could have gotten hurt!" Pupu said.

"As long as we have the camera footage, he won't try to hurt just one of us," he reasoned.

"Still, I think that was dangerous," she said, with a trace of worry in her voice.

"It's OK. Remember how he said he married a wealthy lady? Now that his in-laws and his wife are out of the way, he will probably inherit a lot of money and be able to buy the camera off us."

"Do you think he'll actually pay up? I'm sick of waiting."

"I do. But he said he's going to be busy with the funeral over the next few days so he won't want to talk to us. Will you go with me when the time comes?" Chaoyang asked.

"Of course. You're helping Ding Hao and me, why wouldn't I help you?" she said.

"I actually want to ask him to do something… it's not just for you and Ding Hao."

"What are you going to ask him?"

"I'm not totally sure yet," Chaoyang said evasively, "but it would be great if you help me when I go."

"Of course."

"OK, we'll talk to him together. No matter what I say, you have to support me, OK?"

Pupu thought about it for the briefest of moments and then answered definitively, "Of course. I'll stand by you no matter what." She was quiet, then brought up the difficult topic. "How are things with you and your dad?"

"My dad is dead," Chaoyang said tonelessly.

"Dead? When did this happen?" Pupu looked shocked.

"I mean, he's dead to me," he said, curling his lip. "People came to my house and to my mum's work and splashed us with shit. They also covered the hallways of the apartment building with nasty messages. It was Big Bitch, of course. The police were going to arrest her but they didn't. I couldn't believe the way my dad defended her even when he knew what she did. He doesn't care about me! He only cares about her."

He recounted the events to Pupu.

She squeezed her fists in righteous indignation. "How could she do that! That's horrible! We should drown your stepmother in a giant vat of shit."

"She'll get what's coming to her." Chaoyang smiled coldly.

"So how long did the cops lock her up for?"

"My mum told me they locked her up for a day and made her pay a fine."

"A day? That's so unfair!" Pupu said. "All cops are bad, that's what my dad always said."

"It's not all their fault. They were going to lock her up for longer, but my dad told me not to press charges."

"But she splashed poo all over you! How could he tell you to just forget about it?"

"Just like I said, he only cares about Big Bitch. He said he'd give us ten thousand for damages."

"Well, he should give you money! He should be giving you more—he's so awful to you," she said.

Chaoyang shook his head and laughed bitterly. "I would have dropped charges if he'd just asked. Then he made it about money. The moment he stuffed money in my hands, my dad was dead to me."

"Why? I think if he didn't give you money that would give you more reason to feel like that."

Chaoyang smiled grimly, as if he had suddenly grown up. "You'll understand when you're older."

49

At Professor Yan's behest, Ye Jun had assigned tasks to his officers. They quickly got the results.

"In the two weeks before Xu Jing's death, Zhang Dongsheng never left the village of Lishui. We were able to confirm that with the mobile network operator. The other teachers vouched for him, too," Ye said.

Yan considered this.

"So, Zhang can't be the killer," Ye concluded.

Even though he could think of a few ways of killing someone without being present at the scene, Yan couldn't really contradict Ye as he had no proof. Unfortunately, there wasn't any way to test his own theories because the body had been cremated.

"If Xu Jing's death wasn't an accident, then her lover is a more likely suspect," Ye said, reviewing his notes. "His name is Fu Yifan, he is her boss, and he's married. His relationship with his wife was on the rocks and he started seeing Xu Jing about a year ago. Apparently he has had multiple affairs during his marriage—he's rich, dresses well and is good looking. He admitted that he had been to Xu Jing's house during the two weeks prior to her death. He first claimed it was just to console a bereaved woman following the death of her parents, but he later confirmed that the two had had sex. They used a condom."

Yan nodded. "Zhang said that he found a box of condoms at their house and it made him so angry that he decided to cremate Xu Jing's body immediately. It seems plausible now."

"Furthermore, Fu and Xu Jing had had multiple arguments recently," Ye said. "He admitted that when he was questioned, explaining that he was jealous when he saw that she was sending what he believed to be mixed signals to Zhang. But he was adamant that he would never hurt Xu Jing, and said that the plan was for both of them to divorce by the end of the year so that they could marry next year. Fu said those plans would not have been broken off just because of a few text messages with her estranged husband."

"What's your impression of him?" Yan asked.

"We can't find any evidence pointing to foul play, so there's no change to our initial assessment. Apparently, in her grief, Xu Jing told Fu that if she died unexpectedly, the person responsible would almost certainly be Zhang. But Fu doesn't think Zhang did it because they were together in the days leading up to Xu's death and he never saw Zhang. He also confirmed that she had been drinking more and taking a lot of sedatives recently. Fu is certain that Xu's death was accidental."

Yan absorbed this information and then thanked Ye Jun for the update.

Proving a cause of death such as poisoning would require an in-depth autopsy, which was impossible. Nobody would be able to touch Zhang unless he admitted to his guilt. Yan had little hope that any further investigation would turn anything up. His years of experience told him that not all cases could be cracked—some went cold. More importantly, if Xu Jing really died of natural causes, then Yan's investigation would only harm his relationship with Zhang. Yan sincerely hoped that it was an accident after all and his suspicions were unfounded. He did not want his former student to be involved in such a crime.

50

For the next few days, Chaoyang and Pupu met at the bookstore every afternoon. He did not say a word about his feelings for her and her crush on him, and while she was disappointed, she knew that he had a lot on his mind. She noticed that he was talking less and that on occasion he even forgot to turn the pages of the International Mathematical Olympiad text he was reading.

But about a week later, Chaoyang looked different. His forehead was smooth, he was reading and talking again, and he seemed to be happy. Before they went their separate ways, Chaoyang told Pupu what he wanted to do. "I think Mr Zhang has probably done everything he needs to for the funeral, so we should visit him. Meet me at the entrance to the bookstore at 8 a.m. tomorrow, and we'll go to his place together. No matter what kind of request I make of him you have to back me up, OK?"

She gave him a strange look and asked what it was all about, but he told her to wait. Pupu agreed that she would support him.

The next morning the two kids headed to the Prosperity Bay Luxury Apartments. It was still nearly empty so they only saw a few people. But a damaged red BMW was there, so Chaoyang knew they would find Zhang.

He strode confidently to the number pad and buzzed Zhang's apartment. When they got to his door, the man was still in his pyjamas. His gaze rested on the boy's face for a few seconds. Then he looked at Pupu and smiled. "Come in. Pupu, can I get you a soda? And juice for you, Chaoyang?"

Chaoyang nodded. "Thank you, Uncle."

Zhang handed them their drinks and sat across from them. He reached for his cigarettes. "Mind if I smoke?"

"It's your home, you can do what you like," Chaoyang said.

Zhang chuckled softly and lit the cigarette. "You're here for the money I suppose. I'm basically drowning in paperwork, the inheritance—"

"Uncle, I'm not here to talk about money," Chaoyang interrupted.

Pupu gave him a look, but he ignored her.

"Last time I was here, you told me you used poison to kill your wife. Are you willing to share the details?"

Zhang gave a regretful smile. "You were very insistent. I had to invent something to get you to be quiet before my friend arrived. I'm afraid that my wife really did die of natural causes."

Chaoyang shook his head calmly, looking very mature. "There's no point in deceiving us, we know the truth. Otherwise, you wouldn't have been so panicked when your friend arrived. Maybe he knows some bad things about you?"

Zhang narrowed his eyes. "It was an accident."

"Uncle, don't be like this. You told me last time you would tell me exactly how she was poisoned, and now you're breaking that promise. If you can't keep that promise, maybe you won't buy the camera either. We've been waiting a long time."

Zhang frowned as he attempted to suss out Chaoyang. The boy had changed completely—he was acting and speaking differently. The change gave Zhang a chill. He was used to aggression from Pupu, which was irritating, but he had worked out that it was likely just a defence mechanism to hide her vulnerability. In contrast, Chaoyang seemed to have developed a new malicious streak.

"My wife's death doesn't concern you. I promise I'll give you the money as soon as I can. Listen, you might think that I'm a vicious person for what I've done, but I had no choice. Perhaps you don't understand what it feels like to be a poor wretch

195

marrying into a wealthy family. Let me paint a picture for you. If my parents came to visit me and Xu Jing, she would not let them stay in the house. My parents loved me and took care of me: how could I tell them that they weren't allowed to stay at my new apartment? It was heartbreaking."

Zhang looked at Pupu.

"She didn't let your parents stay at the house?" she asked.

"She complained that my parents did not wash enough. She was clearly prejudiced against country folk."

"I grew up in the countryside, I know people can be mean," Pupu said sympathetically. "But that's not an excuse to *kill* your in-laws."

Zhang gave a hollow laugh. "My wife was sleeping with someone and she wanted a divorce. But if we split up I wouldn't be able to make ends meet. You know I don't have kids. My wife was adamant that she did not want kids. She started seeing another man and then she said she wanted kids with her lover. Now do you understand what she put me through?"

His lie seemed to have struck a chord. "Your wife deserved what she got!" Pupu shouted venomously.

Zhang had only been hoping for some sympathy so they stopped being so careful around him. He was delighted that a bit of embellishment was all it took for the little girl to see his wife as the enemy. After a brief hesitation, he continued, "I don't have kids but seeing you is like seeing my own kids or my students. You haven't told me anything about your situation but I can tell that you are going through a difficult time. I don't want you to suffer like this. You should be studying at school so that you can have a better future. There's nothing to be done about my problems, but you still have your lives to live. I hope that I can support you until you graduate from university. I want you to seize every opportunity that comes your way."

Zhang watched them to see how they would react. Pupu looked sad. Chaoyang seemed to be thinking things over. They were children after all, so he was sure he could win their trust. Just as he was about to congratulate himself, Chaoyang spoke. "Uncle, I didn't come here for a lecture. I need to know how you poisoned your wife," he repeated.

"That's none of your business."

"I have to know. I'm not leaving until I do."

"Even if I told you, what's the point? Do you really think I would use it on you? I'm not going to kill three children to save three hundred thousand."

"It's not about our deal. I have to know," Chaoyang insisted.

"What, do you want to kill someone?" Zhang said, with a contemptuous snort.

"Yes, I do!"

Pupu stared at Chaoyang in disbelief. Zhang's eyebrows crinkled. The boy did not appear to be joking.

"I can imagine that you probably have troubles that seem insurmountable. Remember, at your age lots of kids are bullied at school or have disagreements. When you get older you'll realize that it wasn't so bad as it seemed," Zhang said.

"That's none of your business! Just tell me how you did it!" The boy's tone was menacing.

Zhang sat very still, his cigarette still dangling from his hand. He waited, then looked over to Pupu, who was currently winning the competition for the least irritating brat. "What... happened?"

She turned to Chaoyang and worded her question carefully. "What are you thinking of doing?"

"You said you would back me up, remember?"

"Uh..." Pupu hesitated, but eventually nodded. "Yeah. Umm, please tell us how you did it."

Zhang extinguished his cigarette, stood, paced the living room and sat down again. "Chaoyang, what happened? What do you intend to do?" he asked with concern.

Chaoyang took a breath. "I want to kill two adults. I want to poison them. And I want you to tell me how to do it."

"You want to kill Big Bitch? Who's the other person?" Pupu gasped.

He ignored her and kept looking directly at Zhang.

"That's…" The man now looked seriously concerned. "Who are these people?"

"None of your business. I won't report you as long as you help me. I promise."

Zhang shook his head. "You're young, you're having a flight of fancy. Poison is not as straightforward as you think—one slip-up and the police will catch you. You'd have to get close to them and put it in their food."

"But you weren't there when your wife took the poison. How did you poison her? How come the police never found out?"

"It's complicated, and I got lucky. Otherwise the police would be interrogating me right now," he gloated, unable to help himself.

"Anyway, we already know you killed her so it's not a big deal telling us how you did it," Chaoyang said. He turned to Pupu. "Pupu, you said you were going to help me."

She gritted her teeth. "Uncle, you have to tell him. Otherwise, you know what we'll do."

Zhang looked coldly at the little terrors. Pupu was pleading with him and Chaoyang still looked menacing. If Ding Hao were here, his best option would be to tie up all three of them, find out where the camera was and then kill them. But as always, they had someone waiting for them to come back. It was frustrating that three children had so much control over his fate, especially when the police did not suspect a thing!

He sighed and decided there wasn't any point in hiding the method of killing Xu Jing, given how much the brats already knew. "My wife takes—took collagen supplements for her skin. She took a pill every morning, so I slipped a poison pill in the bottle. Two weeks after I went to Lishui, she took that pill. Since I was not anywhere near Ningbo when she died, the police eliminated me as a suspect."

"What kind of poison was it?"

"Potassium cyanide. I expect you haven't heard of it," Zhang said.

Zhang was right—Chaoyang had never heard of it. "How'd you get it?"

"I synthesized it myself."

"But aren't you a maths teacher?"

"I'm pretty good at physics and chemistry too."

"How long until it takes effect?" The boy pressed.

Zhang sighed, exasperated. "A few minutes."

"That's not possible," Chaoyang said.

"It's true! What would be the point of lying to you now?"

"If your wife took the pill when she was at home, how could she die while she was driving?"

"Well…" Zhang gave up trying to hide details. "The poison was in a small pill hidden inside a larger one. The outer layer dissolved first and the centre took a little bit longer. That's why she was already in her car on her way to work."

Chaoyang nodded. "You were on a trip and your wife was alone in her car when she died. No wonder they didn't investigate you. But what if she didn't take the pill in the morning?"

"She usually did, but even if she died at home in the evening, I would not have been a prime suspect because I was far away. As long as I came home and cremated her body straight away, nobody would be the wiser. It was lucky that she died in the car because the traffic police aren't as thorough. Luck is important. If the person dies soon after eating something, the police will suspect a poisoning. They'll investigate every person who had a connection to the food. That's why you shouldn't attempt it."

Chaoyang frowned as he thought it over. It really was difficult to kill someone without getting caught. He didn't even have the opportunity to get close to his targets—how would he poison them?

"Does the poison have to be swallowed?" Chaoyang asked.

"Yes."

"What if they inhale it?"

"It would take a closed room filled with poisonous gas. Where would you get all that poison?"

"What about an injection?"

"Well…" Zhang frowned too. "Theoretically, yes. But would you want to do that?"

"Would an injection work faster than eating poisoned food?"

"How did you know that?" He stared at the boy.

"We studied the circulatory system at school," Chaoyang said.

"What do you intend to do?" Zhang asked.

"Just give me the poison, I'll take care of this myself."

Zhang knew he couldn't agree to this—mainly because he was certain they would get caught. "I got rid of the poison. I wouldn't leave it lying around the house, now would I?"

"Then make some more."

"I don't have the raw materials," Zhang said.

Chaoyang shook his head. "No way, you can make it again. I don't care what you have to do. You have to help me make the poison. Otherwise you have to kill them for me."

"Kill them for you? Are you insane?" Zhang yelped. "And who could have inspired so much malice in a kid?"

"My dad and his stupid wife!"

Pupu had been uneasy for quite some time. Her expression changed as soon as she heard what Chaoyang said. "You want to kill your dad?" she whispered.

Zhang was equally shocked.

51

When Zhang had recovered, he looked at the boy with a mixture of compassion and horror. "So your father cheated on your mother. I understand your animosity towards him. But that's his business, you don't have to concern yourself with it. You'll feel differently when you're older. Listen, one impulsive act like this will ruin your entire life."

Pupu also tried to talk him down. "I know your dad can be awful sometimes, but he's still your dad. You have to forgive him."

"You promised me that you would support me no matter what!" he snarled, turning on her.

Pupu's eyebrows furrowed. "Yeah, but, Brother Chaoyang, if you do this you'll regret it."

"I won't regret it! I know I won't regret it!" he shouted.

Zhang was certain that something in the child had snapped.

"Your mother would not want you to do this, right, Chaoyang?" Pupu said.

"I'll never tell her."

"But what if you're arrested?"

Chaoyang looked at Zhang. "Uncle is a pro, he can help me. There won't be any evidence."

The man shook his head, trying to sound both firm and caring. "I'm not going to help you. I don't care if you take the camera to the police. This is for your own good; the guilt would punish you for the rest of your life. I promise I will never tell anyone what you told me today. You need to forget that you ever had this impulse, otherwise you'll develop psychological problems. Do you understand?"

Chaoyang glanced at him, then at Pupu. Both of them had tried to talk him out of it. He stood up with a disgusted snort and marched to the door.

"Chaoyang, don't leave," Zhang said.

The child took no heed of him as he ran down the stairs. Pupu hurried to follow him.

"You need to calm him down. Don't let him do anything stupid!" Zhang called after her.

"I know, I know!" she shouted as she raced down.

"Hurry!" Zhang said, seriously worried that the boy would do something rash, like give the camera to the police. That wouldn't benefit Chaoyang or his friends, but Zhang worried that the boy could not act rationally now. When he got to the window, he saw that Pupu had caught up with Chaoyang. They stood talking for a long time. Finally, the boy seemed to relax, and Zhang allowed himself to breathe again.

It looked like he would have to dispatch the three terrors. He wasn't going to let his careful plans be ruined by the recklessness of some kids. The tricky part was finding the opportunity. Killing them would be much more difficult than killing his own wife.

52

Chaoyang had hurled himself down the stairs and run until his breath was ragged. The heat was stifling, and he thought he was going to explode. He slapped a tree trunk several times to release some of his anger, then slowly leaned his forehead against it.

"I'm sorry," a small voice said. He turned to see Pupu bowing her head apologetically.

His tone was severe. "Why won't you help me?"

She looked up at him and then away again. "Killing your dad is not the answer to your problems."

"But you promised! You said you would be there for me!"

"That's because I never expected you to say you wanted to kill your dad! If you want to get revenge on Big Bitch, I'm with you all the way. But your dad is your *dad*."

"He's not my dad any more," Chaoyang huffed.

This time Pupu looked directly into his eyes. "No matter what happens, he will always be your dad. If you do this, you'll never be able to forgive yourself!"

"No way. I would be happy to see him die."

"That's because you've never lost your dad!" she screamed.

Chaoyang was taken aback. He saw that her eyes were red but she was not crying. He had a brief impulse to wrap his arm around her shoulder.

Pupu took a breath and resumed her typical flat tone. "How do you think Ding Hao is doing?"

"What do you mean?"

"Isn't he a happy-go-lucky guy most of the time?"

"Yeah."

"Well, he has been messed up ever since he lost his dad. He has nightmares where he screams himself awake and then curls into a little ball. You have no idea…"

Chaoyang's expression changed. Pupu studied him carefully and then sighed.

"You have it so much better than we do. Why would you want to join the kids-without-dads club?"

"I…" Chaoyang felt like he couldn't speak.

"You never meant to kill Little Bitch, that was an accident. But if you go ahead and decide to kill your dad, everything will be different. If you're arrested, your mum will be all alone."

"But Big Bitch harassed me and my mum. And after the police came, my dad protected *her*!"

"I know your father is selfish, but he's still your dad."

Chaoyang scoffed.

"The way I see it, that attack on you and your mum is kind of like a punishment for what you did to Little Bitch. You weren't arrested, but you were attacked by Big Bitch. They took her to the police station and she learned her lesson. I don't care what your dad does. As long as you and your mum are able to live how you want to live, there's no reason to hurt people like that. You're smart enough to go to university and get a good job. You're gonna make more money than your dad. And when he's old and sees how awesome you are, he's going to be sorry for not being a better dad. Isn't that enough?"

Chaoyang bent his head and thought for a moment. "Thanks," he finally said. He gave her a smile.

"So you're not going to do it?"

"I'll think about it." He smiled bitterly. "Hey, Pupu, aren't you hot standing in the sun? You should come over here in the shade with me."

"Not when you look like you're about to swallow me whole," she said, making a face.

"You're not afraid of anyone, how could you be afraid of me?"

It almost sounded like he was giving her a compliment. She looked at him, not knowing what to say.

"Never mind. Let's go home."

53

"What? Chaoyang asked Uncle Zhang to kill his dad and Big Bitch?" Ding Hao knew it was time to be serious. He quit the game he was playing to hear Pupu explain what had happened.

"Yeah, I guess the stuff with Big Bitch pushed him over the edge," she said.

"But he doesn't really want to kill his dad, does he?"

"I don't think so."

"Did you talk some sense into him?"

"For now, anyway. But from what I can tell, he's still not thinking straight."

"Oh…" Ding Hao frowned. "Let's go talk to him this afternoon."

"Now you have time for your friends!" Pupu said mockingly.

"Of course I do. My friend is in trouble," he said earnestly.

"Listen, I think you need to be a little more cautious around Zhang—he is a murderer, after all. Don't call him 'Uncle' all the time—you'll forget that he's the enemy," she warned.

"I don't think he's all that bad. He gave me a computer and gave you some books. He wants what is best for us," Ding Hao argued.

"He's buying your love, idiot."

"Why would he do that? He hasn't bargained down the price of the camera, has he?"

"Just be careful. Chaoyang says he's dangerous, but also that he hides it well."

"You guys don't have to be so paranoid."

Pupu pursed her lips in exasperation. They were getting ready to go out and get something to eat when there was a knock on the door. Pupu checked the peephole—it was Zhang.

She took her time opening the door. He was carrying a bargain bucket from KFC and a bottle of Coca-Cola and put them both on the table.

"You haven't had lunch yet, have you? I bought you some chicken and some soda. You need to stay hydrated in this heat."

Ding Hao's face lit up. "All right! Thank you, Uncle!"

Zhang smiled and checked Pupu's reaction. She gave nothing away. She hovered by the table, in the same place she always stood when he came to see them. It had been so easy to win over Ding Hao: all it took was the old computer. Still, every time Zhang tried to learn more about his background, the boy would play dumb. Nothing worked on the girl. She would utter a word of thanks but was mute otherwise. He could not find a way to make her lower her guard.

Zhang had hoped that letting the two kids live in this apartment would improve their relationship with him. He even considered installing a recording device so he could learn more about them. But when he discovered the piece of string in the closet door, he gave up on that. He hated to admit that they were more sophisticated than he had given them credit for.

"Pupu, eat something. Don't be shy," Zhang said, as Ding Hao gorged himself.

"Yeah, have some, Pupu. There's some nice bread rolls," Ding Hao said.

"Did you come to talk about Chaoyang?" Pupu asked. She saw right through him.

"Yes," Zhang said. "What happened to Chaoyang to make him so vengeful?"

"Nothing happened."

"But he wants to kill his father. He was relentless!"

"Spur of the moment thing. He's fine now."

Zhang saw that this approach wasn't going to get him anywhere and stopped his questioning. "OK. Well, let's keep talking to him. If he won't give up that senseless idea, come find me.

I'm a teacher after all, I deal with young people's problems all the time."

"OK."

Seeing that Pupu had clammed up, Zhang smiled pleasantly, put a few hundred yuan on the table and left, seething inwardly.

54

Pupu and Ding Hao met Chaoyang at the bookstore that afternoon.

Once again, Ding Hao wrestled playfully with him. He then took Chaoyang aside to have a heart-to-heart. "Hey, Pupu told me everything. Your idea is a little over the top, don't you think? No matter what happens, you have a home and a caring mother. You don't want to change that."

Pupu appeared next to them. "Your parents might be divorced, but at least they're alive. Not having a dad is the worst feeling in the world."

"Pupu's right," Ding Hao agreed. "You had one terrible day when Big Bitch had you splashed with poo, but it's kind of like payback for pushing Little Bitch. She won't try anything else, 'cause the police would totally lock her up. And if your dad wants to protect her, who cares? Eventually he'll stick up for you too. You're his only kid now. He'll definitely stay in contact with you and give you money again."

"He hasn't called me in forever," Chaoyang pouted.

"That's because he's too embarrassed. A lot of things have happened and he doesn't know what to say. Just give him time," Pupu said.

"Oh, yeah, and don't tell anyone that you were thinking about that stuff. If your dad finds out, then that'll be it—he will never call again," Ding Hao added.

Chaoyang sighed.

"You said I didn't support you, but I've always been on your side," Pupu said.

He looked at her for a few seconds, then at Ding Hao. He was filled with warmth. He might not have any friends at school, but at least he had Pupu and Ding Hao. "Thanks," he said softly.

"Hey, that's what friends are for! Right, mate?"

"Right," Chaoyang said.

The three smiled.

55

They stayed at the bookstore until around 4, and then had something to eat and went home. Chaoyang's mother had taken several days off work right after the attack, but now she was back at Sanmingshan, working longer hours to make up for her absence. Chaoyang would be home alone that night. Again. He felt a pang of sadness for no particular reason. He wished his friends could be with him every hour of every day.

His only companion was the maths exercises from the International Mathematical Olympiad. He picked up the book and reread the motivational sentence he had written on the cover: *Work hard and you will achieve your dreams*. He smiled and entered the world of problem sets.

The telephone rang. "Chaoyang, is your mother home?" a familiar voice said.

Chaoyang was thrilled to hear his father's voice but didn't let it show. "No, she's at work."

"I'm waiting for you outside. I have something to tell you."

"OK." He didn't know what his dad could want, but tried not to get too hopeful.

Zhu Yongping was standing on the opposite side of the street from his big Mercedes. He waved at Chaoyang. Chaoyang walked over towards him, but stopped ten feet away. Seeing the boy's expressionless face, Zhu frowned. He stepped forward to put his arm around his son's shoulder, but stopped halfway. A cloud of awkwardness enveloped them.

"How have you been?" Zhu asked.

"Pretty good."

"The thing Wang Yao did the other day… that was dreadful, wasn't it?"

Chaoyang didn't answer.

"She's grieving. She hasn't been the same since Jingjing died. She won't do it again."

Chaoyang still didn't answer.

"It's my fault, I didn't take care of you the way I should have. I love you very much, but it's difficult to be in two families at the same time. Maybe you'll understand when you're older. Wang Yao went off the deep end and we all told her that what she did was wrong. If you have any problems, don't contact me—call Grandma and she'll tell me."

"OK."

"Uncle Fang's daughter Lina will be having extra classes at school. Does that mean that you'll be going to them too?"

Chaoyang made a face. "Yeah, from next Monday. The teachers are worried that we'll forget everything we learned over the holidays."

"You'll be starting your third year of middle school this year, you need to work hard," Zhu said absentmindedly. He looked at his car, and then closed the gap between them, putting his arm on Chaoyang's shoulder. He thrust a stack of bills at him. "This is five thousand for your school fees. If you or your mother need money, just tell Grandma and I'll take care of it."

Chaoyang nodded, letting Zhu's words wash over him. Ding Hao and Pupu were right—his dad really did care about him. His desire to hurt his father evaporated and he was ashamed for even having had the thought.

"Grandpa's not doing very well. We went to the fortune teller to consult on his health, and the fortune teller said he wouldn't be with us next year. You should go see him."

Chaoyang nodded obediently. "I will. I'll see him in a few days."

Zhu's phone rang, and he walked a few steps away before taking the call. He hung up quickly. He tapped his phone a few times and smiled sheepishly at Chaoyang. "It was just a marketing call." Zhu looked like he was trying to gauge his son's feelings. "Son, I want to ask you something. Please forgive me if this sounds insensitive."

"Yeah?"

He struggled for the right words. "When you went to the Children's Palace, were you following Jingjing?"

"No! Dad, how could you even ask that!" Chaoyang exclaimed.

"It's not like that," Zhu Yongping hurried to say. "If you tell me you didn't do it, then you didn't do it. I thought if you followed her, maybe you would have some clues for us. Maybe you would know who her killer is."

"I honestly don't know."

"Umm…" Zhu hesitated again. "When… when your step-mother came to your building, she said that the moment you saw her, you started running away from her. She said you looked guilty."

"I didn't run away from her and I didn't have a guilty look on my face! I go to the Children's Palace all the time, you can ask my friends. Anyway, the police investigated me, and they said I was innocent!" Chaoyang was adamant.

"Don't take it personally. Jingjing was my daughter after all. I just want to find out who did that to her. You do understand?"

Chaoyang nodded again, his face impassive now.

Zhu took a last look at his son and patted his shoulder. "OK, I should go."

Immediately the rear passenger door to the Mercedes opened and Wang Yao jumped out. "Did he confess?" she demanded.

"We'll discuss this later!" Zhu hissed.

"Did he confess or not?"

"Later!"

213

Wang Yao snatched the phone out of his hand and started to play the recording that Zhu had just made: "'Son, I want to ask you something. Please forgive me if this sounds insensitive—'"

Zhu Yongping wrested the phone from her, throwing it forcefully onto the street. It smashed against the kerb.

"What are you, crazy?" she screeched, bending down to retrieve the phone.

Zhu stopped her. "This has nothing to do with Chaoyang. I've made sure. You need to drop this and move on!"

The young boy watched the scene play out in front of him in shocked disbelief.

"Did that bastard confess or not?" Wang Yao screamed. "He didn't admit it, did he? Damn you! You think I didn't notice the money you gave him?" She then glared at Chaoyang. "You like money, don't you? If you admit to what you did, we'll give you all the money you want!"

Even though Zhu prevented her from reaching Chaoyang, she unzipped her purse and pulled out stacks of cash. She started throwing money towards him, aiming for his face. "It's all yours! Now admit it! Either you did it or you know who did! I'll have someone follow your every movement! I'm going to haunt you, you bastard! I'm going to kill you!" Her hysterical shouts started to draw the attention of the neighbours. One stack hit Chaoyang in the face. It hurt, but he remained calm, watching her.

Suddenly, Zhu spun Wang Yao around and slapped her in the face. "How long are you going to go on like this! Enough! I know your daughter is dead, but that's no excuse for this behaviour! We need to go home!"

As he bundled her into the car, Wang Yao continued to whimper. "You bastard, this isn't over yet… I'm going to end you!"

The car drove off and Zhu did not look back. The neighbours busied themselves picking up the bills on the street.

"Don't touch it, it's mine!" Chaoyang bellowed.

He scooped up the money and ran up the stairs. As the day ended, Chaoyang looked out the window at the hazy sky and decided that this really was the worst summer of his life.

56

"I finished it," Chaoyang said to Pupu after turning the last page of *Krabat*.

"What d'ya think?" she asked expectantly.

"It was good. A real page turner."

"It would be nice if there was a place like the Black Mill in real life," Pupu said dreamily.

"What? Every year one of the apprentices from the Black Mill gets killed!"

"Yeah, but they might die if they weren't at the mill. At least they can take things easy on every day except New Year's Eve." Pupu made a face. "But, it's a German fairy tale," she said, seeming to imply that a mill like that could never exist in China.

"That's life, lots of problems and annoying things," Chaoyang sighed.

The two smiled at each other, but his quickly turned into a frown.

"What's wrong?" Pupu asked.

"I think I have a big problem," Chaoyang said in a low voice.

"What's happened now?"

"My dad thinks I killed Little Bitch."

"What?"

"He came to see me yesterday. He apologized for that stuff that Big Bitch did. Then he took a phone call, hung up and said it was a marketing call. Then he asked me if I had been following Jingjing at the Children's Palace."

"What did you say?"

"I said I hadn't, of course!"

"Did he believe you?"

"I'm not sure he did, because he asked me about the day when Big Bitch came to my house. He wanted to know why I looked like I was running away from her."

"What did you tell him?" Pupu asked nervously.

"I said I wasn't running away and Jingjing's death had nothing to do with me. I told him the police were sure that I wasn't involved."

"Then he believed you, right?"

"I dunno, I think he still suspects me. He was going back to his car when Big Bitch came out of it and grabbed his phone from him."

"Why did she do that?" Pupu asked, confused.

His face clouded over. "It looked like she and my dad had a plan. She got him to record the conversation."

Pupu worked it out. "Your dad wanted you to squeal and he recorded you on his phone?"

"Yeah. I don't think he ever got a marketing call—it must have been Big Bitch reminding him to start the recording. If I had said anything incriminating, they would take the evidence straight to the police so they could arrest me."

"Your dad wants you to get arrested?" She was incredulous.

"And that's not the worst part! Big Bitch said either I did it or I know who did. She threatened to have someone follow me and she said she was going to kill me."

"She's vicious!"

"The police took my fingerprints and a blood sample, and they have definitely eliminated me as a suspect. But the evidence would still link Ding Hao to the crime."

Pupu nodded.

"The police don't know about you and Ding Hao; right now nobody knows we are friends. But if Big Bitch finds out, we are screwed. She could easily pay someone to follow me around."

Pupu's face drained of its colour. She didn't look at him and spoke in a low voice. "Do you want us to leave and not contact you again? That... would be the only way to be sure that other people don't find out that we know each other."

"That's not what I mean," he said quickly. "You're my best friends, and no matter what happens we'll always be friends. I can't lose you! You have to stay, I don't want to have to live without you."

Pupu nodded again but looked conflicted. "I want to keep things the way they are, but if one day Big Bitch does find out about me and Ding Hao... you'd be..."

"That's why we need to take action."

"What do think we should do?"

Chaoyang flashed a smile, his voice flippant. "We make my dad and Big Bitch disappear."

"You don't really mean that, do you?" Pupu looked at him— she seemed now to be talking to a total stranger. Last time he brought up killing his father he had worked himself into a rage. This time he was different.

"What do you think?" He spoke calmly, but that only frightened her more.

"That's not OK, Chaoyang, no matter what your dad does, you can't *kill* him. You can hate him and blame him for everything he's done to you, but you can't do that!"

"I know you're worried that I will regret this. But you don't understand." Chaoyang seemed serene and sure of himself.

"Yes I do," Pupu said stubbornly.

Chaoyang switched the topic suddenly. "Oh, yeah, I wanted to ask you something. I have known you for a pretty long time now but I still don't know your real name."

Pupu was a little thrown by the shift and gave him a confused look. "My name is Xia Yuepu."

"What are the characters?"

"Xia as in summer, Yue as in moon and Pu as in ordinary."

"Xia Yuepu. It's a pretty name, who picked it for you?"

She beamed. "My dad. His last name is Xia and anyway

I was born in summer. I was born at ten at night and the moon was bathing everything in a gentle light. So he named me Xia Yuepu."

"From now on, I'm calling you Yuepu, not Pupu."

"Why?"

"Pupu is not your name. It's a dumb nickname from the orphanage. You don't live there any more, and you should dump the nickname too. I'll make Ding Hao call you by your proper name."

Her eyes glittered as she smiled. "So he told you the story about my nickname, huh?"

"Yeah, but that doesn't matter now. You're in a new city and you're starting a new life. You can make a clean break with that nickname. Got it?"

She blinked and looked away. When she turned back, she smiled again. "OK, my name is Xia Yuepu. Not Pupu."

"The anniversary of your father's death is coming up, right, Yuepu?"

"Right."

"What day?"

"The last day of August."

"I have to do summer classes starting on the 12th and they last for two weeks, so I might not be able to be with you. But we shouldn't take the camera to a print shop to print any of the Sanmingshan pictures. That might be risky. Maybe we should just go to a photography studio now and take new pictures."

She smiled. "OK."

57

In the evening Zhou Chunhong returned from work looking livid. She reined in her anger when she saw her son. "Did Zhu Yongping come to see you yesterday?"

"Yeah."

"What did he want? Was that evil woman here as well?"

"So the neighbours told you?" he concluded.

Zhou nodded. Chaoyang recounted the full story. Hearing the details made her even angrier. "He's such a bastard, how could he record your conversation like that? The police said you weren't involved, but he comes here looking for a confession anyway!"

Chaoyang poured a glass of water for her and helped her sit down. "Mum, don't be angry, it's not a big deal."

Zhou looked at him and realized how much he had matured recently. But there was something odd that made her vaguely uncomfortable.

But then the strangeness disappeared. "Mum, I'll focus on my studies, I don't want to disappoint you. You don't need to be worried or angry on my behalf."

She fought back the urge to cry. "You're right, don't dwell on it, you'll be OK."

"I won't." Chaoyang skipped to his room and returned with a thick stack of money. "Dad gave me five thousand yesterday and then that bitch threw three thousand six hundred yuan at me. I picked it up off the ground. You should take it."

Zhou looked sadly at her son. "You deserve Zhu's money, but you shouldn't have picked up the money that that evil woman threw at you. You should have left it on the ground!"

"If I didn't pick it up, someone else would have."

"It would be better to just burn it!"

"Why?"

"Because she was using the money to insult you. Picking it up shows that you're lower than she is."

"Mum, that doesn't make any sense: money is just money." His lips curled into a smile. "You know, if they gave me the entire seafood business, I would take it. It's my inheritance!"

"Your father might plan to have another baby with that woman, to replace their daughter. If they have a boy, then you wouldn't have a chance at the inheritance," Zhou sighed.

"In four years I'll go to university and a few years after that I'll be making money, so you don't have to worry about it. I won't try to contact him any more, and I won't contact Grandma and Grandpa."

"But, honey, your grandparents are good to you. You should visit your grandpa before your summer classes start. I heard he was in hospital just last week. Go see him. We don't want people thinking that you're an ungrateful grandson."

Chaoyang nodded.

58

The following afternoon Pupu met Chaoyang at the bookstore. "Ding Hao is here, he wants to talk to you," she said in a low voice.

"Where is he?" Chaoyang asked as he looked around.

"You were the one who said we should take precautions. He's behind that stack of books over there."

"Did you tell him that the police probably have DNA evidence linking him to Little Bitch's death?"

"I told him yesterday," Pupu answered.

"Is he afraid?"

"A little."

"I think that was a good idea. He needs to understand how serious the consequences are if he is discovered. Let's go talk to him," Chaoyang said.

The two of them looked around before walking nonchalantly to the last stack of books, where Ding Hao was reading a comic book. When they arrived he closed it and put on his solemn face. "Chaoyang, I need to tell you something."

"OK."

"Pupu told me that you're still thinking of doing… that thing."

Chaoyang shook his head. "I'm not *thinking* about it any more. I decided I'm *gonna do* it."

"If you do, there will be major consequences!"

"There won't be any consequences as long as I'm under fourteen."

"That's not what I mean," Ding Hao said. He tried to find the right words. "If you kill your dad… that will weigh on you for… forever."

"No, it won't," Chaoyang said calmly.

"Yes it will!" Ding Hao looked to Pupu for help. "Pupu, it will, won't it?"

"Ding Hao, don't call her Pupu any more," Chaoyang interrupted.

"What am I supposed to call her then?" Ding Hao said, surprised.

"Call her Xia Yuepu."

"I know Yuepu is her name, but that's not that different from Pupu. I've been calling her Pupu for years!"

"Pupu was the name that the bullies at the orphanage gave her. You guys aren't there any more, and you aren't going back. So don't call her Pupu!"

"Ding Hao, call me Yuepu, OK?"

Ding Hao acquiesced, "Fine. But I'm gonna forget sometimes, just so you know."

"I'll remind you," Chaoyang said.

"Looks like your relationship is warming up!" Ding Hao said with a smirk.

Pupu glared at him and attempted to hide her embarrassment. "You idiot, you're forgetting why you came here. Don't change the subject."

"Chaoyang was the one who changed the subject! Why are you putting that on me?"

"I…" she began. "Anyway, don't be stupid."

"Yeah, I'm the stupidest one here, and Chaoyang is perfect," Ding Hao said acidly.

"Let's not get carried away," Chaoyang said. "You want me to change my mind, don't you?"

"Listen, you can't stay on this path. Planning to kill your own dad is not the same as accidentally killing your half-sister," Ding Hao said.

"I'm not just doing this for me," Chaoyang argued. "Yuepu, you remember in *Krabat* how Krabat kills his master in the end? His master is good to him and offers to retire so that Krabat can inherit the mill. He says he'll give Krabat everything."

"Yeah, but if he doesn't kill the master, the master will kill the other apprentices and the girl from the village."

"He kills the master for his friends and the girl that he likes. He doesn't have a choice."

Ding Hao had not read the book and was totally confused. "Chaoyang, are you changing the subject again? This is important."

"I know it is. Big Bitch and my dad suspect me so much that you are in danger now. If Big Bitch hires a private investigator, they might find out about you and Yuepu. She doesn't want to go back to the orphanage, and neither do you, right? You know what will happen if you go back there."

Pupu's face twitched involuntarily. But she continued to look at her friend with concern, still unable to comprehend how his personality had shifted so drastically.

Ding Hao looked vexed too. "But… but if you kill your dad… you'll…"

"I won't get into big trouble. And I won't regret my decision! I don't have a dad any more, I only have my mother and you two. You're my best friends. You're… my only friends."

The other two were shocked into silence. Nothing they said seemed to sway him!

"Plus," he added, "according to the inheritance law, if they both die, then half of the inheritance goes to Big Bitch's family, and half of it goes to my grandpa, my grandma and me. I'm the only grandchild, so basically the money goes to me. Once I have money, I can help you find a better place to live. You won't have to worry any more and it won't matter if we get the money for handing over the camera or not. Once I graduate from university, I'll start a business and I'll make you assistant manager."

Ding Hao smirked. "Let me guess, Pupu—I mean, Yuepu—will be the boss's wife?"

She pushed him forcefully and he immediately stopped his joking.

Chaoyang smiled but didn't respond. "So, are you in?"

"I don't know if we can pull it off." Ding Hao looked at Pupu. "What do you think?"

Her face was expressionless. "As I said before, if Big Bitch finds out about us, Chaoyang's screwed and we're screwed. I don't want that to happen."

Ding Hao wrestled with the decision. "I think we should take out Big Bitch, but your dad is still your dad."

"If Big Bitch has an accident, there's a one hundred per cent chance that my dad will suspect me. They both have to go, and they have to go at the same time."

"If they go at the same time, won't the police suspect you?"

Chaoyang shook his head. "Not if I'm at school all day. They won't think it's me, and they'll think I'm too young to try and hire someone else to do it."

"But if you're at school, who's gonna do the dirty work?"

"The murderer! None of us can do it, but he's already killed three people without getting caught. He'll think of something clever and nobody will catch him."

"But what if he says no?" Ding Hao asked.

"He has to say yes," Chaoyang said coldly.

"But what if he says he can't do it?"

"I've thought of an answer for every possible excuse he could give. It's Little Bitch's birthday on Wednesday. I went to my grandma's this morning and she told me that Big Bitch and Dad are going to visit Jingjing's grave. They'll definitely visit in the morning, because by midday it's too hot outside. Nobody will be around, so he can get them at the cemetery. I'll be in summer school that day, so I won't get in trouble."

"That's…" Ding Hao stopped midsentence. He was afraid of the remorseless look on Chaoyang's face.

"We only have to do this one thing. We have to convince Zhang to help us. He won't want to do it at first, but you have to help me persuade him."

59

Over the next few days, Chaoyang and Pupu met in the bookstore. They talked and laughed frequently, and their lives were peaceful. Yet every once in a while, their continuing anxieties would surface. Pupu kept asking when they would go talk to the murderer, but Chaoyang said that waiting until the last minute would be best. That gave him less time to back out—he would be cornered. Chaoyang was taking a page out of *The Art of War*. He meant to cut off all means of retreat; the only option left for Zhang Dongsheng would be to press ahead.

They decided to visit him on Sunday morning, the day before Chaoyang started his summer classes.

Chaoyang and Pupu agreed to meet at the entrance to the Prosperity Bay Luxury Apartments.

When Zhang Dongsheng saw them, he quickly noticed something was off. "What's wrong? You look stressed."

"We're fine," Chaoyang said. "We're here to do the second-to-last deal with you."

"What? Come inside, I don't want you arousing any suspicion."

The two kids stepped into the apartment but did not sit down.

"Our last deal will be giving you the camera. This one doesn't involve money, it just involves a favour," Chaoyang explained.

"What do you need help with?" Zhang asked uneasily.

"Killing two people."

Chaoyang's nonchalant attitude was totally incongruous with his suggestion—it was chilling to witness in such a young person.

"You're still thinking about that, are you?" Zhang asked.

Chaoyang interrupted him before he could launch into a lecture. "Mr Zhang, I have made up my mind. There's no point in negotiating. You have to help me."

The man looked at Pupu. "I blame you for this! Didn't you say you would talk to him?"

"Uncle, you have to help us," she said in a determined voice.

"You're on his side now?" Zhang yelped. "I don't know what he told you, but this does not qualify as helping a friend."

Pupu avoided his gaze.

Chaoyang remained firm. "Uncle, there's no point in getting her to try to change my mind. I can't turn back now. You have to help me."

"I'm not going to have any part of this!" Zhang shouted.

"You've already killed three people, so the outcome is the same for you if you kill two more." Chaoyang's logic was cruel but rational.

Zhang dug his fingernails into his palms and glared at him.

"You can kill the two of us right now, but Ding Hao isn't here, so you can't get rid of all of us at once. He knows that if he doesn't see us later on today, then we're in trouble. He'll go straight to the police."

Zhang exhaled, his mind racing to find the outcome that would be most advantageous to him. "I won't kill any more people. I had to do what I had to do, but I won't kill anyone in the future."

"Fine. All deals are off. We're handing the camera over to the police. If you can't kill those two people, I'm going to die anyway."

"What do you mean?"

"Let me tell you why I have to kill them. My dad and his second wife had a kid who died at the Children's Palace a month ago. I happened to be there the same day, so that bitch of a stepmother blames me for her daughter's death. The police have already determined that I had nothing to do with it but she doesn't believe anything that anyone says. She attacked me and my mum, then she splashed us with shit and left violent messages on the walls. She has threatened to kill me more than once. If they don't die first, I will."

This was the first time Zhang heard anything about these attacks. "Aren't the police handling it?"

"They've tried to, but she hired someone else to attack us the second time, and there wasn't enough evidence to put her in jail. So she never has to take responsibility for her actions."

"What about your father?"

"He always takes her side. On the day when she had had the shit dumped all over me, he hid her from the police and later he made me drop charges against her."

Zhang looked down for a moment. "That was wrong, but that's no excuse to murder him. Plenty of families don't get along, especially when divorce and remarriage is involved. Sometimes the father will cut off all relations with his previous children, or he will treat the first family as the enemy. Your father is partial to his new family, which is understandable."

"They're going to attack me for the rest of my life! What am I supposed to do, let her kill me?"

"That's just an empty threat, she wouldn't really kill you."

"But they have money and we don't. There's no way that I can get out of this. If you were being attacked every other day, wouldn't you feel like living was worse than dying?"

"Yes... but that's a matter for the police." Zhang spoke slowly, buying himself time.

"I already told you, they tried to do something about it and nothing changed. I don't have evidence to prove that the second attack was her doing, so the police are no use. Plus, if they only lock her up for a few days, that's not really going to change her behaviour!"

"Then you should have a chat with your dad. He could talk some sense into her, couldn't he?"

Chaoyang laughed. "No, he couldn't. He thinks I did it too."

Zhang frowned.

"This is more important to me than getting your money," the boy continued. "You can forget about the money. If you kill them, I'll give you the camera and I'll never bother you ever again. If you decide not to do it, that's fine, but we'll give the camera to the police. You need to decide by noon today. Two of us will come back in the afternoon to go over the plan."

"You're being reckless, Chaoyang," Zhang warned.

"No, I'm not. I have been thinking about this for weeks now. I know you don't want to do this, but you don't have a choice." He was menacing.

Zhang smiled through gritted teeth. "I won't do it. Go ahead and give the camera to the police. I'll be arrested and I'll tell them you're planning on killing your father and his wife. What do you think would happen then?"

The boy smiled back coldly. "Go right ahead! *Talking* about killing someone isn't a crime, is it? Things can't get any worse for me."

"Leave any time you like. I'll wait for the police," Zhang snorted.

"I'm not kidding!"

Zhang gnashed his teeth, as Chaoyang turned and left.

"He's really going to do it," Pupu threatened, leaning against a wall. "I know what he's like."

Zhang heard footsteps echoing in the stairwell. He frowned for a second. "Um... can you come back, please?"

60

Zhang Dongsheng had asked Chaoyang to return, but the footsteps were getting softer and further away. He shouted twice more, but there was no response. The boy had already left the building. Zhang cursed angrily and chased after him. When he caught up with Chaoyang outside, he spun him around. "Let's go upstairs and discuss this."

"There's nothing to discuss. I'm not changing my mind."

"Listen to me, please."

"No thanks."

"Let's talk about the deal then," Zhang growled.

"Are you in?"

"Wait, listen—"

"Then forget about it."

"OK, OK!" he said, exasperated. "This isn't going to be easy, we need to plan everything carefully. Now, will you come upstairs?"

Chaoyang nodded and they returned to the apartment.

Zhang pulled a cigarette out as he started to speak again. "You want me to kill two people that I have never met before. How am I supposed to do that? I have only killed family members that I knew well—that made it easy to gain their trust. I don't know your father or his wife, and they will be suspicious if a stranger tries to get too close to them. When am I supposed to get an opportunity to do this?"

"That's what you're most worried about?" Chaoyang's tone was derisive. "You'll have an opportunity on Wednesday when they visit the grave of their little girl. Dahe Cemetery is on the eastern outskirts of Ningbo, next to a mountain. People don't visit much in summer because it's too hot. At the cemetery first thing in the morning, you won't attract any attention."

Zhang looked at the boy in horror. He had been about to argue that he would be unable to kill them without getting caught. He did not expect Chaoyang to have a date and location ready for him.

"But don't you think they'll be a little guarded when they see me? I can't do martial arts and I never trained with the special forces. I won't be able to kill two people at the same time."

"All you need to do is poison them." Chaoyang smiled.

"And how do you expect me to *poison* them in a cemetery?"

"There's got to be a way," Chaoyang said stubbornly.

"There isn't always a way."

"I can help you!" Pupu said suddenly.

Zhang looked appalled. "You want to help him kill his father?"

"I do," she said confidently.

"This is not helping him. He'll regret this and he will hate you for it."

"She's my best friend, I wouldn't blame her for anything. It's all my plan anyway," Chaoyang replied quietly.

Zhang couldn't understand how the boy had convinced her to commit such a serious crime, and he was surprised at the amount of planning that had already gone into it. He began to suspect he was the last part of an elaborate scheme with no way to back out. He had built up resentment for years before he thought that murder was the only option for him. This thirteen-year-old had concluded that murder was the best way of dealing with his father and stepmother in the space of a month.

"You know that you would be the top suspect if they both died," Zhang said.

"No I won't. I have class on Wednesday, I'll be at school."

"You're not going to be there?"

"Of course not. Otherwise the police would suspect me, you said so yourself. The police don't know that I know you."

"But they know about your two friends."

"No, they don't," Chaoyang shot back.

"The police will definitely question you. And when they do, you'll talk," Zhang taunted.

"No, I won't, I know how to deal with them!"

"Cops can see through the lies of a child."

"You're not the only one who can act in front of the police! As long as I stick to my story, they'll rule me out!" he said, raising his voice.

Zhang said nothing.

Chaoyang forced himself to calm down. "Uncle, if you help us, you'll know our darkest secret and we'll know your darkest secret. Then neither of us will betray the other. We won't threaten you with the camera any more either."

"We have a low chance of success if it's only Pupu and me at the cemetery."

"Why?"

"She's not strong enough to fight an adult. What if the situation gets out of control? Even if I do manage to kill them, do you think she could help me move two adult bodies? I don't. I'm not doing this unless you convince Ding Hao to go with us."

Zhang was fully aware that the other boy was a big softie and confident that he would not agree to commit murder. If Ding Hao refused, it would give Zhang an out.

"Fine. Ding Hao, me and you will go to the cemetery," Pupu declared.

"Wait, did Ding Hao agree to take part in this?" Zhang cried.

"Oh, he will," Pupu said.

"Stop making excuses. In three days, you'll take care of things and we'll give you the camera. That's the best—and only—option for you."

Zhang's cigarette had burned itself out, but he took no notice. He did not move a single muscle as he focused all of his attention on the kids. He was silent for fifteen minutes. They stared right back at him. Zhang was deliberating whether he should kill these two harassers now and deal with Ding Hao

233

afterwards. But he ultimately abandoned that plan because Chaoyang had come prepared. He knew they had already instructed Ding Hao, and Zhang reasoned he might not get to the boy before the camera was handed to the police.

Chaoyang claimed that his life could not be any worse, whereas Zhang was ready to start a new life. If Zhang didn't placate the stupid brat, everything he had worked so hard to attain would disappear. He would face the death sentence. On the other hand, if he did manage to kill Chaoyang's father and stepmother, he would finally gain the trust of the three rotten kids. He wouldn't have to worry about them and their camera in the short term. Of course, in the long term, he would have to use a permanent method to wash his hands of them. Zhang knew that there were risks involved. Chaoyang would certainly be seen as a person of interest even if he had an alibi. He had no confidence that Chaoyang's acting would hold up against police scrutiny. Once they broke down his defences, he would almost certainly tell them everything.

For this to work, they would need to make it look like the couple had gone missing for as long as was possible. The police tended to neglect missing persons cases and they would not interrogate Chaoyang so long and harshly if they did not suspect foul play. It sounded like Dahe Cemetery would be an ideal place for it. They could bury the bodies in an empty tomb on the mountainside. It would take months, perhaps years, before the bodies were discovered, and it would be unlikely that anyone would suspect him. After carefully weighing the pros and cons, Zhang finally nodded his head. He would do it.

But Chaoyang was still a little worried when he and Pupu left Zhang's apartment. "There's still one more problem."

"What's that?"

"He wants Ding Hao to go with him, so we now have to go convince him!"

"He'll go to the cemetery," Pupu said confidently.

"Yeah, but you know he's a coward."

"Doesn't matter! This affects all three of us, and I'm not going to let him mess up my future."

61

"Are you serious? You want me to help out with a murder?" Ding Hao said.

"Idiot!" Pupu whispered, yanking his arm. "Don't broadcast it to the whole park!"

Ding Hao looked anxiously around, but they were in a deserted corner and nobody seemed to be looking at them. "No way, I'm not doing it."

"But you already agreed to the plan!" she said.

"I agreed to the plan when it was letting Uncle do the dirty work. I never said I would help."

"So you've decided you won't help?"

"That's right, I'm not going to get involved," he said stubbornly.

"Excellent!" Pupu said with a glare. "You want to be selfish, fine. I'm not going to be friends with a selfish brat like you!"

Ding Hao looked hurt and angry in equal parts. "Are you forgetting all the times I helped you at the orphanage? I helped you fight bullies, and when Wang Lei made fun of you, I punched him so hard a tooth fell out. They put me in the naughty room for two whole days! How can you call me a selfish brat?"

"You're a selfish brat and a coward," she taunted.

"But, this isn't like fighting people… this is… killing people!" he protested.

Chaoyang decided to intervene before their argument got out of control. "It's my fault. It was my idea, and I'm the reason you're fighting now."

Neither of the others spoke.

Chaoyang's expression was sincere. "Ding Hao, I'm begging you, will you help me?"

The boy shook his head sadly. "I can't."

"If you're afraid, just say so!" Pupu challenged him.

"Mm," Ding Hao turned his head, ignoring her.

"Don't be too hard on him, Yuepu," Chaoyang said. "Ding Hao, this all happened because of me. If I hadn't pushed Little Bitch out of the window, I wouldn't be asking you to do this. But we can't turn the clock back, and if we don't get rid of them, the police will find out about us eventually. Then I'll go to the youth rehabilitation centre and you'll go back to the orphanage."

Ding Hao pressed his lips together and remained silent.

"I don't want to go back! I've had enough of that place," Pupu said.

Chaoyang backed her up. "You don't want to go back to the orphanage, do you? All I want is for you to think about it—for me and for Yuepu."

"You're not even fourteen, remember? It doesn't matter if you get in trouble. Even if you killed someone, you'd only go to a juvenile rehabilitation centre or whatever. That's got to be better than the orphanage," she said.

"We just need a helper. You're not killing anyone, you're just moving the bodies," Chaoyang added.

Ding Hao looked down, not wanting to engage in this discussion.

"Come on. I'm not scared of going! Why are you so scared? You're a boy!" Pupu said.

"Are you going?" Ding Hao said, surprised.

"Yeah. I'm great at pretending and kids make people less wary."

"What are you gonna do?"

"You'll see. My job is harder than yours, so stop being such a weakling," she said ominously.

"Listen. If you don't go, we're all in deep trouble," Chaoyang said. "If you go and something goes wrong, Uncle Zhang will be in trouble, but we won't. The death sentence is for adults, not

237

kids. And if you go and everything goes right, then I'll have a lot of money from my dad's inheritance. Then I can start a company and you'll have a job and we'll all get married and the four of us will play mah-jong."

"Sounds like Yuepu is already halfway to being your wife," Ding Hao joked.

She kicked at his shin but he dodged it skilfully.

"So are you in?" Chaoyang asked.

"Yeah but promise me that I'm not going to mur—" He stumbled on the word, "—the death stuff is not my responsibility. I'm only lifting."

Chaoyang gave him a hug. "Fantastic! We just have to get through this, and then it will be smooth sailing."

They said their goodbyes and Chaoyang started walking home. When he was out of earshot, Pupu looked at Ding Hao. "We're his ride or die. We support Chaoyang no matter what."

62

That afternoon, Pupu and Ding Hao went to the Prosperity Bay Luxury Apartments. They found Zhang Dongsheng leaning against the red BMW, reading his phone.

He spoke calmly. "I've been waiting for you. Let's talk."

They entered his apartment and Zhang made a last-ditch attempt to persuade the children not to go ahead with the murders. "Killing one's own father is morally wrong, even thinking about it is wrong. I'm sure that in your heart of hearts, you are against it. Sometimes teenagers have stupid ideas, but we cannot let them ruin their lives. You have to convince him to give up this wicked plan."

"Uncle, we both support Chaoyang," Pupu said.

"Why? You're his friends, aren't you? What kind of a friend would do this?"

"Uncle Zhang, it's not just for—" Ding Hao began.

Pupu pinched him before he could say anything else.

"Ah, there's another layer to this? What else is going on here?" Zhang asked tentatively.

Ding Hao hung his head and said nothing.

"Yeah, there's another reason. It's money," Pupu said.

"Money?"

"Yeah, Chaoyang doesn't look like he's rich, does he?"

"Judging by his clothing, no," Zhang admitted.

"That's because his parents are divorced. He lives with his mother, who is poor. But his dad has more money than you do!"

"That's not saying much. You thought I was rich just because I was driving my wife's car."

Pupu ignored his remark. "His dad's kid died last month,

239

so there are no other heirs. If his dad and his dad's wife die, Chaoyang would inherit the family fortune."

Zhang was surprised that they would think so carefully about financial matters. He had only started worrying about money in his thirties. Why on earth would an eleven-year-old be thinking about money?

Pupu seemed to read his thoughts. "You're the one who taught us to think like that."

Zhang glowered at them but said nothing.

"I don't see how you're going to convince him, unless you can give him a million yuan. He has three good reasons to do this: pure hatred, protecting himself and money," she said.

"But it's morally wrong!" Zhang repeated.

"You did it."

"I never killed my own father. I never killed my own flesh and blood."

"Chaoyang has already cut off his relationship with his father. The situation is worse than you could possibly imagine."

Zhang shut his eyes in irritation.

"If you help us with this, we won't need your money. We'll just give you the camera. But if you don't, Chaoyang is still going to go through with this. And if he does a sloppy job, the police with lock him up and he'll end up squealing about the murders you committed. You don't want that to happen, do you?" Pupu said.

The man was quiet and then changed tactics. "Ding Hao, I won't be able to subdue two people at once. You'll have to help me do it. Are you prepared to do that?"

"Uh-huh," Ding Hao said, looking down.

Zhang gave a bitter smile. "Once you do this, you won't be innocent. You'll be like me."

This warning seemed to have its intended effect. Ding Hao wavered.

"I'll be with you," Pupu reminded him.

Ding Hao nodded. "Relax, Uncle Zhang, I'm not gonna back out."

Zhang reluctantly admitted to himself that he saw no way to change Chaoyang's course of action. He looked at the two kids. "Fine," he muttered.

63

On Wednesday morning, Zhu Yongping and Wang Yao drove to the cemetery to visit Zhu Jingjing's grave. The little girl would have been ten years old today. Zhu kept repeating what he had told his wife before. Even if the police never found Jingjing's killer, they were going to have to move on. He had stopped smoking and promised to eat a healthy diet so they could try for another baby soon. Zhu had only turned forty and Wang Yao was still in her thirties; it would not be difficult to have another child. Wang Yao knew that she should be grateful for the way her husband had been tolerant about her extreme grief and terrible behaviour. He had been patient and tolerant for more than a month.

When Wang Yao first met Zhu, he was just starting his business and Zhou Chunhong was pregnant. He had borrowed money to buy land and then used the land as collateral for a bank loan to build the factory. In the early years, Zhu seemed to be living the extravagant lifestyle Wang Yao wanted. But eventually she learned that it was all an elaborate scheme to make himself look good; he was actually in a lot of debt.

Wang Yao was beautiful and had many suitors. Zhu fell madly in love with her and set out to win her affection by any means necessary. She did not choose him because he was rich— she knew that it was all borrowed money. She almost split up with him when she learned he was married, but Zhu Yongping promised to divorce his wife and be faithful to her, removing one reason for her to say no. Somehow, he convinced her to

242

marry him. True to his word, Zhu divorced Zhou when his son was only two years old. It was not long before he and Wang Yao were married. After that the real estate market boomed all over China, causing Zhu's land to increase significantly in value. His business grew and eventually his net worth reached tens of millions of yuan.

Zhu Yongping was totally committed to Wang Yao. Everyone said that he had thrown himself at her feet, but he didn't care. He had been indifferent towards his first wife, but Wang Yao seemed to be his one true love. Maybe her relationship with him was true love. She didn't know.

After a month of constant consolation by her husband, Wang Yao was finally able to deal with her emotions. Even though she was certain that Zhu Chaoyang had something to do with her little girl's death, she had no evidence, and the police had no reason to arrest him. She buried her hatred at the bottom of her heart after Zhu promised not to speak to his son or his first wife again. At least the boy had effectively lost his father—that settled the score a little in Wang Yao's eyes.

There wasn't a single cloud in the sky. It was going to be a scorching day. The couple had arrived at the cemetery at about 6 a.m. The sun was not too punishing so early in the day.

Dahe Cemetery had been built recently. Like most cemeteries, it was out of the way, and nobody lived nearby. Wang Yao hadn't seen anyone when they drove there, except for a few farmers who were toiling away while it was still relatively cool. They parked the car and when they got out, Wang Yao carried a basket of paper money folded into ingots that they would burn for Jingjing. Tears streamed down her face as she walked towards her daughter's grave. "Stay strong. We'll stay with her for a few minutes and then we'll go home," Zhu said. Wang Yao nodded and tried to be brave.

When they arrived at Jingjing's grave, Wang Yao stared dumbly at it, while Zhu busied himself with the paper money they had brought. He noticed two children walking on a path, carrying their own basket of paper money. The boy looked like he was a teenager and the girl younger, but Zhu wasn't sure. They stopped at a grave about thirty feet away. He lost interest in them and began to help take the folded ingots out of Wang Yao's basket, one at a time.

A few minutes later, the girl scurried over. "Uncle, we don't know why, but we can't get the fire to light. Would you help us, please?"

"Didn't you bring a lighter?" Zhu said, offering his lighter to her.

"We have a lighter, but the flame keeps going out." She pouted with concern.

"You're lighting it at the top, aren't you? You need to light them in the middle, then the paper will catch fire." He mimed the motion for her.

The girl looked distressed. "We tried lots of times, but it won't work! Please, Uncle, can you come and help us? My brother is stupid, he can't get it to work."

Zhu looked at her innocent face and was reminded of Jingjing. "OK, I'll help you." He turned to his wife. "Wang Yao, I'm going to help this girl with her paper money. I won't be long." He walked behind the girl and asked, "Whose grave are you visiting today?"

"My mother's. It's her birthday today."

Zhu immediately felt a connection with the poor girl whose mother had died. "Why is it just you and your brother? Isn't your father coming?"

She spoke very softly. "My dad died last month in a car accident."

Zhu Yongping couldn't help asking her more questions. "Who do you live with?"

"Nobody. We live on our own."

"On your own? Don't you have any relatives?"

244

"My dad owed money to a lot of people so our relatives didn't want us. Everything in our house was taken away," the girl said in a quiet voice.

"What are you going to do?" Zhu asked as they arrived at the other grave.

The girl shook her head. "I don't know. But I learned how to make mochi rice cakes. I'm going to sell them to make money. Do you want to try one?" She presented him with a fresh mochi rice cake wrapped in cling film. Zhu hesitated. He instinctively wondered if this was a scam—scams were a scourge in big cities. Then again, what kind of a scammer would take advantage of people in a cemetery?

The girl seemed to understand his hesitation. "Just try it, you don't have to pay for it. I'm worried that they don't taste good and I won't be able to sell them. Tell me if they're sweet enough."

Zhu felt guilty for suspecting a young girl, so he smiled and accepted the mochi, unwrapping it and popping the whole thing in his mouth. He chewed it briefly and swallowed. "It's delicious! Just the right amount of sweetness."

"Oh, good! Then I should be able to sell them," she said with a smile.

Zhu admired the photograph at the top of the dead woman's headstone. He looked at the girl's older brother. His head was bowed and he looked deeply unhappy. Not knowing them, Zhu did not know what to say. So he simply kneeled and helped them light the paper money. It only took a few minutes. He felt dizzy when he stood up, but assumed that was because he had been kneeling for so long. He gathered his strength and started towards his wife. Within seconds, he felt his leg muscles twitching, although he tried to hide it. After a few more steps, Zhu was certain that his legs would give out. He wondered if he had high blood pressure and it was causing him to faint. "I think I'm going to fall."

As he spoke, his knees buckled and the boy came to his side to help him sit on the ground. The girl called to Wang Yao. "Auntie! Excuse me! Uncle just fainted."

"What?" She had not paid much attention when her husband went to help the children. She ran over to see what was wrong. Her husband was breathing rapidly and his face was bright red.

"Yongping! What's wrong? Talk to me!"

Wang Yao felt a tiny prick on her neck and turned her head. The girl was standing just a foot away from her, syringe in hand. She looked coldly at the dying couple.

"What are you doing?" Wang Yao asked, clearly dazed.

Ding Hao stayed close but did not dare to look at them. Wang Yao collapsed next to her husband, the poison taking effect almost immediately. Once he was sure that the poison had done its work, Zhang Dongsheng jogged over from his hiding place. He was already wearing latex gloves and handed some to the kids. His voice was a little shaky. "Ding Hao, take the woman. I'll take the man. We need to drag them to that tomb and bury them right now."

They dragged the bodies about a hundred feet, until they reached a row of recently constructed tombs, which were sheltered from view as they were at the top of a steep hill. Two folding shovels were resting against one tomb—Zhang was nothing if not meticulous. He manoeuvred the corpses into the empty spaces. They were small, about 3 feet long and 1½ feet wide, designed to house ashes. Zhang bent the knees of the corpses so they would fit. "Take their watches, rings, necklaces and any cash," he instructed the boy.

"Are we going to give them to Chaoyang?" Ding Hao asked.

"We're making it look like a mugging. Work now, talk later!"

Ding Hao quickly took all the valuables and Zhang used a switchblade to remove their clothes. Not a scrap of fabric was left. He stuffed the clothing into a woven plastic bag.

"That's all you need to do. Go hide behind those trees and keep a lookout. I have to do a couple more things," Zhang said.

"I'll help," Pupu offered.

"It'll be too upsetting. Go and keep a lookout, both of you," he said firmly.

Pupu relented and followed Ding Hao to hide in the copse of trees. Zhang finished the job and covered the bodies with earth, which was already piled on the side of one tomb. It was easy to cover them and the entrances to both tombs. In five minutes, Zhang walked towards the kids with the bag. "Did anyone walk by?" Zhang had tried to keep an eye out while he was working, but he did not want to take any chances. The copse was a better vantage point.

Ding Hao stood listlessly, his eyes vacant. "Not a soul," Pupu said.

Zhang checked his watch. "It's only 6:40. I'm going to break their car windows and take anything valuable. Then we can go back the way we came." He noticed that Ding Hao was not himself and patted him on the shoulder. "It's all right, it's over now."

Ding Hao looked down and grunted a response.

"Uncle, are you going to give those things to Chaoyang?" Pupu asked.

"Of course not. I'm going to destroy them."

"But they're probably worth a lot of money."

"I'll give you the cash in a few days. But you need to forget about this stuff, you can't keep it and neither can I. It has to be destroyed. It's time for us to finish this. You need to give me the camera. We will never speak of this again. Understand?" Zhang said, looking intently at them. He looked at Ding Hao. "It's all in the past now. You have a clean slate."

"OK. It's all in the past now. I won't think about it," the boy said.

"Me neither," Pupu agreed.

The end was in sight. Zhang Dongsheng had held up his part of the deal and he knew what he had to say to pacify the kids until he got rid of them once and for all. "We all need to make a break with our past lives. I'm worried that if I give you the three hundred thousand yuan in one lump sum, you'll spend it irrationally, but I promise that I will take care of you and pay for your expenses until you're old enough to work. How does that sound?"

The two looked at each other and then gratefully at Zhang. "Thank you, Uncle!"

64

"Psst. Psst," Lina Fang, Chaoyang's desk partner, whispered, tapping her fingers lightly on the wood. "Hey."

"What did I miss?" he said, slightly out of it. He was absolutely unable to concentrate.

"Did you leave the classroom because you got in trouble again?" she asked softly.

"What? No, I just went to the toilet. Does Mrs Lu want to see me?"

"I was just guessing because you seem not quite with it today," Lina said, glancing at his pen, which had not moved in several minutes.

Chaoyang smiled weakly.

"Are you upset because of your dad?" Lina asked, keeping her voice low.

"My dad…" he began, looking nervously at her.

"My dad told me how you and your mother were attacked. Don't worry, I won't tell anyone. Mrs Wang is a monster."

"You get used to it," Chaoyang said.

"Don't be sad, OK?"

"OK." His lips twitched into a tiny smile and he turned his focus to his workbook.

By the time the last study session of the day had ended, the sun was starting to set. He hopped on his bike and raced home. He looked around, but he didn't see anyone at all. That worried him, but then he heard a light cough. He turned and saw Pupu crouched in the shadow of an awning. Chaoyang swiftly locked his bike, looked around again and led her to a quiet alley where they could be sure nobody was eavesdropping.

"How did it go?" he asked urgently.

Pupu pursed her lips and looked hard at him. "It's done."

Chaoyang felt several emotions at once, but his face was shrouded in shadow, making his features indistinct, so she could not see his reaction. He took a deep breath and tried to get himself under control. "They're both dead?"

"Dead and buried. Nobody will know."

He looked up to the sky, admiring the early stars and letting his mind wander, then looked back at her. "How did you do it? Tell me everything."

Pupu went over every detail of the morning.

"My nightmare is finally over."

"Uncle Zhang keeps asking when we'll give him the camera," Pupu said.

Chaoyang realized that her fear of Zhang Dongsheng had abated. "You're not starting to trust that murderer, are you?"

"I don't think he's that bad," she argued.

"You still need to be careful."

"It's fine, he won't do anything."

After a moment, Chaoyang nodded. "I hope not."

"So when should we give him the camera?"

"In a few weeks. Once everything has blown over, I'll hand it over to him and thank him. I should be thanking you: you've done so much for me today."

Pupu blushed. "No big deal."

"How is Ding Hao?"

"He was really nervous this morning, I thought he was going to screw it up. But he's already back to playing computer games."

"He can't live without his games," Chaoyang laughed.

"Yeah, and if we went back to the orphanage, he wouldn't be able to play any more. I think that's why he helped us," she said, laughing too.

"OK, from now on we don't have to talk about all that stuff. Including the orphanage. Those people can go to hell."

"Yeah, they can go to hell," Pupu said with a smile.

"So you said they're buried in tombs at the top of the hill, right?"

"Yeah."

"I want to go see them."

"Maybe after a few days you won't like what we did... maybe you'll hate me... he was your dad... and I was the one who did it, after all..." Pupu said, her voice as thin as an insect's hum.

"That won't happen!" Chaoyang said, looking earnestly at her. He gripped her shoulder as he spoke. "Don't ever think that. You're the most important person to me and I'm never going to hate you. I will never regret what you did, I promise! I know you didn't want to do it and you only did it because I asked you to. I was the one who killed them. I just want to see them one more time. Don't tell Ding Hao or anybody. I'll go on Sunday. Then it will be over."

Pupu nodded and left.

Chaoyang walked slowly up the stairs, with a faint smile on his face and tears streaming from his eyes. He looked up at the inky sky and hummed a tune to himself.

65

When she arrived home on Saturday evening, Zhou Chunhong saw that the door to Chaoyang's room was closed and the light was on. She knew he was studying—he was always studying.

Despite the sacrifices her son made, the hard work was clearly paying off. He was the top student in his class. All of his teachers praised him, especially the maths teacher, who believed that Chaoyang would almost certainly win first place at this year's China Mathematics Competition. Zhou's heart swelled with pride every time she thought of him. It was quite a feat to raise such an outstanding son while being a single mother with a low-paid job and an average education. Everyone thought Chaoyang was a treasure, everyone except for his own father, who had never been emotionally available for Chaoyang. Zhou couldn't help scoffing at the way he treated them. She promised herself for the thousandth time that she would give her son more love to make up for his father.

The only thing she wanted to fix about him was his height. Chaoyang had been frustrated about being so short for the past two years. Then again, she supposed every teenager worried about some aspect of their looks. She poured a big glass of milk and went to his room to give it to him. She entered without knocking and found him at his desk, facing away from her. He was scribbling furiously and he hadn't even turned on the fan. Beads of sweat dotted his bare back.

"How about a glass of milk and a little break?" Zhou offered.

252

He started and turned to look anxiously at the intruder. "Mum, don't sneak around like that! You scared me!"

Zhou smiled apologetically. "You were concentrating so hard you didn't hear me. What are you working on?" She flicked her eyes at the notebook and saw pages filled with characters. "Oh, you're writing an essay."

Chaoyang mumbled a reply and closed the notebook.

"Drink up. You need more calcium in your diet."

"Just put it down, I'll drink it later," he answered.

"Why don't you turn the fan on? You're sweating all over the chair!"

"The fan is too noisy."

"You never said it was noisy before," she complained.

"I have a lot of summer school homework, and I haven't even started some of it yet."

Zhou relented. "Has your dad called while I was away?"

Chaoyang looked up, surprised. "No, he hasn't. Is something wrong?"

"Your grandmother called and said that Zhu Yongping is missing. What nonsense!" she said with a disdainful sneer.

"M-missing?"

"He hasn't shown up to work and neither has his bitchy wife. Their phones are switched off and your father missed an important meeting. Your grandmother has tried everything, even calling me."

"Why would she ask you?"

"She hoped that I would know where they might have gone. As if I care what they get up to."

"How long have they been missing?" he asked after a pause.

"A few days now. Apparently nobody has spoken to them since Wednesday."

"What were they doing on Wednesday?"

"Who knows."

"Do you think something has happened to them?"

"I don't care if they had an accident. Your father doesn't care about you, so why should you care about him? You don't get anything out of the relationship except to be ridiculed by that evil woman."

He nodded.

"You should go to bed soon. Tomorrow you have a day off, enjoy it while it lasts! When school starts again, you won't have many days off until university."

"I know, I know. You can go now."

Zhou left but was a little hurt by the way her son quickly closed the door on her.

She woke up in the middle of the night to use the toilet and discovered that the light in her son's room was still on. She could vaguely hear a pen scratching away. "Chaoyang, it's one in the morning, go to bed. You can finish that essay tomorrow," she said to the closed door.

"I will stop soon," he answered.

Zhou waited until his light went off before going back to sleep.

66

A few police cars were parallel parked on a street leading up to Dahe Cemetery. A Mercedes SUV was also parked there. Captain Ye Jun emerged from one of the cars and looked into the Mercedes. He then walked up to the cemetery with the attending officer.

The bodies had been discovered at the top of the cemetery, in a row of empty tombs. They had now been dug up and a temporary canopy was erected to protect them from the heat. A foul stench permeated the air. Ye looked at the bodies until he could stand the smell no longer, and moved several steps away. Dr Chen, the tireless and hard-working coroner, joined him to have a grumble. "I can't take it! How could anyone be so cruel as to subject us to a double homicide in the middle of summer? Couldn't they wait until winter to do this? Honestly!"

"Work is a bitch, but the pay is good," Ye said wryly.

"It's not too bad once your nose adapts to the smell. Stand over there for a few minutes, you'll see what I mean," Chen teased.

"I'll pass. What can you tell me about the two victims?"

"They were both stabbed to death and their faces were viciously mutilated: a male and a female. I estimate the time of death to be a couple of days ago, but that's difficult to pinpoint in this weather. One interesting detail is that they were stripped of all their belongings, even their underwear. I'm afraid it will take a long time to identify the victims."

255

"I don't think it will take too long," Ye replied. He pointed towards the parked cars.

"What am I looking at?"

"See the Mercedes? It was the only car near the cemetery when we arrived. Why else would an expensive Mercedes be parked in the middle of nowhere?"

"Good point," Chen said.

"I've asked the traffic police to check the plates. We'll see what turns up."

A few minutes later, Ye Jun took a call and then hung up. "Looks like this will be a massive case."

"Somebody mutilated two people, of course it's going to be a big case!" Chen answered.

Ye scoffed. "Want to guess who owns that car?"

"Tell me."

"Zhu Yongping."

"Who is Zhu Yongping when he's at home?"

"The father of Zhu Jingjing."

Chen's jaw dropped. "You mean that's Zhu Yongping... and that's his wife?"

67

That evening there was a meeting at the police station. A couple of detectives gave a briefing to the rest of the team. They explained that the double homicide had been discovered by a group of mourners. Just before 9 a.m., a group of about seventy people arrived in two coaches for a funeral. They set off firecrackers, then a monk performed religious rituals that were fairly time-consuming. The friends and relatives of the deceased were a little bored, so a few wandered up to the new tombs. One discovered part of a foot. At first it was assumed that someone had flouted the law and buried their loved ones instead of cremating them. But as more people came to look, they agreed that they should report the bodies to the police.

The bodies were identified as Zhu Yongping and Wang Yao, who had been missing since they visited their daughter's grave at the cemetery on Wednesday. The family had reported them missing when they were unable to contact them.

The initial autopsy suggested that the time of death was Wednesday morning. The bodies had decayed rapidly over the course of less than a week and were nearly unrecognizable when the crime scene investigation team arrived. Unfortunately, there was no hope of getting evidence such as footprints after so much time had passed, and especially after the large group of mourners had tromped everywhere.

Another detective explained the coroner's report. The coroner believed that the cause of death was loss of blood due to stab wounds. There were cuts all over both bodies and they were buried in tombs, so it seemed that the perpetrator attempted to destroy all possible evidence. Initially it looked like robbery and murder, since the victims' valuables were missing. Some valuable personal effects from the car were also taken, such as cash and cigarettes. Investigators dusted for fingerprints in the car, but the results had not come back yet.

The murder weapon was not found at Dahe Cemetery, despite the squad looking for it all day. The exact location of the murders was not identified either; too much time had elapsed. The police were working with zero clues, apart from the approximate time of the murder and the identities of the victims.

Ye smoked a cigarette as he listened. The atmosphere in the room was very pessimistic. Some officers had experienced challenging cases, but everyone knew that some were never solved. For example, there were a lot of factories in Zhejiang, which attracted workers who sometimes became drifters. So almost every year, bodies would wash up on the beach, and there were dismembered bodies that were never identified. Cases that had no leads would collect dust until they were quietly filed away. The only advantage here was a time of death and the identities of the victims, but without any other information, clues, CCTV footage or witnesses, the police were at a loss. Hardly anyone visited the cemetery. If it weren't for Zhu Yongping's foot being spotted, the bodies might have gone undiscovered for months, or even a year.

Still, Ye had a gut feeling that there was something really dodgy about Zhu Jingjing's parents being killed just over a month after their daughter. The whole family had died. Even though the double homicide looked like a robbery gone wrong, there might be something much more sinister going on.

Could the two sets of murders be related?

68

Only Chaoyang's year had to attend the extra classes over the summer. Qiushi Middle School felt emptier than usual.

None of the students were that interested in studying and none of the teachers were that interested in teaching. Only one teacher monitored the evening independent study classes. Unsurprisingly, people chatted, passed notes and joked. When it got too loud, the teacher would enter the classroom and give everyone a stern look. The noise would subside until they left the room again.

The evening self-study sessions were especially chaotic. Fang Lina wasn't interested in boosting her grades. Her parents exhorted her to be more like Zhu Chaoyang, and it got on her nerves. Still, she did not bear any hard feelings towards him, unlike some of her classmates. Chaoyang was a thorn in the side of the girls who would be top of the class if it weren't for his stellar scores. This was not true for Lina, though. She was certain that if he fell really ill and had to take his exams from a hospital bed, he would still beat her. Chaoyang frequently let her "borrow" his homework, and sometimes even let her copy his test answers. He was an expert at finding the angle that allowed her to see his test without letting his nemeses catch a glimpse.

Lina had spread a large workbook on her desk and kept her pen in her hand, as if she was in the middle of writing an answer. Meanwhile, she immersed herself in a love story hidden underneath. Reading it made her immensely happy. But when the second session rolled around, she remembered that she had not written a single character for the homework assignment and would need a favour from Chaoyang again. Lina turned and was surprised that he was bent low over his desk, writing like a madman. She peeked under his arm and saw that he wasn't answering questions. His workbook, like hers, was covering something else. He was writing as if his life depended on it.

"Hey," she said.

"What's up?" Chaoyang asked, as he covered his work. He quickly assumed the pose of a thoughtful scholar, answered one question and then turned his head slightly to speak to her.

"What are you writing?" Lina smirked.

"I'm answering questions, of course."

"Yeah," she said with a knowing glance. "And what about the other thing?"

"I don't know what you're talking about."

"Come on, let me see!"

"It's an essay."

"An essay?" Lina said, clearly not fooled. "The teacher didn't assign any!"

"I'm just practising," Chaoyang said.

She laughed softly. "That's not what you're doing."

"Then what am I doing?"

"Writing a love letter," Lina said confidently.

"Hey, don't make accusations like that!" Chaoyang said casually.

"You know what else? I know who it's for."

"Who?" Chaoyang asked, but now he was really nervous.

Lina was proud of her detective work and gave him a meaningful look. "You sure know how to pick them, Chaoyang. How did you fall for a bully like Ye Chimin?"

His muscles relaxed. "Where'd you get that idea? She has a twisted mind!"

"You can't say that, she's your crush!"

"I have always said that. I'm not going to stop now."

"That was before. You shouldn't say she's twisted if you're writing love letters to her," Lina said.

"Never in a million years would I go out with her."

She frowned. "So it's not for Ye Chimin? But I could swear that I saw her name!"

Chaoyang narrowed his eyes. "What else did you see?"

"Don't worry, I only got a teeny-tiny peek. I promise I won't tell your secret. I can deliver the letter for you, if you tell me who it's for," Lina said nonchalantly.

"It's not a love letter."

"Then what are you writing?"

"A journal."

"But we don't have to write journal entries over the summer," Lina said.

"I'm just writing a little bit each day so I can improve my writing skills. I'm not handing it in."

"How disappointing," she said, deflated. Her mood quickly brightened. "So you've already mastered Maths, English, Physics and Chemistry, and you're working on an essay to perfect your Chinese. Ye Chimin and the other girls don't have a chance! If they try to sabotage your exam scores, it won't work… and oh, yeah, can I borrow the homework for today?"

At the exact moment when Chaoyang handed his notebooks to her, Mrs Lu entered the classroom. She walked straight towards them, her eyes fixed on him. The two students froze, petrified. Mrs Lu spoke to Chaoyang in a low voice, "Come with me."

Chaoyang asked for his homework back, stuffed the journal in the middle of a stack of books in his desk and followed Mrs Lu to her office. A few minutes later, he returned to the classroom, his eyes red. He silently gathered his things. Everyone watched him; some with curiosity, some with *Schadenfreude*.

Lina looked guiltily at him. "She's making you go home just for lending me your homework? That's unfair."

"It's not that."

261

"Was it them?" Lina whispered, motioning towards Ye Chimin and her clique.

Chaoyang shook his head. He passed a few booklets to Lina, and quickly zipped his backpack. "Would you hand in my homework for me tomorrow? You can copy it, I don't mind."

"What's going on?" Lina asked, certain that Mrs Lu was punishing him unfairly.

Chaoyang wiped the tears from his eyes and whispered in her ear, "My dad has died. My family wants me to go straight home."

Lina was dumbstruck. Eventually she nodded. "I won't tell anyone, I promise."

69

Chaoyang's home was filled with people. Zhou Chunhong's brother and sister had come with their families, as had Fang Jianping and several other bosses. Seeing Chaoyang's tear-stained face, they comforted him for a few minutes. Then Fang got down to business.

"The bodies of your father and Wang Yao were found at Dahe Cemetery three days ago. The police say the motive for murder was robbery, but they're still investigating. We can't let our emotions affect us. We have to go to Yongping Seafood right now. You're Yongping's only son, and most people would see you as the rightful inheritor of his estate, but according to the law Wang Yao's family has a claim too. We need to occupy the facility and make sure they don't start removing valuables."

Chaoyang agreed that they shouldn't let Wang Yao's family get to the premises before they did. The group hashed out details and went straight to the factory.

When they arrived, they met Zhu Yongping's mother and his other relatives. There were also business partners of Zhu's and more bosses from the neighbouring cold-storage facilities. Anticipating a showdown, the bank, the police and government officials were already there. The building was surrounded by people, but Fang Jianping knew almost everyone and greeted them individually. He suggested that the immediate family should discuss the matter in Zhu Yongping's office.

Listening attentively, Chaoyang learned about his father's financial situation: the main tangible assets were the factory, two automobiles, a villa and three apartments; other assets had not yet been calculated. Fang Jianping stated that Zhu Yongping had taken out a 15,000,000 yuan loan, and that he and some of the other bosses were the guarantors. Since his estate was worth more than that, the bank agreed not to freeze his accounts.

The next question was how to divide the assets. Zhu Yongping's mother was a kind woman and wanted everything to go to her surviving grandchild, Zhu Chaoyang. Once this was done, she wanted nothing more to do with the Wang family. Still, according to China's inheritance law, Wang Yao's parents, as well as Zhu Yongping's parents, had a valid claim on the inheritance. The Wang family would certainly want to maximize their share, but they lived far away, and before they arrived, the Zhu family could set the terms of negotiation.

Zhou Chunhong simmered with rage at the mere mention of the Wangs. She wanted her son to get as much of his father's estate as possible. She urged Fang Jianping to use any means necessary to prevent the other family from taking advantage.

Fang presented his plan to Zhu Chaoyang and Zhou Chunhong. They would have control of all important documents, including official company stamps, accounts and certificates of ownership, thus gaining the upper hand. They would convert all of Zhu Yongping's liquid assets before the Wang family even arrived, then haggle over the fixed assets such as the factory and the cars. When the Wangs requested a fair division, the Zhu family would have a court arbitrate for them, where the Wang family would be at a distinct disadvantage due to their not knowing the total value of the fixed assets.

As for the seafood inventory, Fang and the other bosses knew that Zhu had purchased a significant amount of fish in the last month that was still in cold storage. The other bosses wanted to buy the whole lot at half price and transfer the money directly to Zhou Chunhong. The price did not sound a good deal to her, but she reasoned she wouldn't have to share any of it with the Wangs. Fang had a contract in hand and said they could sign it if they were happy with the terms. Then his people would move the fish to his storage facility, working through the night if necessary. Zhu Chaoyang was worried that a factory worker might tell the Wang family about the deal, which would lead to nasty arguments. If the Wangs asked, Fang would explain that he owned the inventory all along, and Zhu had simply been storing it for him. They had often rented storage from each other in the past, and now that Zhu Yongping was dead, Fang needed to recover his goods. This all sounded feasible. Fang had a larger factory than Zhu and a sterling reputation, so it was unlikely that he would cheat them. Chaoyang signed the agreement without further hesitation. The adults praised him for his maturity and stoicism at such a difficult time.

When they calculated everything, they estimated the total value of the factory assets at 20,000,000 yuan, but since the company owed 15,000,000 to the bank, it was not as much as it had seemed at first. When the real estate, the cars and the other assets were included, Chaoyang could expect to inherit 10,000,000 yuan. The Wang family would get a few million at most. If the Wang family decided to file a lawsuit about the division of assets, Fang would provide help to Chaoyang and his family. The funeral arrangements could be decided at a later date.

It was a long night, but the boy felt like it was the chance for a fresh start.

70

Ye Jun had not made any progress on the case.

The farmers who regularly went past the cemetery had seen the Mercedes parked, but they did not remember when it arrived, who was driving, or if anyone suspicious had passed through the area. Nobody in their right mind would drive out from Ningbo to stroll through the cemetery on a hot day in August, so the chances of finding a witness were virtually nil. The police had searched everywhere for the weapon but had found nothing. There was a pitiful amount of physical evidence.

The task force held a meeting that night and it was clear that no one was optimistic about finding the murderer. It was frustrating, but not as frustrating as finding DNA and not being able to use it, as in the Children's Palace case. It was challenging to work in the scorching heat—they were human after all. They had knocked on door after door. After so many disappointing interviews with locals, they were losing their fighting spirit. The task force was also investigating whether Zhu Jingjing's death was linked to her parents' deaths, but the majority thought it was not. The victims were related, but the MO, course of events and other details were completely different.

In Zhu Jingjing's case, the perpetrator was violent and perverse. It was harrowing that anyone would assault and kill a child at a public place and in broad daylight. The killer carelessly left his DNA and the fact that he had not been caught was down to sheer luck.

The double homicide was different because the perpetrator was clearly motivated by money. They stole everything, even the valuables locked in the victims' car. A description of the watch, platinum necklace and rings Zhu Yongping and Wang Yao were wearing was sent to the jewellers and pawn shops in the area, and they were instructed to notify police if any of it turned up. Ye was aware of the unlikelihood of catching the criminal through such a method—criminals who knew what they were doing sold their loot in a different city or even a different province. And if the jewellery did turn up, it would not necessarily bring the police closer to the killer.

Ye Jun felt exhausted as he trudged home. He had been handed two serious cases two months in a row, and there was no hope of solving either. His wife handed him a steaming mug of ginseng tea. He flopped on the couch and took a sip. He ached for a cigarette, but just as he was about to light it, his wife scolded him. "Chimin's doing her homework now, so don't fill the whole house with smoke. She's told me a hundred times that it irritates her."

"Why doesn't she tell me herself?" Ye asked, shoving the cigarette back in its pack.

"Do you really not know the answer to that question?" his wife said. "She's already thirteen but you treat her like a toddler. You shout at her all the time. It's no surprise that she's terrified of you."

Ye had worked in criminal investigation for years; the hours were brutal. Sometimes he couldn't go home for days and at other times he had to leave in the middle of the night. When work did not go well, he would take it out on his family. Acting like a tough general at home was the only way he knew how to deal with the pressures of his job.

He knew she was right but he still scoffed at his wife. "I only shout at her when I need to teach her a lesson! If she didn't do things wrong, I wouldn't criticize her. I haul troublemakers into the station every day. You know what they have in common? No discipline at home!"

Ye Jun went to his daughter's room. When he opened the door, he found her doing her homework. "Dad," she said. It was clear from her nervous expression that she had heard the conversation.

He grunted a reply, his face stern. "You were supposed to take a mock test this summer, right?"

"Yes."

"Did the scores come out?"

"Yes..." she stammered.

"Why haven't you shown them to me? Did you get a low score?"

"We only got the scores today. I was going to show you when I finished answering these questions." Chimin leaned over to her backpack, pulled out her mock test papers and handed them to her father.

Ye Jun looked briefly through her papers, focusing on her total score for the maths test. She got 96 out of 120.

"How did you get so many wrong?" he said, pointing.

"This test was super tricky... My classmates scored about the same as I did."

"What did you rank for this test?"

"Top ten in the class?" Chimin's voice faltered.

"And in your year?"

"They didn't give the year ranking this time."

"How did Zhu Chaoyang do?"

"He..." Chimin began in a panicked voice. No matter how hard she tried, she never scored better than that overachiever. Once she lied and said that Chaoyang scored less than she did and her father actually went to the school to check. Then he gave her a tongue lashing for lying and she thought he was going to hit her, but he didn't. She knew not to lie, but she hated admitting that classmate's score. "He got 120."

"Why did you do so much worse than him?" Ye Jun demanded.

Chimin hesitated and within seconds tears were streaming from her eyes.

Her mother dashed in and scolded him. "You made her cry again! She's not a criminal! It was only a mock exam; she just needs to try a little harder next time."

Ye frowned but he knew he was being too harsh. He hated to see her cry. "Never mind. Don't cry, just do better next time."

"Don't cry, honey. It's fine," Ye Jun's wife said. She gave her husband a stern look. "This is what your disciplined approach gets you! Don't you have something better to do? Go brush your teeth."

"I need to have a quick chat with Chimin, I'll brush my teeth right afterwards," he said to his wife. "Chimin, please don't cry. I'm sorry for being so strict."

Chimin's mother only left when Ye Jun promised he wasn't going to talk about test scores. Finally he could ask Chimin the questions he had been wanting to ask: "Did Zhu Chaoyang take any days off from school recently?"

Chimin nodded.

"What about yesterday?"

"Mrs Lu called him into her office, and then he took the rest of the evening independent study class and today off. Is something wrong?" She looked at her father, her curiosity growing. She fervently hoped that Chaoyang was in trouble, although she couldn't say that to her dad.

"Something happened to someone in his family, but you can't tell anyone," Ye Jun said, deliberately being vague.

"Oh."

"Did Chaoyang take any days off last week?"

"No, he didn't."

"He came every day? Are you sure?"

"I'm sure, he never ever takes days off."

"What about the evening independent study classes?"

"He was there."

"Did he arrive late last Wednesday, by any chance?"

"No, he's always the first to arrive. He's awfully energetic in the morning."

Ye Jun did not notice the condescension in his daughter's voice and continued, "Are you certain that he did not take the day off last Wednesday?"

"Yeah, we had a chemistry mock. He was there."

"And you're certain that he did not arrive late?"

"I'm certain."

"How can you be so sure?"

"He sits in the front row and I'm in the third row. I stare at the back of his head all day."

"Oh," Ye Jun said. "Have you seen him in contact with anyone at school recently? Any new friends, perhaps?"

"No. He never talks to anyone in the entire school."

"Why is that?"

"He acts like he's better than everyone else, but all he knows how to do is read books. Books aren't that great; they're just dead trees."

Ye Jun missed his daughter's subtle dig. "Do you think his behaviour has changed recently?"

"Like what part of his behaviour?"

"Anything you can think of."

Chimin shook her head. "I can't think of anything. He's always been a loner and he never talks to anyone. He studies hard, but he'll always be a big dork."

She was hoping to inundate her father with reasons why being a dork was terrible so that he would stop comparing her with Chaoyang, but he stood up before she had the chance to say anything else. The conversation was over, and it didn't seem like any of her comments had their intended effect.

Chimin asked in a rush, before he closed the door, "Dad, did Zhu Chaoyang commit a crime? Did you arrest him?"

Ye Jun looked intently at her. "No, why would you say that?"

"Because you're asking questions, loads of questions."

"Oh, I was just curious. Time for bed, Chimin. Study hard like Chaoyang and the others, and you'll do better on your next test," he said as he left.

Chimin pouted at the closed door. Clearly her dad didn't get any of her cunning messages!

71

From the day that the police notified him of his father's death, Chaoyang was absent from summer classes. His mother thought it was best that he avoid the stresses of school and wait until classes started in September.

The Zhu family had successfully gained the upper hand. Yongping Seafood was going to be sold to Fang Jianping and a couple of the other bosses. This understanding was advantageous to both Zhu Chaoyang and Fang: one contract would be shown to the tax authorities and the other one would be the real contract. This allowed Fang to give Zhu Chaoyang money without it being taxed.

Chaoyang was present at the inheritance battles at Yongping Seafood but was not required to say anything. The Zhu family had possession of nearly all the property already, and the Wangs had nothing to show for their efforts, even after they called the police. The latter recommended a formal lawsuit, and the Zhu family agreed: let a judge decide how much the Wangs deserved. They would not get a *fen* more. After several days of clashes, the Wang family went home. They had little hope that the impending court case would get them more from the estate.

The two bodies had not yet been released, so the families would have to wait before they could hold a funeral.

That afternoon Chaoyang and Zhou Chunhong left Yongping Seafood and went home. He spied Pupu sitting in her hiding place outside the apartment, so told his mother that he was going to buy an ice cream after the stress of the morning. Zhou went to the apartment without him. Chaoyang ran into a little alley and Pupu tailed him.

After they emerged on the other side, Chaoyang suggested they walk and talk. "Did you wait a long time?"

"It wasn't so bad, I had a book to read. Did the police question you?"

Chaoyang was surprised but continued walking. "How did you know?"

"Uncle Zhang guessed they would."

"Really?"

"He saw that the bodies were discovered on the news. He asked me if you touched them."

"What did you say?" Chaoyang asked.

"I said I didn't know."

"Oh."

A while later, he asked, "Why did he think that I went to the cemetery?"

"He thought it would take at least a month before the bodies were found, so when they were found so soon, he suspected that you had messed with them."

"What would happen if I disturbed the bodies?"

"You actually touched them?" Pupu gaped.

Chaoyang quickly denied the accusation. "No, I just looked."

"He said you might've left footprints or something like that. He was mainly worried about the CCTV."

"Are there cameras in the cemetery?"

"Not in or around the cemetery, but definitely on the main roads."

"I took the bus and then I stayed on the path next to the mountain. I didn't see anyone," Chaoyang protested.

"There aren't any cameras there. It'll be fine," she said.

He thought about it and said, "Yes, it's probably OK. Otherwise the police would have arrested me already."

"Didn't the police question you?"

"Yeah, but it wasn't a big deal. My mum and some other relatives were questioned too. They asked if my dad or Big Bitch contacted us, and they wanted to know where we were last Wednesday. I was in class and my mum was at work. We're both in the clear."

"That's good." Pupu was relieved.

"You and Ding Hao and Uncle Zhang don't have a connection to my dad, so the police will never suspect you. We just have to wait for things to quiet down. It will be better soon, and then we can actually hang out."

"The sooner the better," Pupu smiled. "One other thing. Uncle Zhang wanted me to ask you when you're going to give the camera to him."

"How about once the police stop asking questions? By the way, how are you and Ding Hao? Is he still frightened?"

"He forgets all his problems when he's at the computer. But I'm kinda worried because we aren't living in that little studio any more. We're living in Uncle Zhang's own apartment now."

Chaoyang stopped short, and his brow creased. "Why did you move?"

"After we came back from the cemetery, Ding Hao let some things slip, like the fact that we aren't enrolled in any school. Uncle Zhang doesn't care about the camera any more. He says we should be going to school, but if we wanted to go, we would need to get a *hukou* register, 'cause right now we don't belong anywhere and we don't have the right documents to go to school in Ningbo. He said he would get us a *hukou* and then get us enrolled. He is gonna sell the little apartment to get money for our *hukou*."

"You just said the camera's not important to him now. Why do you think he's being so selfless?" Chaoyang asked.

"He doesn't want us on the streets. If we're out there, the cops might pick us up. Then I guess he is worried that one of us might talk."

Chaoyang heard a hint of reproach in her voice and hurried to explain. "I mean that's great that he's being so generous!"

"Do you think it's risky, living with him?" Pupu asked.

"No. He didn't look like he wanted to kill you before and he has already said he doesn't want to kill more people. He's a rational person."

She nodded, satisfied. "He's not all that bad. He's a teacher, and teachers are good. He said we should all forget about the past and just live our lives."

"Yeah, I just want to hurry up and start living my life," Chaoyang said.

"OK, I'm going back now. In a few days you can drop off the camera. Uncle Zhang has some of your dad's stuff, by the way. He says he can't give you your dad's watch or any of the jewellery but he can give you the cash later."

"I don't know what I would do without you, Yuepu."

She shook her head modestly with a hint of a smile.

"Oh, yeah, when is the anniversary of your dad's death?"

"Saturday."

"Are you going to burn a photograph for him?"

"Yeah."

"Want me to come?"

"That's OK, it's not a good time just now to get together. You can come with me next year," Pupu said.

"OK, I'll do that," he promised.

72

Summer classes ended, just in time for the school year to start. The third year of middle school was a critical year for exams, but Chaoyang had been allowed to stay at home and mourn until the beginning of the new school year. Zhou Chunhong had taken time off work to manage family affairs. Even though Chaoyang's inheritance was life-changing, she did not quit her job. She planned to set up a bank account in her son's name and then buy him a house and a car when he graduated from university. After less than a week, Zhou went back to work at Sanmingshan, and Chaoyang took the opportunity to meet with Pupu. He told her he would give Zhang the camera the next morning.

It was Chaoyang's first night alone in a week. He leaned over his desk and wrote until well past midnight. Then he quickly stretched, closed his notebook and sighed deeply.

He put the notebook on his bookshelf, tidied his desk and arranged his workbooks on one side, placing *Home Remedies to Increase Height* on top of the pile.

He closed his eyes and leaned back in his chair. When he got up, he dug out the camera and its memory card from their hiding place. He had bought another memory card at an electronics mall that afternoon. He inserted it into the camera and fiddled with some buttons. Then he removed the old memory card and tucked it into an internal pocket of his backpack.

When he finished, he gazed out the window at nothing in particular. He looked older now. With another sigh, Chaoyang got ready to go to sleep.

Tomorrow was going to be a big day. He hoped that Pupu and Ding Hao would be all right.

The next morning Chaoyang put on his backpack and made his way to the Prosperity Bay Luxury Apartments. When he rang the doorbell, Zhang Dongsheng spied him through the intercom. His eyes crinkled as he smiled to himself.

"Ding Hao, Pupu, Chaoyang is here," he called over his shoulder as he buzzed him in.

Ding Hao greeted his friend at the door. "I haven't seen you in weeks, mate!"

"Come in, have a seat," Zhang said.

Chaoyang sat down and chatted with Ding Hao for a few minutes. Everyone avoided talking about the murders.

Eventually, Chaoyang decided it was time to hold up his end of the deal. "Uncle, I brought the camera," he said, removing it from his backpack and handing it over.

Zhang turned it on and checked it. "The video is still on the camera, but you don't have another copy on a computer somewhere, do you?"

"No," Chaoyang said.

Zhang looked carefully at all three kids. "You never saved a copy of the video?"

"Never," Chaoyang said firmly.

"I promise, Uncle, I never saved it anywhere," Ding Hao said.

"There's no point in tricking you now. We don't need the video any more," Pupu said.

The cautious murderer removed the memory card and smashed it in front of their eyes, then smiled and threw the pieces away. "Now we can start anew."

Ding Hao had a genuine smile and even Pupu's lips turned upward. Chaoyang struggled to join in their happiness, and Zhang noticed his grim expression. "It's done now. There's no point in regretting it. Just forget about it."

"I don't regret it. It's just a lot has happened recently…" Chaoyang murmured.

"Time heals all wounds," Zhang said.

"I'll feel better eventually."

Zhang tried to lift the small boy's mood. "Chaoyang, now you can live in peace, and Ding Hao and Pupu are going to get a *hukou*. Then we can find a school for them and get them enrolled. It might take some time, but I'll take care of it."

Ding Hao smiled again at the thought of going to school again.

"We have been through a lot over the past few weeks. I think it's time to celebrate. How does that sound?" Zhang announced.

"Let's get pizza!" Ding Hao suggested excitedly.

"Maybe another time. I have a treat for you," Zhang said.

"Is it the cake in the fridge?" Pupu asked.

Zhang faked surprise. "Did you see me when I hid it yesterday?"

"I saw it too, I just didn't say anything," Ding Hao said.

Chaoyang laughed at him—Ding Hao never wanted to be left out. Even though Zhang's surprise was spoiled, the three kids were excited about the gorgeous cake studded with fruit and chocolate.

"This is amazing!" Ding Hao said, smacking his lips.

"I'll get you something to drink. Juice for Chaoyang, I presume? What about you two?"

"Anything is fine with me, just make it snappy," Ding Hao said, stabbing a strawberry and eating it before Zhang returned.

Zhang shook his head and smiled when he discovered Ding Hao had already started eating. He served them their drinks and poured a glass of wine for himself. "Bottoms up, everyone," Zhang said.

"All right!" Ding Hao, as usual, was greedy and drank over half of his soda in one gulp.

Pupu drank about a third, while Chaoyang had a small sip and coughed into a tissue. He took another sip and coughed again. "I really need to pee," he muttered. He took a big gulp and held the liquid in his mouth as he dashed to the toilet. Zhang glanced at his glass: one third was gone.

"Time to cut the cake!" Zhang declared, and when the boy returned, the man asked, "Chaoyang, do you want a piece with chocolate or with fruit on top?"

"No cake for me, thanks. I had stomach problems last night and I still feel awful."

"OK. Ding Hao, do you want this slice?" Zhang asked.

Ding Hao accepted it and took several bites. Then he winced. "Ugh, I think I have stomach problems too. It hurts real bad!"

Pupu gave him a look. "That's what you get for wolfing down your food."

"Be nice, I'm dying over here," Ding Hao joked. But seconds later, he was clutching his stomach and howling in pain.

"Ding Hao! Ding Hao!" Pupu's first thought was that he was just being dramatic but then he slipped to the floor, his face twisted in agony.

Chaoyang and Pupu rushed to prop him up. Zhang came over and helped Ding Hao back onto his seat. "What's wrong? Do you have gastroenteritis?"

"What's going on?" Pupu said, alarmed. She watched as Ding Hao twitched. Moments later, her own face contorted with pain.

"It must be gastroenteritis. I have some medicine for that," Zhang said. He turned as if to get something out of a drawer. But instead, he picked up the remote control for his new electronic door lock. Ka-chunk!

Chaoyang staggered back to his seat, complaining loudly. He fell to the floor, writhing and moaning, and turned onto his stomach. Ding Hao twitched and Pupu rocked back and forth on the floor. She turned her gaze to Zhang, who was perfectly calm. Suddenly she remembered how Chaoyang's father had died. "You're… going to kill us!" she gasped.

He said nothing. He stood and watched their bodies spasm.

Eventually they were quiet. Five minutes later, Zhang exhaled triumphantly. "You made me do this. You thought this was finished? You don't understand that as long as one person knows my secret, I can't rest."

Zhang calmly pushed Ding Hao's eyelids back with his fingers. He was dead, although his body was still warm. The multiple murderer planned to take the three brats to the beach and throw them in the ocean. He felt carefree. As Zhang turned to retrieve the plastic bags for the bodies, he felt a pain in his torso. He didn't understand what was happening. He felt the pain once, twice, three times, four times. He touched his back and was shocked to find blood. When he turned back, Chaoyang was holding a long knife. He recognized it as his knife, the one that Chaoyang had taken when he and Pupu discovered it lying under the maths magazines. Chaoyang watched Zhang topple over and slowly bleed to death. Finally, he too was still, his lifeless eyes staring up at the boy.

After a long time Chaoyang recovered from his shock and looked at his friends. He knelt next to Pupu and called her name. "Yuepu, Yuepu, wake up…" Too late. Chaoyang gently held her hand, feeling a trace of warmth there, which was comforting.

"Yuepu, time to get up. We need to leave, OK?" Chaoyang held her hand tightly, then stroked her fine hair. "Yuepu, please get up. Please?"

Giant tears rolled down his cheeks. Chaoyang started wailing, but Pupu did not move. She would never move again. Chaoyang leaned forward and kissed her forehead. It was the first time he had ever kissed a girl.

He looked at his friends and cried for a long time. Eventually he sniffed, got to his feet and examined his surroundings.

He pulled a tissue covered with spit and orange juice out of his pocket, then pushed it back in while he picked up the bottle of orange juice and his glass. He tossed the tissue in the toilet, then emptied the glass and the bottle into the toilet. With one flush, it disappeared. He went to the kitchen to wash them. He brought the empty glass back to his seat and filled it halfway with the poisoned soda. The broken memory card was next. It went into the empty juice bottle. He walked to the balcony, checked that nobody was around and threw the bottle as far as he could. Returning to the living room, he reached for the camera, took the original card from his backpack and inserted it into the camera.

Next, he took the knife into the bathroom and washed and wiped it thoroughly with a towel. Using the towel to avoid fingerprints, he returned to the living room and dipped the blade in Zhang Dongsheng's blood. He placed the handle first into the man's hand and then Ding Hao's, making sure to get fingerprints both times. He took the knife, using the towel again, and standing near Zhang's body, clenched his teeth and slashed his own chest and his arms. The cuts were shallow but they made bloodstains on his T-shirt. When he was finished, he threw the knife next to Ding Hao's body, dropped the towel, overturned chairs and pushed the cake to the floor.

He took a deep breath and went to open the door. It wouldn't open. Chaoyang realized the door was fitted with a new lock and remembered hearing the ka-chunk sound earlier. He needed to find that remote control. There it was, on the table. He almost grabbed it, then changed his mind at the last second. Instead he ran into the kitchen, opened the window and shouted with all his might: "Help! Help! He's going to kill us!"

73

A security guard for the apartment complex heard cries for help and scanned the windows. He spotted a kid covered in blood and immediately called the police. Other guards ran to the third floor to help Chaoyang. They couldn't open the door—it could not be opened on either side. Finally, the police broke down the door. They were shocked by the macabre scene.

The living room was a mess, the floor slick with blood. An adult male and two children were lying on the floor. The boy who had called for help was lying in the kitchen. He was covered in blood and had several injuries. He had fainted from the shock but was quickly revived. Nobody could understand what he was saying, so two officers rushed him to hospital. The others stayed behind to secure the crime scene.

A doctor examined the boy and said his injuries were not life-threatening. Chaoyang was probably in shock, but there was nothing much wrong with him. The assistants bandaged the wounds and he was kept in the hospital for observation. The police phoned his mother.

Ye Jun was out of town when he received news of a triple homicide at the Prosperity Bay Luxury Apartments. He sighed. When had Ningbo become such a hotspot for violent crime? But when he learned that the only survivor was a boy called Zhu Chaoyang, he double-checked the name carefully. Sure enough, it was the same Zhu Chaoyang, son of Zhu Yongping. It was strange that these serious cases had this young boy in common.

Ye Jun went straight to the hospital. Chaoyang was in a private room, surrounded by police officers, and looked very distressed. He had bandages on his arms and around his chest, and he was sobbing quietly when Ye Jun entered. His eyes were red and his expression was grim. An officer comforted him, offering him water.

The police were anxiously waiting for him to speak, because he was the only survivor and therefore the only person who knew what had happened in that apartment. Half an hour later, Ye Jun judged that Chaoyang was able to answer questions. "How are you feeling? We called your mother, she's on her way from the nature park. Can you tell us what happened?"

Chaoyang opened his mouth and attempted to speak. His eyes were filled with despair. "A murderer… he wanted to kill us. First he killed Pupu… I mean Yuepu… he killed her… he killed Yuepu, and then he killed Ding Hao… they're all dead…"

"But how did it happen?"

"He… he wanted to kill us."

"How did you know this man? Why did he want to kill you?"

Chaoyang hyperventilated, making himself incoherent. "We… we had a video of him killing people. He was a murderer… we knew… he wanted to silence us… with poison."

"Did you say he poisoned you?"

"He poisoned us… that's how he killed Pupu and Ding Hao."

"So the boy's name is Ding Hao and the girl's name is Pupu?"

Chaoyang nodded. "Her real name is Yuepu… everybody calls her Pupu."

"Tell me more about the video."

"We went to Sanmingshan… we … we were making a video… and in the background, you can see him pushing his parents-in-law off the mountain."

Ye Jun was shocked. He remembered Yan Liang suggested that perhaps the death of Zhang Dongsheng's in-laws was not an accident, but it seemed too far-fetched.

"Where is the video?" Ye asked urgently.

"It's in the camera. We gave it to him. It's in his house."

"Why didn't you give it to the police?"

"Because…" Chaoyang said, hesitating, "… we couldn't report it because Ding Hao and Pupu would be taken away."

"What do you mean?"

"They ran away from the orphanage. They didn't want to go back… but now… but now they're dead! I didn't want this to happen!"

Ye Jun couldn't put what Chaoyang was saying in order, but he tried to be patient. "So you had this video. How did the man find out about it?"

"We…" Chaoyang hung his head. "We were going to sell him the camera."

Ye was astonished. Why would they blackmail a murderer?

"So you brought the camera to him and he tried to kill you, so you wouldn't tell anyone?"

Chaoyang nodded.

"Tell me what happened in as much detail as possible."

Chaoyang looked scared as he recalled the morning. "He… he tried to poison all three of us, and Ding Hao and Pupu were poisoned. We realized what was happening. And we… tried to fight back. He was going to kill us. Ding Hao found a knife. I held him still with Pupu's help, and… and Ding Hao stabbed the man."

Ye Jun could not believe that after Zhang Dongsheng poisoned the kids, the tallest kid had somehow managed to summon the strength to stab him to death. It was extraordinary.

"How did he poison you? And why didn't *you* die as well?"

Chaoyang wailed before answering. "He gave us some soda— it was in the soda! Pupu and Ding Hao drank it, but I didn't. I have a book called *Home Remedies to Increase Height*. It says that carbonated drinks leach the calcium out of your body. When I remembered that, I didn't swallow the soda, and I spat it out in the bathroom. When I came back, my friends were clutching their bellies. Pupu said the soda had poison in it and the man laughed. I tried to run away but the door was locked. The man was about to finish me off when Ding Hao took out the knife. He would never go down without a fight. He stabbed the murderer to death and then my friends… my friends… they died!"

Chaoyang broke down and cried again. The police knew that the deaths had been profoundly disturbing for Chaoyang. The officer next to Ye Jun made a concerted effort to comfort him. Gradually, he calmed down.

Now he had a summary of the attack, Ye Jun felt he understood pretty well the sequence of events. He changed the subject and began, "So, Ding Hao and Pupu ran away from the orphanage?"

Chaoyang nodded.

"Which orphanage was that?"

"I don't know. It's in Beijing."

"Beijing?" Ye Jun said, surprised. "How did you meet your friends?"

Chaoyang's lip trembled as he spoke. "They were my best friends. They were my only friends."

"How did you meet your friends?" Ye repeated.

"Ding Hao was my friend in primary school. Pupu and Ding Hao had known each other so long, they were practically brother and sister. They both came to my home."

"When did they first contact you?"

"Last month."

"When exactly?"

"I dunno," Chaoyang said. "When the summer break started. I would have to check my journal."

"Journal?"

"I write in a journal every day. I can't remember now, I'm too tired. I don't want to stay here. I want to go home. Please, Uncle, I want to go home!" Chaoyang broke down again, then coughed and coughed until his face turned red. He closed his eyes, genuinely exhausted.

Ye knew that they wouldn't be able to continue the interview after the poor boy had experienced something so traumatic.

"Let the boy rest, Captain," one officer suggested. Ye nodded. He was desperate to get to the bottom of this, but he needed to wait until Chaoyang was able to speak to him.

Ye reminded the hospital staff to take good care of Chaoyang and let him sleep. He told an officer to find the journal as soon as Zhou Chunhong returned home. Hopefully, it would explain what had happened over the last two months.

74

That evening an officer came to Ye Jun's office. "Zhu Chaoyang is still sleeping at the hospital. He woke up a few times but went right back to sleep. We'll have to wait to interview him further; he's still too frightened to talk more. Zhou Chunhong, the mother, went to visit him and also helped us look for the journal at his home. We found it and we found *Home Remedies to Increase Height*." He handed them to Ye.

The book was cheaply printed and the title took up half of the cover. It was a jumble of spurious facts, clearly a gimmick. Still, Ye wasn't surprised that Chaoyang fell for it, given how short he was. Ye flipped through the thin book. Some paragraphs were underlined—Chaoyang seemed to treat it like a textbook. The tip about avoiding carbonated drinks was marked with a star.

Ye turned to the journal. The pages curled upon themselves due to the large amount of ink on almost every page. The paper looked somewhat old and the first entry was from December of the previous year. The first half of the journal was yawn-worthy, with the two main topics being studying for tests and being targeted by bullies. Some of the entries were just a few sentences long, while others were over a page. The most recent one was written just last night.

Ye Jun was uninterested in the early parts. As he searched for the first mention of Pupu and Ding Hao, Dr Chen and a high-ranking detective interrupted him.

Ye put the notebook down. "What do we know so far?"

"Zhang Dongsheng's cause of death was definitely stabbing. The knife had Ding Hao's fingerprints on it. There is no external trauma on his body or the girl's. Their cause of death was poisoning; I think it was cyanide but I will have to do further tests to confirm that. We didn't find any cyanide in the apartment. We'll comb through the apartment as soon as we can."

"Good," Ye Jun said.

"We also found a camera there, with a video that shows the three kids playing around. In the background, you can see Zhang Dongsheng. He clearly pushes two people over the wall. The report from the nature park said it was an accident, that the father-in-law must have fainted and grabbed his wife as he fell. Without the video, it would have been impossible to uncover the truth," the detective finished.

Ye Jun remembered his conversation with Yan about Xu Jing's death. It seemed much more likely now that Zhang had killed his wife too.

Dr Chen interrupted Ye's train of thought. "We found one other thing. I bet you'll never guess."

"What?"

"We found a bag of jewellery and other valuables in a closet, including a distinctive platinum necklace that belonged to Wang Yao."

"How could those be in Zhang Dongsheng's house? Did he kill them?" Ye was astounded.

"I don't know," Chen said. "Zhang doesn't appear to have any connection to the couple. The only link is Zhu Chaoyang. It's odd that he didn't report the murders, unless he took part in them. Anyway, that's your job."

Ye frowned and nodded.

"And if you think that's strange, wait till you hear this! Remember the fingerprints at the scene of Zhu Jingjing's murder that we couldn't identify? I took the initiative to check them against the fingerprints of the dead children and they match. The hair in the girl's mouth might belong to Ding Hao; we're comparing the DNA now."

Ye's face froze in shock.

"There must be a lot of things that Zhu Chaoyang hasn't told you," Chen said. "I hear he hasn't woken up yet, but I would recommend that you question him before he goes home."

Ye was still frozen. The nine murders were connected somehow. It was incredible.

"It looks like Zhang Dongsheng was prepared to snuff out the kids so they wouldn't talk," the other detective said. "The door to his apartment had a remote-controlled lock, and that explains why Zhu Chaoyang was unable to get away. We looked into the knife, which was extremely unusual. It turns out it was a gift: Xu Jing's uncle bought it for her while on holiday in Germany. Based on what we know now, the knife must have been stashed near the table as part of Zhang's backup plan. Ding Hao must have discovered it while Zhang was distracted by Chaoyang."

"We need to verify the identities of Ding Hao and Pupu. Hopefully that will clear things up," Ye said. "We should make a photocopy of the journal—it's valuable evidence."

Once Dr Chen and the detective left, Ye sat alone in his office. His instinct told him that Zhu Chaoyang had to know something about the deaths of Zhu Jingjing, Zhu Yongping and Wang Yao. He might even be connected to both cases. Ye had asked the boy about all of the deaths, but he had claimed that he knew nothing. Chaoyang had lied to him.

Did he commit patricide, then?

Ye shuddered involuntarily.

Ye took a breath and opened the journal again. He found the entry where Zhu Chaoyang first met Ding Hao and Pupu, dated 2nd July. The entry was long. After reading a few pages, his hair stood on end.

75

Two days later Ye received a surprise visit from Yan at the station. He went to reception to meet him. "Professor Yan?"

"I'm sorry to bother you," Yan said, looking sorrowful. "A family member called and said that Zhang Dongsheng was killed. Two children died as well. Are you able to share anything about this case with me?"

Ye sighed and brought Yan into his office, closed the door and poured him a cup of tea. "Professor Yan, Xu Jing and her parents were killed by Zhang Dongsheng, just like you said."

"Oh?" His voice sounded a little off; he had really been hoping that his favourite student was not a murderer.

"We have a video of Zhang Dongsheng pushing Xu Jing's parents at Sanmingshan. We still don't have physical evidence proving that he killed Xu Jing, but we have a witness statement."

Yan was quiet for a moment. "How was Zhang killed in his own home? And what did the children have to do with it?"

"It's a long story," Ye said.

"I want to know."

"It will probably be easier if you read it yourself. Zhu Chaoyang's journal explains everything. It's a photocopy though—we want to keep the original safe."

Ye passed it to Yan, then leaned back and looked out the window.

Yan started at the beginning.

Saturday 8th December 2012

*Every time I start a journal I keep it up for a few days and then stop.
Mrs Xu says that I shouldn't treat a journal like an assignment. She
says short entries are OK as long as I get into the habit of writing every
day. I want to improve my writing so I do better on the writing part
of exams. This time I'm going to stick with it. I'm going to write every
day, even if I have to stay up late. That's all for now.*

Goodnight!

Yan kept reading. Most of the entries just recounted what
had happened that day, but a few were personal. There was a
record of every single day, making it a valuable resource for the
investigation.

Chaoyang usually wrote shorter accounts whenever he was
busy, such as when he had been studying for a test. He wrote
a sentence like "It's the New Year and I don't want to write,
but I need to stay in the habit." Some of the longer entries
described how he was subjected to teasing and had to pay protection money to an older kid.

Yan realized that Zhu Chaoyang was diligent, hard-working
and very self-conscious about his height. He worried that none
of the girls in his class liked him. He liked to keep himself to
himself. He never wrote about any friends, only about people
who had been nasty to him. He lived alone with his mother, but
he only saw her every few days because her job was so far away.

Yan spent an hour and a half reading the first part of the
journal while Ye did paperwork. Prying into Chaoyang's personal
life compelled Yan to think about his own schooldays. Even
though his own experience was different, he was sure that every
adolescent had their own secrets and anxieties. Yan had been a
genius at maths, physics and chemistry when he was Chaoyang's
age. Unfortunately, in the 1980s, people dismissed bookworms.
The girls seemed to prefer boys who were interested in the arts;

so-called young intellectuals were especially popular. Yan was lonely as a teenager, like Chaoyang. Yan empathized with the boy.

Yan smiled briefly as he reminisced. He turned to the entry on 2nd July, where the entries exploded in length. His expression went from blissful to serious.

76

Tuesday 2nd July 2013

So much happened today.

Ding Hao and his sworn sister Pupu visited me out of the blue. He was my friend in primary school, but I haven't seen him for the past five years! We used to be the same height but now he's really tall. I wish I had known about Home Remedies to Increase Height *before. I will never drink soda again.*

Ding Hao asked to stay at my place for a few nights and I said yes. Then he told me the truth about why he moved away from Ningbo: his mother and father were convicted of murder! First he went back to his hometown and then he went to an orphanage in Beijing. He met Pupu at the orphanage. She's also the daughter of a murderer. They ran away and they want to stay at my place so that nobody tries to send them back.

They seemed all right at first. When I got the full story I was worried. Pupu said her father was forced to confess to a crime he never committed. She told me she wanted to take a photo of herself so she could burn it on the anniversary of her father's death.

My dad called and asked me to go see him that afternoon. I was worried that Ding Hao and Pupu might steal something while I was gone, but they left the apartment with me and said they would only stay there when I was home.

My dad and some of his friends were gambling while my dad's wife and her daughter were at the zoo. Then that bitch who married my dad, Wang Yao, showed up. She said that the camera battery was dead so they left early. I tried to hide but she spotted me. Jingjing, who gets her bitchiness from her mother, asked who I was. I couldn't believe it, but rather than explain that I was her half-brother, my dad claimed that

I was Uncle Fang's nephew. His explanation that it would negatively impact her emotional growth is utter bullshit.

Then Uncle Fang said my clothes looked tatty so my dad should take me to buy new clothes. Wang Yao shamelessly announced that she was coming with us. My dad gave me 5,000 yuan when nobody was looking and then I asked for his old camera, so I could help Pupu take those pictures for her dad. He gave it to me. At the mall, I asked for a new pair of trainers, but Jingjing screamed for attention and my dad left me to see what she wanted. He didn't pay attention to me. That little girl even spat at me! I think Wang Yao put her up to it.

I went home by myself, I couldn't spend another minute with them. I tried to hold it in, but I ended up crying on the bus. It was dumb to cry like that. Why do I even care?

Ding Hao and Pupu noticed that I had been crying and they thought that I wanted them to leave. I told them what happened. Pupu was filled with righteous anger, and she immediately nicknamed Jingjing Little Bitch. She said she would toss Little Bitch into a rubbish bin and make her cry. She even asked me where Little Bitch went to school. But I don't know where Little Bitch goes to school, so I don't think we'll ever be able to teach her a lesson.

Then we talked about the orphanage. They said they ran away because they kept getting locked into the naughty room whenever they got in trouble. Ding Hao stole the director's wallet before they left. It had 4,000 yuan in it! Just thinking about all the things they've done terrifies me.

Ding Hao told me that he's stolen a lot of things before. He used to steal things in his hometown. When he got caught, they sent him to the orphanage. At the orphanage, he stole money to play games at the internet café.

Ding Hao made a name for himself beating up the other kids. He wants to be a boss of a triad when he grows up. That's why he wrote the characters for "person" and "king" on his arm.

After Pupu's dad was executed, she went to live with her uncle,

294

but she got in a fight with a classmate who said mean things about her dad. She hit her classmate, and then on the same day that classmate was found dead in a reservoir. Everyone blamed Pupu and the police arrested her. They eventually let her go due to a lack of evidence. The classmate's family kicked up a fuss and Pupu's aunt didn't want to take care of her any longer. So she went to the orphanage.

I got really angry when she told me that story. The way the adults treated her was so unfair.

Then she smiled and I asked her what was so funny. She said she was the one who pushed the girl, and that girl deserved what she got.

I was scared out of my skin! How could someone as sweet as Pupu kill someone? She could read my mind because she promised me that she would never hurt me. She said she and Ding Hao would protect me from bullies.

Maybe she was too young to understand that pushing her classmate into a reservoir would lead to her death. Pupu has had a tough life. As her friend, I am going to keep her secret.

They're both asleep in my room while I'm writing this. I'm sleeping in my mum's room to keep an eye on the money from my dad. I really want someone to talk to, so I'll pretend that they're my real friends. I just hope they don't steal anything from me or my mum!

Yan closed his eyes after reading this entry, when the introverted Chaoyang was accosted by these troubled youths.

According to the journal, the Ding Hao character committed petty crime on a semi-regular basis. He aspired to be the boss of a crime ring, of all things! Then there was the little girl who had pushed her classmate in a reservoir just because of an argument. Yan was shocked to think of the little girl being investigated and not admitting to what happened. What caused her to think like that?

Their difficult upbringing undoubtedly caused them to spiral. Stealing, fighting, tattoos, pushing classmates into reservoirs and running away from the orphanage—it was one bad thing after another. Then they met Chaoyang, a vulnerable child who was used to being bullied. Yan was genuinely worried for Chaoyang as he turned to the next entry.

77

Wednesday 3rd July 2013

I'm afraid. I don't know what to do or who to talk to.

I took Ding Hao and Pupu to Sanmingshan to take some photos and we made a video for fun. Then an old couple had an accident. Someone had screamed for help, but it was too late.

We went home and later when we connected the camera to the computer, we noticed a shocking detail in the video. The old couple didn't have an accident. They were pushed by the man who screamed for help!

I called the police as soon as I saw the video. I started to explain the situation when Pupu disconnected the call. She said we couldn't report that man to the police, because they would ask questions about her and Ding Hao. Then they would have to go back to the orphanage. The police called back and Pupu told them we called the number by mistake. They shouted at us.

Someone's life was taken away. How can we not report it?

I'm going to report the murder as soon as my friends leave. But I'm worried that if the police send them back to the orphanage, they'll hold a grudge against me. Would they seek revenge on me? I know that Ding Hao would hold a grudge.

Pupu came up with the crazy idea to look for the murderer. She wants to sell the camera to him. It would be blackmail, but Pupu and Ding Hao have no money and everyone needs money to live. She had noticed that the murderer was driving a BMW and thought that he was probably rich. She even said she would share part of the money with me.

I told her I didn't want anything to do with it. I've never broken any rules, not even rules at school. Why would I blackmail someone? I refused, but Ding Hao said he wanted to do it.

I tried to convince them not to do it, but they didn't listen.

That evening I went to the bookstore with Ding Hao and Pupu. My dad was there with Jingjing. He pretended not to see me, which made me incredibly angry. Pupu noticed and said as long as I agreed to sell the camera, she and Ding Hao would get revenge for me by beating Jingjing up. I refused.

I'm exhausted. Having two children of murderers as guests is terrifying. I definitely regret my hospitality, I can tell you that.

I don't know what to do. I'm afraid that Ding Hao will hurt me if I try to contact the police. If we don't report it, will I have to keep this camera for the rest of my life? I don't want to blackmail anyone. I don't want to commit crimes.

After finishing the entry, Yan sighed.

The writing style was a little childish and unrefined, but he could still tell that Chaoyang was in a difficult situation. He was a good student, and he was naturally inclined to contact the police when he saw evidence of a murder. The two orphans refused to report the evidence because they did not want to go back to the orphanage. That was understandable to Yan. Still, the fact that they decided to blackmail a murderer seemed too wicked for such young children's minds. Yan turned the page.

78

Today was the worst day ever.

I was worried they would talk about blackmail again so I took them to the Children's Palace to help everyone relax.

Pupu saw Jingjing when we arrived. She said she would help me get revenge after Jingjing spat on me and my own dad ignored me. I said it was a bad idea because there were too many people. If someone saw me and told my dad I would get in big trouble.

Ding Hao said they would take care of it and I could watch from a safe distance.

They went in first and I waited because I was afraid that Little Bitch would see me. Pupu discovered that she was studying calligraphy, so she went to the fifth floor and told me to wait by the stairs. Pupu and Ding Hao waited outside the toilets to see if Little Bitch would come out by herself. If she did, they would beat her up. I was worried that she would be seriously hurt, but Ding Hao promised me nothing bad would happen.

Of course something awful happened. A few minutes after Little Bitch was pulled into the toilets, Pupu and Ding Hao came running. They said Little Bitch fell out of the window.

They only told me the truth later. They pushed Little Bitch into the men's toilets and when Little Bitch spat on them Ding Hao was so angry he pulled out some hair from down there and stuffed it in her mouth. She was so disgusted that she stopped screaming for a while, but then she bit him. That's when Ding Hao pushed her out of the window.

I told him off and he said he regretted it. Pupu said there was no point blaming anyone. She was certain that nobody would find out.

She told me to check if Little Bitch had died from her fall and give the all-clear signal if she was dead.

I couldn't push through the crowd around Little Bitch but they could see that she was dead because they were watching the scene from the first-floor window. So I left the Children's Palace then and the two of them left after me.

None of us said anything that night. I was scared, even though it wasn't my fault. Would people think that I told them to do it? I never wanted her to die, I just wanted her to cry. But I didn't think anyone would believe that story. If my dad found out he would never speak to me again.

Pupu said she and Ding Hao would try to get money from that man and then leave Ningbo as soon as possible. I thought about it for a long time. At the time, Pupu's plan seemed like the only option. If they were caught, it would be impossible to explain what had happened. But how would we find that murderer?

I feel terrible.

Yan's heart sank. They had only planned to hit her until she cried, but then the situation spun out of control. Suddenly the children had a death on their hands. It did not seem that the three meant to kill little Jingjing, but the thought of the vile tactics Ding Hao used to stop her from screaming made Yan extremely uncomfortable. Because Jingjing fought back and bit Ding Hao, he pushed her out of the window. How did he become so violent? Was he accustomed to using violence to get his way?

Yan could understand Chaoyang's worry, since he had brought them to the Children's Palace. Neither the police nor his father would believe that their intention was to simply make Jingjing cry.

Reading between the lines, Yan saw that Chaoyang was deprived of love from his father. Time and time again, his hopes were shattered. Naturally, Chaoyang was fearful that his father would find out about his involvement in Jingjing's death. Although the two things were indirectly related, Yan felt that his craving for love from his father led to his fear of being blamed for the girl's death.

Yan felt a creeping sense of dread—what would he find next?

79

Friday 5th July 2013

We know the murderer is from Ningbo because of his licence plate. But Ningbo is huge, how will we find him?

We don't have a solution. My mum is coming back from work in a few days, so we need to hurry. This is so frustrating! What if Ding Hao and Pupu are arrested?

Saturday 6th July 2013

We found the murderer but I don't know if this is good news or bad news.

We happened to run across him at a supermarket. I didn't remember what he looked like but Pupu did. He was about to leave in his car so Pupu stopped him by saying she saw him kill someone. The murderer glared at her. I was afraid, but Ding Hao said he had my back. The murderer didn't attack us, he just tried to leave. When Pupu threatened to give the video to the police, he glared at us again. Ding Hao and Pupu made me go home and get the camera.

The murderer watched the video and his face turned green. He said we needed to talk someplace else. Before we got in his car, Pupu made me take the camera home again. She said if the murderer didn't have the camera he wouldn't try to kill us.

The man took us to a café. Pupu explained that she would sell the camera with the video to him. The murderer asked how much, but Ding Hao and Pupu had not decided how much they wanted. The three of us discussed it away from the murderer. Ding Hao said he wanted 30,000 yuan. Pupu asked me how much money she would need to live on her own for the next five years, including rent, and I said 100,000. So she decided she wanted 300,000. I said it was too much and the murderer would never agree. But she was stubborn. She said he would pay because it was a life-or-death situation for him.

Pupu asked for 300,000 and the murderer got really angry. I was scared, but Pupu and Ding Hao weren't. Sure enough, he agreed to the price, but he said we would have to wait a few days before we got the money. He gave us his phone number.

When we left Pupu made us run fast, because she didn't want the murderer to follow us. Ding Hao bragged that he would beat that man in a fight. Pupu said that the murderer would probably have a knife, and then Ding Hao would lose the fight. I thought the deal we made might be dangerous and Pupu agreed. But she said the murderer wouldn't hurt us as long as we kept the camera away from him. So we decided that we would always leave one person at my house so that if something happened at the murderer's house, we could still contact the police.

The plan might work, but I'm not sure.

Sunday 7th July 2013

Pupu decided that Ding Hao should stay at home because he's tough but dumb. He attacks people without thinking.

She's totally right. If he hadn't been so hot-headed at the Children's Palace, Jingjing would still be alive. I'm worried that they'll get arrested, but I'm even more worried that my dad will find out. If he does, he will hate me forever. I hope everything goes smoothly tomorrow and that they leave Ningbo as soon as they get the money.

Pupu's so smart. She knows how to prevent the murderer from hurting us. She has a plan for everything. She's really nice to me, too.

At least now I have two friends I can depend on.

Monday 8th July 2013

Pupu and I went to the murderer's house today. Pupu said that we shouldn't bring the camera this time because he would probably try to play a trick on us. He said he didn't have the money. He's so devious, telling us to bring the camera when he didn't have money for us.

He clearly is rich but he says that his wife and her family have control of the money. He told us to wait until he could get the money.

Pupu asked why he wanted us to bring the camera when he didn't even have the money. He said we might not keep the camera safe. He's trying to outsmart us.

Pupu wanted part of the money now but the murderer said we might spend it all at once and attract attention. Then she said she needed to rent a house, and the man agreed to let her and Ding Hao stay in his other apartment.

Pupu agreed. She told me to keep the camera safe so that she and Ding Hao wouldn't get in trouble. She really thinks of everything.

Now Pupu and Ding Hao are living in an apartment owned by a murderer and I'm all by myself. I hope nothing bad happens to them!

Tuesday 9th July 2013

The police came to my house today. They asked about Little Bitch. They knew that I arrived at the Children's Palace after she did.

I didn't know what to say. Pupu instructed me not to tell the police anything, otherwise Pupu and Ding Hao would be arrested. The police were intimidating but I was mainly afraid of my dad and what he would do if he found out I was involved in Jingjing's death.

I lied to the police and said that I went to the Children's Palace to read. I said I had only met her once before and I didn't see her when I went to the Children's Palace.

I'm not sure if they believed me. They took a blood sample and fingerprints. When my mum came home, she argued with the police. I feel really bad for my mum, she's really upset.

If I could turn back the clock, I would never have gone to the Children's Palace.

Pupu came looking for me that afternoon. She told me that as long as I didn't confess the police wouldn't find out who did it. She said she wouldn't come to my house any more, just to be on the safe side. We decided to meet in the afternoons at Xinhua Bookstore.

Wednesday 10th July 2013

Big Bitch came to our house. She attacked my mum and hurt her badly. Later that day, my dad slapped my mum. When I grow up, I'll make them pay for what they did!

My dad's wife said she was going to kill me. I'd like to see her try.

Thursday 11th July 2013

When Ding Hao and Pupu found out that Big Bitch injured my mother, he said he would get revenge for me. They would beat her up and then run off and I wouldn't have to do anything. Of course, I would love for her to pay for what she did to my mother, but if Ding Hao got arrested for beating her up, the police would find out about what happened to Jingjing. So I told him not to do anything.

Pupu thought Ding Hao's idea was risky too. She asked me if Big Bitch knows that I was involved in Jingjing's death. I don't know how much Big Bitch knows, but I think she suspects that I'm involved.

Pupu says that if Big Bitch keeps harassing me, maybe they should make her pay in a permanent way. Pupu asked me if I would be happy if Big Bitch died. I was scared and asked her what she wanted to do. She said it was possible that Big Bitch would actually hire someone to follow me, and that would put her and Ding Hao at risk. She didn't want the police to send her back to the orphanage, but she said that she read one of my books that said the age of criminal responsibility is 14. Pupu and Ding Hao are both under 14, so they wouldn't go to prison for their crimes.

I told her she had to stop thinking such crazy ideas. I said I wouldn't tell anyone about what happened to Jingjing. Then Pupu said she was just joking. I think she was serious, but it's OK because I don't think Pupu or Ding Hao have what it takes to kill an adult.

Pupu told me that the murderer said he was going on a trip. So the camera deal is being pushed back again.

Yan turned the page to the next entries and quickly realized that nothing important happened for several days. Chaoyang recorded that he met Pupu at the bookstore every day, listed the books that he read and what he talked about. These accounts were short and trivial.

Chaoyang had revealed his innermost feelings in his journal. Yan could see that he really cared for Pupu, which is why he spent so much time writing about her. He would even note down what books she had read. Apparently Chaoyang never told her he liked her because he was afraid she liked Ding Hao. He never told anyone his feelings about Pupu.

Things picked up again on 27th July and Yan read on.

80

Saturday 27th July 2013

Big Bitch is a slut! She's the worst person ever!

She paid someone to attack me with a washbasin full of shit. The same people attacked my mum while she was at work. They even painted threatening messages outside our apartment. Captain Ye took me to the seafood factory so I could watch her get arrested. But my dad thought protecting her was more important than anything. Even when everyone around him told him to stop being an idiot, he protected her! He said he would give me 10,000 and told me to drop the charges. My dad gave me hush money.

Big Bitch means the world to him and I'm worth exactly 10,000 yuan.

I hate them! I hate them more than anything!

Wednesday 31st July 2013

Ding Hao came to the bookstore today instead of Pupu. He said he saw the murderer on TV. His wife had just died, and the news called it a sudden death. Technically the murderer was far away, but Pupu still thinks he was responsible for his wife's death. Pupu said she would ask the murderer how he did it when he got back, but I didn't want her to take that risk, so I went to his apartment and asked him instead.

The murderer kept saying his wife's death was an accident. Then someone came to visit and he got really nervous, so he told me to pretend to be his student. I refused unless he told me what happened to his wife. So he told me that he poisoned her. He put the poison in a mini capsule and put it inside one of the capsules of beauty supplements that his wife took every day. That's why she died later on in the car.

Pupu says as long as we have the camera and the three of us don't visit his apartment at the same time, he won't hurt us. She smiled at me and I quickly asked her if she likes Ding Hao or not. She said Ding Hao was like a brother to her. Then she said she likes smart people.

I wonder if she thinks I'm a smart person.

Eventually I told her about Big Bitch's latest attack. She asked me what I wanted to do and I said I wanted to see how she liked being splashed with shit. Pupu said she would think of something.

Over the next few days, nothing important happened, as Yan skimmed the early August entries.

Tuesday 6th August 2013

My dad suspects me.

He came to my house and he gave me 5,000 yuan in the street outside. He said he would try and be a better dad and I almost believed him. Then he asked about Jingjing and whether I followed her into the Children's Palace. I said no.

Big Bitch jumped out of their SUV, taking me by surprise. She took my dad's phone and played back a recording. It was the conversation I just had with my dad. They were trying to get me to confess!

Big Bitch said she knew I was involved in her daughter's death somehow. She said she would pay someone to follow me until she had her answer.

This is unbearable. I don't know if it will end.

I don't want a dad like this. I'm officially disowning him.

Wednesday 7th August 2013

I told Pupu about the visit from my dad and Big Bitch. She's worried that Big Bitch will actually pay someone to investigate me. If they learn about Pupu and Ding Hao, we'll all be in trouble.

When she asked me if I still loved my dad despite what he had done, I said no. I told her he wasn't my dad any more. Big Bitch has made my life miserable and he always takes her side. I just want to splash them with shit so they know how it feels.

Pupu said she would take revenge for me.

Thursday 8th August 2013

I don't want to visit my grandparents, but my mum says just because my dad doesn't know how to be a dad, doesn't mean I can't be a good grandson. So I went. Grandpa has been sick for a really long time and everyone says he doesn't have long to live. Grandpa has always been nice to me. Grandma is getting older too, so I hope I'll be able to keep visiting her when school starts.

Grandma says that my dad has done some terrible things but he is in a bad place. Grandma says dad and Big Bitch are going to visit Jingjing's grave on Wednesday and after that they will try to move on from her death. I think my dad will treat me better because I'll be his only child again. I'm not going to hold my breath though, because Dad has disappointed me too many times already.

I spoke to Pupu and told her everything Grandma had told me. Pupu thinks that even if my dad wants to be nice to me again, Big Bitch will never let him. She's probably right.

She asked me which cemetery they will be going to, saying that there wouldn't be many people there so she and Ding Hao could attack Big Bitch when she goes to Jingjing's grave. I really want to get revenge on Big Bitch, but I'm worried that Ding Hao will get arrested. Pupu said it would be fine, Ding Hao is faster than the average cop.

I hope the splashing goes well!

The next few entries were again short, and not of interest, so Yan concentrated on the one dated the 14th of August. It was so unexpected that his glasses tumbled off his face.

Wednesday 14th August 2013

Big Bitch is dead and so is my dad! They really messed up this time!
I was on my way home from evening independent study when I saw
Pupu in the street. She said they both died. I asked why they didn't
follow the plan we had agreed!

She apologized and said she was lying when she told me that
plan. She said if she told me the truth, I would convince them not
to do it. She was really worried that Big Bitch would pay someone
to investigate me. Killing Big Bitch was the only option in her mind.
I don't know how she persuaded him to do it, but she even got the
murderer to poison Big Bitch! Pupu only wanted to kill Big Bitch,
but the murderer killed my dad too. He said otherwise we would all
get caught.

How could they do this? I never wanted this to happen! I was
disappointed by my dad, but he's still my dad after all. I don't know if
I should report them to the police. I don't want to get Pupu in trouble.
I feel awful.

I think the murderer has found a way to threaten us. Now that
Pupu and Ding Hao were involved in killing people, the camera is not
so dangerous to him. I hate him! I hate myself too. Why did we ever
approach the murderer in the first place?

The next few entries recorded Chaoyang's inner turmoil, so Yan
skipped to the 18th.

Sunday 18th August 2013

I asked Pupu where my dad and Big Bitch were buried and went to
see them.

I don't know how to describe my feelings. I desperately wanted her
to suffer, but I never ever wanted my father to die.

How could everything end this way? What's going to happen to me?
How am I going to keep living after all this has happened?

Someone will find them eventually, won't they? What will happen when someone discovers them buried like this?

I'm worried. Not just for myself, but for Ding Hao and Pupu.

I kneeled at their tombs and hoped that my father would forgive me. This is not what I wanted.

Wednesday 21st August 2013

Somebody finally found Dad and Big Bitch. The police are going to question me any day now. Should I tell them the truth? Should I tell them what Pupu taught me to say? She said that I had an alibi because I was in class.

I don't want to keep lying like this. But if I tell the police what really happened, Pupu and Ding Hao will be taken away. I don't want to get them in trouble.

What should I do?

Saturday 24th August 2013

Pupu visited me last night. She said it was time to give the camera back to the murderer. But she didn't call him the murderer, she called him Uncle Zhang. She says he's not really that bad after all.

Uncle Zhang is going to sell the extra apartment to pay for a hukou *registration for Pupu and Ding Hao. That would mean they could go to school and start a new life in Ningbo. They're now living in the spare room of his apartment.*

What about me? Can I start a new life?

I hope that everything settles down soon.

I promised to go to his apartment in a few days. We all agreed that we won't talk about this ever again.

Tuesday 27th August 2013

Tomorrow I'm going to give the camera to Uncle Zhang. I am on edge. I really want to get rid of that camera.

The police aren't asking me any more questions, and things are almost back to normal. Tomorrow, after I give him that camera, I'll be able to start a new life.

The school year is about to start. We'll get a fresh start.

I want to be a new person.

81

It took three hours to read the entire journal. After Yan finished the last page, he closed his eyes. The harrowing account left him with a pain in his chest.

Ye said, "I bet you never would have guessed at that backstory to the three kids and Zhang Dongsheng," Ye said.

Yan nodded in agreement. "How did Zhang die?"

"When Chaoyang took the camera to him, all of the kids were in the same place with the camera. That was the 28th August."

"So Zhang would have been able to silence all of them and destroy the evidence," Yan commented.

"Chaoyang was the only survivor and he was unable to get away because of the lock on the door. It had been recently installed, suggesting that Zhang was just waiting for the right moment to act. He wanted to make sure nobody escaped." Ye continued, "When Chaoyang finally calmed down, he told us that Zhang asked him several times if they made a copy of the video. Then he brought out a cake for everyone to enjoy. He poured soda for the kids and a glass of wine for himself. The poison was in the soda. Potassium cyanide. Chaoyang said Zhang had told him that he used the same poison to kill his wife. So we have now done in-depth autopsies of Zhu Yongping and Wang Yao. Potassium cyanide poisoning was the cause of death for both. We never suspected poisoning because of all the knife wounds. Zhang must have done that to mislead us."

Yan was pained to learn that Zhang had used his brilliance to commit such wicked deeds. He had committed so many murders and hoodwinked the police multiple times! It was incredible.

Yan had another important question. "Why didn't Chaoyang die of poisoning?"

"He briefly forgot that he was never going to drink soda again. He had read a book called *Home Remedies to Increase Height*, and underlined it throughout. Who would have thought that a crummy little book like that would save his life! He took a sip, remembered that he wasn't supposed to drink soda and went to spit it out in the bathroom. By the time he returned, the poison was already acting on Ding Hao and Pupu, and it was clear that Zhang was very dangerous. Chaoyang tried to run away but the man came after him. Ding Hao used the last of his strength to stab Zhang with a knife. He wouldn't have gone down without a fight, but it was three against one, with Pupu and Chaoyang preventing Zhang from fighting back. Chaoyang's chest and arms were cut but they weren't too deep. It's crazy: if Chaoyang had died, we would have never learned the truth."

"It's ironic that Zhang had been so careful for the other murders, but he was thwarted by three children," Yan agreed.

"Potassium cyanide is fast-acting but some people get a burst of adrenaline right before they die. I don't think he ever suspected that Ding Hao would try to take him down."

"What are you going to do about Chaoyang now that you have the journal?" Yan asked.

"That hasn't been decided yet," Ye said. "We had a meeting with the Ningbo Public Security Bureau. Director Ma, the top city official at the meeting, believes in education and rehabilitation. Zhu Chaoyang was not directly involved in any of the deaths, even though he perverted the course of justice. The boy had told the police at the time that he did not know anything about his half-sister's death, but he was protecting Ding Hao and Xia Yuepu, aka Pupu. Given the circumstances, his behaviour is understandable. Then when Zhu Yongping and Wang Yao died, he was too afraid to go to the police. He's an excellent student and he doesn't have any prior convictions. It seems he was simply mixing with the wrong crowd, and was overly influenced.

Ding Hao was a petty criminal and Xia Yuepu was devious. Also Director Ma has confirmed that perverting the course of justice only applies to people over the age of sixteen, and Chaoyang is thirteen. Given his age, we probably won't charge him with anything."

Yan nodded. The laws had not changed since he was a cop.

"Typically, the family is expected to educate and monitor the child. In more serious cases, the child is sent to a juvenile rehabilitation centre. Nobody thinks Chaoyang should be sent there—he would be thrown in with another wrong crowd. I'm liaising with Zhou Chunhong and the school about the education part. He will need therapy, but we're hoping that he can still attend school as normal. This is all confidential of course—we don't want this to affect his future."

Yan nodded again, relieved. "Your job isn't just to catch the bad guys, but to save the people who might otherwise choose the wrong path. It's good that you're helping Chaoyang rather than condemning him." He stood to leave. "I should probably go. Thank you for explaining what happened to Zhang Dongsheng, I know you made an exception for me, but he was a close former student. You have a lot of work to do, don't you?"

Ye gave a bitter smile. "That's just the way it is when we get so many cases back to back. The Xu family cases were chalked up as accidents, but we have had to reopen the files. Zhu Yongping and Wang Yao's deaths became a sensation after that big group discovered the bodies, so their case is high priority. Then we have the follow-up with Chaoyang."

"That will keep you busy for a good while," Yan commiserated sympathetically. But just as he was about to leave, he registered what Ye had just said. "Hang on, you said a large group of people discovered the two bodies?"

"That's right," Ye said.

"What happened exactly?"

"The mourners had been at the cemetery for half an hour, and some got bored and walked along the new part when one person saw half of a foot sticking out of a tomb."

"Half of a foot, sticking out of a tomb?" Yan repeated.

"Yeah, it was Zhu Yongping's foot. The tombs were designed for cremated remains, so are small. It's not surprising that a foot was pushed out."

"Impossible," Yan said. "It would be in Zhang's best interest to hide the bodies carefully; he would never be so careless."

"But that's how it was."

"May I see the crime scene photographs?"

Ye located the case file and handed it to Yan.

"There's something wrong here," Yan said, flipping through the photos.

"What? What's wrong?"

"There are slashes on both faces, right?"

"Yeah, Zhang Dongsheng must have done that."

"And their clothing and valuables were missing?"

"Yeah. We found them in Zhang's apartment—"

"Why do you think he took all their possessions and cut up their faces?" Yan asked, taking on the role of the criminal logic professor once more.

"He wanted to make it difficult for us to investigate. If we couldn't identify the victims, it would take ages to solve the case," Ye responded promptly, a good student.

"Exactly. Even if you discovered the bodies, you wouldn't be able to identify them. But if he took the time to do that, why wouldn't he check that the bodies were properly buried? Wouldn't it be a waste of time to do all the rest if he left a foot close to the surface? Every other crime he committed was flawless."

"Maybe he was in a rush at the end," Ye suggested.

"Zhang would have planned every last detail of their disposal. He would never do a sloppy job, he was extremely logical and thorough."

316

"Maybe the rain washed the surrounding soil away. We might have had a few thunderstorms around that time," Ye said.

"But there wasn't that much rain," Yan said, as he knew it had rained little in Zhejiang in the months of July and August.

"That's true..."

"Nothing could have washed that much dirt away except for a huge storm."

"Professor Yan, what is your point?"

"Maybe somebody dug it out," Yan said.

"Who would do that? What are you trying to say?" Ye asked, perplexed.

Yan paced the office, his voice soft. "Everything we know about these cases comes from one source: Zhu Chaoyang."

"Do you think he is lying?"

"I don't want to jump to conclusions either way," Yan answered.

"He's just a middle school student! He couldn't lie so successfully to that many cops," Ye said.

"He's lied before," Yan countered.

They were both quiet for a moment.

"Did you ever check the facts in his statement and his journal?" Yan asked.

"Yes! We've checked everything that we could." Ye pulled out a thick stack of files. "We contacted the orphanage director, who confirmed that Ding Hao had stolen money to play games. He got into fights and made a bit of a name for himself. He had a crude tattoo on his left forearm, just like the journal said. He arrived at the orphanage after stealing from a shop. Xia Yuepu was the brains behind Ding Hao's brawn. Apparently she didn't boast and was quite quiet, so people didn't realize how wicked she was. Ding Hao protected her from bullies. Eventually they became isolated from the others. The director thinks they ran away because they were punished so frequently. They stole the director's wallet before they left."

"So you think the portrayals of Xia Yuepu and Ding Hao are accurate?"

Ye nodded. "If you ask me, Ding Hao could probably have learned to control his aggression as he matured, but Xia Yuepu was genuinely dangerous. We spoke to the police from her hometown. They said she pushed a child into a reservoir but never admitted to it. They let her go due to lack of evidence and her age."

"What else did you check?"

"We know that Zhu Yongping was playing cards with the bosses of the other seafood businesses on 2nd July, and that when Wang Yao and her daughter arrived at the office, Zhu Yongping made Zhu Chaoyang call him Uncle rather than acknowledge him as his son. This would have a profound impact on a young child. We went through the call logs to the police on 3rd July and heard Chaoyang say a few words before the call dropped off. The operator returned the call, and Xia Yuepu answered. She said that they called by accident.

"Xia Yuepu's and Ding Hao's fingerprints were in the men's toilets where Zhu Jingjing was attacked when we compared the prints after their deaths," Ye continued. "The hair in the little girl's mouth was a match for Ding Hao's pubic hair. I was the attending officer both times when Wang Yao attacked Chaoyang and his mother. I know that everything that he said then actually happened."

"Have you checked the times where possible?" Yan asked hesitantly.

"Yes, and they match. We even checked the Xinhua Bookstore CCTV, so we could see when Yuepu met with Chaoyang," Ye said.

Ye continued to load Yan with facts. "We combed through Zhang Dongsheng's apartment and finally found the poison he used in a small plastic bag, which was inside a container of bathroom cleaning powder. He might have bought the chemicals on the black market or synthesized it himself. As a teacher, he would have access to the school lab."

"What about that knife? Did it belong to Zhang?" Yan asked suddenly.

"We checked the knife!" Ye said, losing his patience.

"I see," Yan said quietly.

"Professor Yan, what do you think happened?"

Yan was hesitant again. "I firmly believe that Zhang Dongsheng would not have made such a basic mistake at the cemetery."

"So what you're saying is…" Ye said.

"You're not going to like this, but I think that Chaoyang must have dug out the foot."

"I remember he said that he visited the cemetery on the Sunday after they died. Perhaps he wanted to see the body so he dug it out a little bit and then covered it back up but one foot wasn't buried deep enough."

"He mentions visiting the grave but he never says anything about moving the soil or the body," Yan retorted.

"For goodness' sake, it's just a journal! He's not going to write every last detail down."

"Do you know if he is at home?" Yan persisted.

"He went home yesterday."

"Could you call him for me?"

"What are you going to ask him?" Ye was wary.

"Just one question. I want to know if he moved the dirt by his father's grave."

"Is it that important?" Ye asked.

"Of course it's important!" Yan shouted.

82

Ye dialled Zhu Chaoyang's home and switched to speaker-phone. Zhou Chunhong answered. Ye asked for Chaoyang, and when he answered, Ye asked Yan's question. The line was quiet. "I moved the dirt and I saw a foot… and I was afraid," the boy finally said.

"Why did you want to move the dirt?" Yan said, leaning towards the telephone.

"I wanted to see him."

"Why did you go to the cemetery on that day?" Yan asked.

"I… I wanted to see my dad… one last time," Chaoyang said.

"What was your *other* reason for going there?"

Yan's tone was menacing and Ye gave him a look that said *that's not how you speak to a child suffering from trauma.*

The line was quiet again. "I didn't… I didn't have any other reason, I just wanted to see him," Chaoyang burst into tears. Zhou came to the phone explaining that her son was still upset and it would probably be easier to answer questions in person. Ye apologized for distressing her son, and after hanging up, gave Yan a reproachful look.

Yan looked chastened but unbowed. "His answers were perfect. There's no reason to suspect Chaoyang."

"Tell me, what were you thinking he did?" Ye demanded.

"This is going to sound despicable, too despicable for a child to come up with. But in the final analysis, who benefits the most from all these deaths?"

"Well, who?"

"Zhu Chaoyang!" Yan exclaimed. "He is bound to inherit a large share of Zhu Yongping's fortune."

"But Zhu Chaoyang didn't kill him. He never wanted his father to die."

"Let's ignore the emotional side of things for just a moment. Financially speaking, he would benefit the most from his father's death."

"What the hell does that have to do with the foot?"

"If the foot wasn't visible to a passer-by, those bodies would have gone months without being noticed. Do you agree?" Yan asked.

"There aren't that many visitors to the cemetery. They might not have been discovered until one of the new tombs was put into use."

"Zhu Yongping and his wife would just have been listed as missing. Without a death certificate, Chaoyang wouldn't get his inheritance. The factory would keep operating and the Wang family would probably have taken over. None of the assets would have gone to Chaoyang."

Ye was unconvinced.

"Chaoyang had to move the dirt so someone would discover the bodies and he could get a death certificate! That way he would have access to his father's estate!" Yan concluded.

"That's absurd! He's just a little kid!" Ye said.

"It is a hypothesis." Yan shrugged. "We can never know what a person is really thinking, can we?"

"So what if he had those ideas? Everyone is greedy. If his father died, he couldn't change that fact."

"If he had those ideas, everything you think you know about this case is wrong," Yan said emphatically.

"I don't understand," Ye said.

"If Chaoyang deliberately exposed his father's foot so it would be discovered, this would not be a simple case of perverting the course of justice. We couldn't be sure if Yuepu orchestrated the murder—or if Chaoyang did. We would have to re-evaluate our assumptions."

321

"But he went to the cemetery *after* he found out that his parents were killed. He didn't think about his father's fortune before he was killed."

"Journals are personal, the writer does not have any reason to hide anything about themselves. We can expect the writer to record the things that are extremely important to them. If he exposed the foot to get his inheritance but he never wrote that down, then we can conclude that the journal does not reveal all of his thoughts. That suggests that Chaoyang did not write the journal for himself, but you, the police."

Ye stared at Yan.

"There are two things that I find suspicious about the journal," Yan said, warming to the topic. "First, it is too detailed. I gained a full picture of the past six months by reading it once. Things were recorded that Chaoyang would not need to explain to himself. Why would he explain who Ding Hao or Wang Yao was? Second, he went into detail about rather mundane days, but on the day when his father's body was discovered, he only wrote a few sentences. He wrote just a single sentence about the division of his father's assets. That would have been the most important thing in his life for those days, but he barely says anything."

"Perhaps he was traumatized by the news of his father's death and he didn't want to write about it?" Ye proposed.

"Yes, but there are other things he is hiding. I imagine that the Zhu family has taken steps to control more of the assets than they are entitled to. Why did he not write about that? I hesitate to say this, but I think if he wrote what really happened, the authorities would know that the estate was not being divided appropriately." Yan took a breath and continued. "There are two other things that do not add up. First, nine people died who were all connected to Zhu Chaoyang. Somehow, none of their murders is *directly* connected to him. Second, right at the moment when Zhang would have realized his plans, he was stabbed to death by a boy he had poisoned. That might be

322

possible in your eyes, but I knew Zhang Dongsheng. It boggles the mind that he would fail to anticipate something like his own knife being used against him."

"So you think Chaoyang wrote the whole journal in advance and left it for the police to read?"

"It's my hypothesis. So many people have died that we are forced to rely on his version of events."

Ye flipped through the copy of the journal, shaking his head. "He couldn't have made all this up, there's too much detail. Plus, there are parts that talk about Chaoyang's inner emotions."

Yan agreed with Ye that there were too many small nuances for it to be completely fabricated.

That settled it for Ye. "You might have your suspicions but that's not evidence. He would have to be a clairvoyant to make this up. He'd have to know Zhang would poison them, know that it would be in the soda, know that Ding Hao would try to stab Zhang and know that Ding Hao and Xia Yuepu would die, so he would be the only one left. Zhang wouldn't have told Chaoyang where the poison was, would he?"

"You're right," Yan said. "Zhang wouldn't tell any of them that poison would be in the soda. Logically speaking, I have no reason to suspect Chaoyang any more."

Ye breathed a sigh of relief. The thought that the journal might have been written especially for the police scared him. How could a thirteen-year-old plan something so wicked?

"Have you returned the journal to him?" Yan asked.

"No, it's kept here at the station, in the evidence room. He agreed to let us keep it."

"Mind if I take a look?"

"Isn't it the same as the copy you just read?"

Yan smiled an endearingly awkward smile. "I just want to examine the original."

"Fine," Ye said. He made a quick phone call and a junior officer brought the journal and waited.

Yan studied the document carefully. The pages looked old and were so full of ink that they puffed out slightly. The spelling mistakes and ink smudges were exactly the same as in the copy. Yan turned casually and raised his voice to cover up a small sound he was about to make. "Chaoyang must be an extremely diligent student to keep up this habit for so many months. This must be at least twenty thousand characters long!"

"He's the best in his class and the entire school. He is the most disciplined student I've ever met."

"OK, that's all I wanted to see. Thank you," Yan said, handing the book back to the other officer.

The junior officer took the journal and trembled with panic. "Aiya, where did the rest of this page go?" He had turned to the second page, where a corner of the page was missing.

"It was like that when I examined it," Yan said.

"You ripped it when you came up here!" Ye bellowed. "How can you be so careless? Don't ever let me catch you doing something like that again or you'll pay for it!"

The humiliated officer gingerly stepped out of the office. Yan felt a tiny bit guilty. "I have one more favour to ask. Can I speak with Chaoyang face to face?"

"What do you want to talk about?" Ye asked warily.

"I won't be so aggressive this time, I promise. You can join us, if you like."

83

1 SEPTEMBER

Chaoyang and his mother came to the police station. Since this was not a formal interrogation, Zhou waited in an empty meeting room while Yan asked the boy some questions.

"Hi, Uncle Ye," Chaoyang said politely.

Ye smiled and poured a glass of water for him. It was clear that he liked the boy very much. Chaoyang looked closely at Yan and seemed to remember him. "You teach mathematics, right?"

"Yes. We've met before," he said kindly. "I am sorry for your loss."

Yan explained that he had gone to visit Zhang Dongsheng when Chaoyang happened to be there.

"That was so cool when you found the error in the maths problem that day," the boy said.

"You're not too bad yourself. I look at problems every day so it's not surprising that I can spot an error. But to see a mistake in a high school level problem while still being in middle school is quite something!" He shook his head. "When I first met you, I really thought you were Zhang's—"

Ye coughed loudly, hinting that Yan should not be so obvious, and Yan broke off with a smile.

Chaoyang's expression changed slightly. He changed the subject: "Do you teach at a university?"

"Yes."

"Which university?"

"Zhejiang University."

"Zhejiang University!" the young boy said with awe. "I really want to study maths there. It's my top choice!"

"We'll see how you do on your university entrance exams," Yan said faintly. "I had a question to ask you about the ongoing cases in which you were involved. I've read your journal and wanted to ask: how did Xia Yuepu convince Zhang Dongsheng to help kill your parents?"

Ye coughed again, but Yan ignored him, focused on Chaoyang's reactions.

"It's just like I said to the police before, I don't know how she did it," he said, his eyes downcast.

"She never told you?"

"Yuepu… Yuepu only told me what happened to my dad… after the fact. She and Ding Hao must have threatened Zhang Dongsheng and then convinced him somehow. But I don't know how."

"Then let me ask you something else. I believe that Zhang Dongsheng would not want to keep killing people. Even if he were threatened, he would think of a way to get out of it. But surely the best way of doing that would be to tell you, so you could stop your friends. Didn't he come and talk to you?"

"He didn't know my address," Chaoyang stated.

"Good answer," Yan said with a smile.

Ye sounded like he was about to cough up a lung.

Yan was undeterred. "How did they poison your father and Wang Yao?"

"Like I said before, I don't know. Yuepu wouldn't tell me the details."

Yan was about to fire off another question when Ye interrupted, "Professor Yan, I think you've asked enough questions, don't you?"

Chaoyang turned to him. "Uncle Ye, I don't really want to talk about that stuff any more. I just want to be a normal person like everybody else."

326

"Have you had enough, Professor Yan?" Ye pressed.

"I just have one more question—" Yan began.

This time Chaoyang interrupted, his voice low and beseeching, "Uncle Ye, I'm supposed to register for school tomorrow. Will I be allowed to go to school?"

"Don't worry, you'll go to school just like normal."

"Can you help me with something?" the boy continued.

"Just say the word," Ye said.

"Please, don't tell Ye Chimin about what happened; she can't know what happened," Chaoyang said, looking afraid. "If she knew... I... I would be in big trouble."

"Chaoyang, what do you mean?" Ye asked, his curiosity piqued.

The boy explained that last term, on the day before the exams, Ye Chimin had claimed that he had broken her camera lens and told teachers that he had poured water all over her head. If she knew about everything that happened to him, she would make his life miserable. He would be bullied so much that he would be compelled to switch schools.

Yan remembered reading about a girl called Ye Chimin bothering Chaoyang at school in the early journal entries, but he had never guessed that she was Ye Jun's daughter! He looked at Chaoyang, startled. Based on Ye's reaction, it seemed that he had not taken that information in either. His eyes flashed. He slammed his palm on the desk, startling Yan and Chaoyang, and got to his feet.

Ye did not look like he was going to show mercy. "I apologize for what she did to you! And I promise, Ye Chimin will never bully you again! I won't let anyone at the school know what has happened, not even the teachers. It's my job to protect innocent people, especially children, so if you ever have problems with anyone, you tell Uncle Ye!" He was so furious that he was ready to leave immediately to confront his daughter.

"What are you going to do?" Yan asked.

"I'm going to smoke! When my shift is over I'll sort her out!" Ye stomped out of the room.

"Does your mother know of all the impressive things you can do?" Yan asked, his face unreadable.

"What?" Chaoyang asked, puzzled.

"I should go." Yan stood. "Keep your nose to the grindstone."

84

2ND SEPTEMBER

It was the first day of Chaoyang's third year in middle school.

He didn't have any classes today; it was just a registration day. Still, he arrived bright and early. Everyone was excited to chat with each other and nervous about starting the new term. His classmates were busy talking about what they had done that summer—nobody noticed him. Fang Lina said hello, which was better than nothing.

Ye Chimin was late. She gave Chaoyang a nasty look when she entered the classroom but didn't say anything. She opened her book and started reading.

"What's Ye Chimin doing, looking at you like that?" Lina whispered.

"No idea."

"We just started term! You better watch out for her."

"I'll just ignore her."

"Good plan," Lina said encouragingly.

When it was time for assembly, Mrs Lu led her students to the playing fields. As Chaoyang was leaving the classroom, he heard a tiny voice behind him. "It's all your fault."

He turned around and was met with an icy stare. Chaoyang rolled his eyes. "What?"

"You don't want to admit to what you did? Fine," Chimin said with a toss of her head. "From now on, I'm going to leave you alone, and you're going to leave me alone."

"Where did this come from? I've never done anything to bother you."

"Pshaw." Chimin quickened her step and left Chaoyang well behind.

They arrived at the fields where the other students were bubbling with energy. Chaoyang stood with the others, but apart. He thought about Pupu, about Ding Hao, and how nice it had been to read at the bookstore every afternoon. A sigh escaped.

His two friends were gone.

He would never have any friends again.

Pupu's father wouldn't receive a photograph of her any more.

His throat constricted. He looked up at the sunshine and felt a little better.

It was a new term. It was a new day. He was a new person.

Standing outside the fence was a middle-aged man wearing glasses, his eyebrows knit tightly together. He quickly spotted Chaoyang, one of the kids standing slightly apart from the others. He was alone, always.

Yan reached for his phone. He read the text message: *Professor Yan, the analysis of your paper sample, received yesterday, shows that the text was written within the last month. It is not possible to confirm exactly when the text was written given the technology we have.*

"That's my answer," Yan said to nobody at all.

He had ripped off a corner of a page that was supposed to have been written in December, nine months ago. Then he sent it to an old friend at a forensics lab, calling in a little favour. Yan's hypothesis was true: Chaoyang had written the journal for the police. The notebook was not new, so he must have used one that he had had for a few years. That would look more authentic. But, apparently Chaoyang had not taken account of the fact that it was now possible to use ink analysis to estimate roughly when something was written.

How much of the journal was fabricated?

Not all of it, clearly.

The police had checked facts and they were correct.

There were fingerprints proving that Xia Yuepu and Ding Hao were at the scene of Zhu Jingjing's death, but nothing showing that Chaoyang had been there. He was in class at the time of his father and stepmother's deaths—he was blameless once again. The details of the strange deaths of Zhang Dongsheng, Xia Yuepu and Ding Hao matched perfectly with his statement.

So what was the point of going to the effort of writing the journal?

Yan did not know.

The thing that shocked him the most was that if the journal was fake, it would mean Chaoyang had predicted what would happen at Zhang's apartment. How could he have known that the murderer would try to kill them, that the poison would be in the soda, that both Pupu and Ding Hao would die of cyanide poisoning, and crucially, that Ding Hao would stab Zhang Dongsheng to death?

Yan could not think of any explanation.

Yan *knew* that Chaoyang was lying about something. The journal was fake, after all.

There had to be an important secret, something Chaoyang would have to hide for the rest of his life.

Would the fact that the entire journal was written in the past month or so be enough to convict Chaoyang of murder? There wasn't any evidence that he had been involved in any of the murders. And if he had been, he was only thirteen, so he would not be punished too severely.

If Yan uncovered his darkest secret, it would pierce through the armour that every person needed to go through the world. Psychologically, Chaoyang would not only have to live with the terrible deeds he had done, but also live with the stigma of being a criminal. Yan was deeply worried. What kind of trauma would be inflicted on Chaoyang if everyone looked at him with a mixture of caution and fear? How would he react?

How would it affect his ability to finish his education and get a decent job?

The national anthem played out of speakers at the edge of the field. The children stood to attention. The sun shone cheerfully. Chaoyang looked up, his face towards the sun. From where Yan stood, every child looked healthy, happy and full of hope.

Yan brought up Ye Jun's number on his mobile. His finger hovered over two buttons. The button on the left said Call; the one on the right said Cancel.

His eyes returned to the children in the sunlight. Yan was suddenly reminded of the last sentence of Chaoyang's journal: *I want to be a new person.*

Surely that sentence was true. Wasn't it?

Yan was torn. Chaoyang might be turning into a new person already. If he called the police with his findings, wouldn't it destroy the boy's life? Yan's finger remained one inch away. Call. Cancel.

One inch to the right and a young person would be able to seize the opportunity to live a completely different life. One inch to the left and his life would collapse like a house of cards. The distance between the buttons represented two totally different realities.

It was the longest inch in the world.

AVAILABLE AND COMING SOON
FROM PUSHKIN VERTIGO

Jonathan Ames

You Were Never Really Here
A Man Named Doll
The Wheel of Doll

Sarah Blau

The Others

Zijin Chen

Bad Kids

Maxine Mei-Fung Chung

The Eighth Girl

Amy Suiter Clarke

Girl, 11

Candas Jane Dorsey

The Adventures of Isabel

Joey Hartstone

The Local

Elizabeth Little

Pretty as a Picture

Jack Lutz

London in Black

Steven Maxwell

All Was Lost

Louise Mey

The Second Woman

Joyce Carol Oates (ed.)

Cutting Edge

John Kåre Raake

The Ice

RV Raman

A Will to Kill
Grave Intentions

Paula Rodríguez

Urgent Matters

Tiffany Tsao

The Majesties

John Vercher

Three-Fifths
After the Lights Go Out

Emma Viskic

Resurrection Bay
And Fire Came Down
Darkness for Light
Those Who Perish

Yulia Yakovleva

Punishment of a Hunter